ROOM OF CLOTH

R. H. GRÜND

R. H. Gründ Works

R. H. Gründ Works
www.rhgrundwriting.com

Book Layout © 2017 BookDesignTemplates.com

Room of Cloth/R. H. Gründ. -- 1st ed.
ISBN 979-8-9876458-0-2

ROOM OF CLOTH

1.

Who would have thought, out of the whole world, Sebastian Creed would be the one chosen?

He paced around the diner restroom, thin and negligible in his black jacket and jeans, clutching his ragged backpack to himself with white knuckles. He was more nervous with every second, torn between exhilaration and despair. It was on him—a bloody, hard-fought past and a blissful, jubilant future. It was on *him*, the most vanished of the wasted, the most wayward of the lost. He wasn't prone to self-reflection, but the thought fell on him now with devastating clarity. A drugged-up, psych-case dropout was responsible for protecting what was likely the most valuable thing to ever exist, the only thing worth a goddamn in this fucked-up, self-polluting, self-destructing wasteland. Who would have thought?

He produced the bag of cocaine, the last he had from Boston. He had made a deal with himself: no more drugs now that he was chosen. No more dope in the failing light of the evening as he prepared to float away into sleep. No more coke in the morning as he prepared to endure another aimless day. But where there had been chaos before, now there was design. Where there had been thoughtlessness, now there was purpose. If he was to protect the room of cloth, if he was to protect the future, he needed a clear head. He needed focus. But there could be exceptions. If the drugs were needed. If the drugs were essential.

He poured a line on the sink and snorted. He rubbed his gums. He waited.

There was the paradoxical, conditioned calm after a moment. He breathed. He saw. He smelt. Calm down, he told himself. Be ready. He made for the door, prepared to continue the mission, prepared to keep going—and then the room changed. He looked around himself in alarm. He screamed. His jeans grew damp. The lousy, little restroom with its piss-yellow walls and shit-caked toilets disappeared into smoke, and in its place was a room of red and black, the walls wheezing out hot, blood-drenched breath, undulating as though alive, enveloping him in heat. A room of flesh and bone. A room of cloth.

He fell to his knees. He spread his hands over the bloody floor and lifted them up as if he were at a church service. He laughed. Never before, not with any weed or powder at least, had he felt such a quickening in his chest, such a sudden reverberation throughout his body. The closest had been taking a square of acid in some hazy, green-lit apartment, launched out of his body into noise and color without the comforting framework of time and space to keep him together. So frightened had he been, so fucking scared, that he swore never to take anything like that again. Trembling, teeth clacking, running dirty fingers through greasy hair and over pimpled skin. He swore to himself, over and over. Never again. Never again.

That was a vivid memory, him stumbling off the sofa and dropping the little paper-wrapped tablets with the cranes into the toilet, watching them eddy into darkness. Never again. Never again. But this was different. When his mother had stared at those crosses on the wall, when she touched them like she was touching the skin and sweat of a lover, he had scoffed. He had scorned her prayers, disregarded her admonitions about Heaven and Hell. But now he understood. This was what she meant. All those years, the dumb bitch had been onto something—of course, she'd been praying to the wrong god. She'd been listening to the wrong sermons, following the wrong traditions. Now, he was the one reaching out, hoping there would be a hand to take his own, to take him away, to take him out of the red and black heat into something golden, something sweet-smelling. But his fingers latched onto only air. His grasp came back empty.

All of it came back—the walls, the toilets. Him kneeling there, pale and bloody-eyed, lips smeared with the telltale chalk. Mouth open, almost crying, like when his father abandoned him in the middle of the supermarket when he was four years old. Weeping and wailing and groping. Daddy, Daddy. Where are you? Where did you go? The man coming out of nowhere, seizing his hand, calling him a bitch, ordering him to stop crying. Sebastian groped that same way now, whispering under his breath. Daddy, Daddy.

He felt so lonely then, whisked from his vision, stolen from his paradise. Was that how his mother had felt when she rose up from praying? Was that why she cried afterwards? God only graced her for a few measly seconds. Except that wasn't God. Just a comforting lie dreamt up to help her and the other sheep sleep at night. They had no fucking idea what was really up there, and they never would. They would never be chosen.

"Jesus Christ," he laughed. "You're really fucked if you're thinking about them." Mother and father, both dead, both pieces of shit. They had no place in what was coming. He got to his feet, wiped the leftover coke off the edge of the sink, splashed water on his face. Of course he was fucking nervous. Why wouldn't he be, ferrying what he was? For the first time in his life, actually responsible for something—entrusted with something. It was more than he could say of his good-for-nothing parents. More than he could say of his sister.

He put his sunglasses on, pulled up his hood. He took hold of the backpack again.

He ate a couple of slices of cherry pie in the diner, drank a milkshake. Truckers came and went, men in ball caps and flannel shirts, women in sweaters and torn jeans. Sebastian knew they were all looking at him. He didn't cut a pleasant figure even next to them. Ratty jacket. The same black jeans he'd been wearing for months, so worn one could see his pinstripe underwear through the holes in the back. Sneakers—also black—scraped and bruised. Half-beard that needed trimming. Ragged bandage around his pasty, jittery hand. Scrawny and waifish, as though made of twigs, ready to fall apart from the slightest breeze.

But, no, they weren't looking at him. They were looking at the backpack. What was in the backpack.

An hour later, he was on the bus, watching the dark pass by. He checked the backpack again, the fifth time he had done so since getting in his seat. He rummaged through the shirts and socks until he unearthed the mailroom envelope, coffee-splotched, covered in black ink. He touched it briefly, almost undid the string, but he pulled his hand back. No. It wasn't safe. The pages inside begged to be read, demanded that he just look at the words—but he couldn't. "Too many eyes," he whispered, more sweetly than he had ever whispered. "But soon. Soon."

After a while, he saw lights in the distance, little orbs in the black. His hometown of Lorraine, Maryland. He couldn't help but laugh. Back to the dump. Back to the beginning. Maybe his sister Sarah wasn't even there anymore. Maybe she'd met someone or just moved out of that little apartment. A part of him hoped she had—always hoped she had. But he needed her to be there, this time more than ever. Sarah's was the safest place he could crash.

The bus station was crowded and noisy. So many people waiting around, talking on phones, poking at tablets. Every television had the news on. There were reports of heavy rains across the Northeast, videos of flooding. Cars going under, whole houses swept away. There was a picture of another aid worker found dead in some backwater, desert shithole. Gagged and blindfolded. Head cut off. Probably tortured and raped. Big, brown eyes. Long, dark hair. Young. He couldn't stand looking at her. Better to see the drones and mines tearing up dirt and sand. At least then there weren't any faces. None left to see, anyway.

On the cab ride to Sarah's apartment building, he pulled off the gauze around his hand. The flesh underneath was tender and pink, faint enough to be unnoticeable. The long scar across the palm was almost invisible if he kept it out of the light. It was hard to remember exactly how he hurt himself—he must have been so high at the time—but he could recall the pain just fine, the way the blood washed over his knuckles and down to his wrist. Didn't matter, anyway. Could say he cut his hand moving a shelf. Could say he dropped a plate and had to pick up the pieces. Just as long as Sarah didn't ask questions. Just as long as he kept her off the scent of the manuscript.

Inside the apartment building, it was all battered, white walls and cracked, green tiles. Pale, sickly lights led the way up the stairs, past roaches scurrying from one crack to another, past graffiti announcing the end of the world. Yelling from another hall. Music from a television. A phone ringing from the floor above.

Sebastian walked faster.

As he got closer to his sister's room, it dawned on him that Sarah might actually, really have left, and he wouldn't know because he lost his last cell phone months ago in a bar fight. For all he knew, she could be dead. Gagged and blindfolded with her head cut off like the aid worker. Stuck in some filthy, underground room. One or the other. Both. Christ. Fucking Christ, he wanted to run, but he couldn't. He couldn't. Fucking remember, he thought. What you saw. What you were shown. How you were chosen. Fucking remember and just do it.

He rang the buzzer.

2.

Sarah snapped awake at the screech of the buzzer. She sat in a daze at her coffee table, for a moment unsure as to where she was, what she was doing. The tabletop was strewn with essay pages smeared with blemishes of ink and chocolate, the stains indistinguishable from one another in the poor light. She peeled away one such page from her cheek and surveyed the splotch of saliva still wet on its bottom corner. The filaments of the paper were especially noticeable, a criss-cross hatch of off-white and near-gray that would crumble with a sudden poke of her finger. Wiggle it through, she thought absently. Tear it apart.

The buzzer rang again. She shuffled away from the table, wrapping her cardigan around herself the way a woman twenty years her senior might have done. She was only thirty-two, but she had been mistaken on more than one occasion for forty or even fifty. By her students. By her coworkers. By drunkards on the street. Slim and gaunt, hair so light as to appear gray when the sun was dim, eyes so faded as to resemble budding cataracts. "A strong wind'll blow you over," her fellow teacher Louisa once said. "Need some meat on those bones."

Her apartment stank with darkness. Only the light above the stove buzzed, spotted with the dark shapes of flies long dead. Only the neon sign across the street burnt red, washing her table and her dead plants with a milky luridness. She was past being scared of the apartment and the phantoms she sometimes thought dwelled in those shadows. Even if they were there, they were nothing. Just pretend things that hid in the dark, dispelled with the simple flick of a switch.

Her heart was steady now after the initial shock of the buzzer. No one visited, not the neighbors, not even the landlord. Only one person would be here, especially in the dead of night. Only one person would be clawing at the door, begging to come inside. She thought of him and was not even relieved—just tired. Her breath left her in a sigh, and she reached for the doorknob.

On the other side, Sebastian waited, waited, waited. After the second ring, the anxiety returned again tenfold. She's gone, he told himself. She really did move out. She really did get married. She's fucking shot full of kids even though it wouldn't have happened, couldn't have happened. No one would want to date Sarah, let alone marry her, get her fucking pregnant. That was a crazy idea, the craziest he'd had recently. But he couldn't help it. Too much was on the line. Or what if she was dead? What if there was an unmarked grave somewhere, no one to visit, no one to make pretty? What if she was rotting underneath, really the corpse that she sometimes looked? What if the person living here was someone else? What would he do? Where would he take it? Where would he unveil the pages, touch them tenderly, read them sweetly, like a parent reads to a child before bed and after a nightmare?

After that vision in the diner, this couldn't be it. He'd seen it at last. The room of cloth. He'd touched it, tasted it. For the first time, everything in its place. For the first time, at peace.

This couldn't be it. This couldn't be all there was—

Then the door cracked open, and everything was fine, everything was back to normal, perfect, the way it should be, because it was just Sarah standing there, staring at him, bags under her eyes, unkempt hair down her bony shoulders, looking like a cartoon character who got hit with a falling piano. Flattened. Worn out. A thousand times dead, deader than he was.

In other words, same old Sarah.

"Sebastian?" she asked, though he couldn't tell if she was surprised, confused, or something else between the two.

"Hey, Sis." He took off his sunglasses and pulled down his hood. "Gonna let me in?"

Something in her face flickered, something like anger or frustration—he never knew with her, never knew when to expect a lashing-out or a sermon—but she pulled the door back. The place was exactly the same. The little kitchenette with the old stove and all the pots and pans stacked on top. The dead flies in the light fixture. The tiny table. The white window drapes she took from the old house. The same crosses on the wall to which their mother used to pray, also from the house. Everything right where he remembered it being. Nothing had changed.

Darker, if anything. Dirtier. Like he could reach out and touch the ugly red light from the window and smear his face with it. Like he could grab a clump and crumble it in his hand, scatter it over the shadows and their endless miles. Or was that heaviness something else, neither dark nor dirty? Something alive that waited for him? Something expecting his arrival?

He felt her behind him, fidgety like she always was, wispy and small. He didn't know what to say, so he just said the same thing he always did.

"Been a while, huh?"

"One year," she said, eyeing him, kneading her hands. "One year, Sebastian."

"Yeah. Well, I'm back. Aren't you happy to see me?"

He waited for the attack. This, too, was always the same, no matter the amount of time that might have passed. He could have left for a week, a day—hell, even an hour—and he would have still been treated like the fucking prodigal son, capable of no right and all wrong. But he couldn't expect much else from Sarah. Both of them were just playing their parts, and he needed those parts to stay the same. He needed the stability and consistency. He needed her to follow the script, color between the lines. So, fine, she could be her usual uptight, bitchy self. He wouldn't fight her so much. He needed her bitchy. She was more predictable that way. Easier to control.

"Of course, I'm happy," she said. "Of course, I am. But you should've called me. You should've told me where you were—you should've told me *anything*, not just up and leave one day. For a year." She repeated it. "For a *year*."

He looked away in an effort to appease, to accelerate the charade. "Okay. You're right. I'm sorry. I lost my phone, so I wasn't able to call you. It's my bad."

She drew a breath. "All right. Come here." She pulled him into a hug. "I was worried about you. I was so worried—by God, you *stink*." She reared back. "When was the last time you took a shower?"

"I don't know. A week?"

"Well, we're going to fix that right now. I'll wash your clothes, too."

"What, you gonna strip me?" He laughed. "Let me unload my stuff. My room the same?"

She nodded. "I cleaned it up, but that's all. Go ahead. I'll get the water running."

"Okay." He turned around, saw a stack of red-inked papers on the nearby chair and the layer of black-blotted pages blanketing the coffee table. "You know, I was expecting like a guy to answer the door, a boyfriend. Thought maybe you'd even moved. But I guess everything's just the same. You're still looking at papers. Still teaching the same little assholes."

"Don't call them that," Sarah said.

"It's what you used to call 'em."

She fixed him with a glare. "Just don't call them that. I have a responsibility to those kids, Sebastian, to my job. I can't just do whatever I want whenever I want. You do something, and it affects people—"

"Okay, okay! Jesus. I'm sorry." He hated that look she gave him, the same self-righteous scowl she always had. The same look their mother always gave him, too.

"Fine," she said, trying a smile. "You're right. I should be happy you're here. I'll get the shower ready."

After she went into the restroom across the hall, Sebastian hurried to his room. Just like she said, it was exactly the way he left it: tiny cot in the corner, old Pantera posters on the walls, broken desk with a cheap robot toy on top of it. It was too perfect. Too easy.

He set the backpack down and took out the mail-room envelope. He caressed the envelope's edges, gently felt the shape and weight of the pages within. The manuscript. The room of cloth. Safe at last, safe from all those jealous, hungry stares. He was safe, too, and now, he could do the thing he was chosen for. Now, he could write. Now, he could finish it.

He pushed the toe of his shoe into an off-center floorboard. Underneath was a hollow space, big enough to store the bags of pills and weed he usually crammed inside. And it was big enough for this. He squashed the envelope into the space. He hurt to see it crushed and folded, abused, but he had to do it. No one could know it was here. No one. Not even Sarah. *Especially* not Sarah.

He replaced the floorboard. He knelt there, basking in that triumphant feeling, letting the manuscript's sweet cinnamon scent wash over him. Then he went to go take that shower.

With Sebastian squared away, Sarah meanwhile returned to the coffee table. She picked up her pen, straightened the nearest essay, but against the sound of the running water and the droop of her bleary eyes, she was powerless. Sebastian. Back again, what could've been the tenth time, the hundredth. But for how long? And why now?

She fingered the now-dry patch of saliva on the essay she had put aside. Like a scab, the gray patch was rougher, more callous than the rest of the paper. A wound, she thought, forever stuck, unable to heal. A cut in the skin that lingered for years.

3

The next morning, Sarah was on her second cup of coffee, eyes away from the cold glare of the windows, nose wrinkling at the hot smell of bacon sizzling on the stove. Unsurprisingly, she hadn't slept at all during the night. Sebastian. Her little brother. The druggie. The dropout. The embarrassment. Even before the psychiatric hospital, before the night that changed everything, he'd been called all sorts of names by their father, mother, neighbors, teachers, other kids. Sarah was ashamed to include herself among their number. Weirdo, creep, pest—what hadn't she called him while they were growing up? And when, after coming back from the hospital, he started getting home late, started skipping school, started leaving behind the needles and pills and joints, hadn't she sat in the tub late at night and screamed into a bag, wishing he had never been born? Hadn't she done that more times than she could count?

Things hadn't changed much since then. He was still doing the drugs, still dropping off the face of the earth. This time was a new record, though. For over a year, he had been a ghost. Not a single call, text, or e-mail, either from him or the police. Just a hole cut in her life, rippling at the edges like a magazine page after a class project. Now, he was back, acting like he never left, like she hadn't spent countless nights awake and anxious, wondering if he was dead in a ditch somewhere or lying on the cold metal of an autopsy table, seconds away from the knife.

The pop of burning grease brought her back. She turned off the stove. The rest of the table was already set: a platter of toast and fried eggs, a pitcher of orange juice, a pot of coffee. As picturesque as she could manage. The bacon was burnt, the eggs lumpy, the tablecloth splotched and wrinkled, but better than nothing. A homemaker she was not.

He probably needed money. She would suggest a job, like always, and he would try it for a little while, like always. But nothing ever stuck with Sebastian. Packing groceries, taking calls, making lattes, whatever it was never lasted. He'd stop going, or he'd tell someone off, or he'd simply check out, and the boss would fire him. Sometimes, she would get a call from the police, or, worse, he would come home with a black eye and a swollen jaw, maybe even a broken rib. Something had to give, she knew that. She had to keep him here, keep him clean, whatever it took. She was responsible for him, the only person he had left now that their parents were gone. It wasn't a responsibility she took lightly, and it certainly weighed on her, but she wasn't going to let it go. There was an opportunity here to change things, to make them right. But no matter what she tried, what she promised herself, things always ended up the same. Their relationship was like a ritual they just kept repeating, their roles crystallized, their fates unalterable.

As she prepared their plates, he came out of his room, eyes wet, long-sleeve shirt undoubtedly covering fresh track marks. He looked okay otherwise, better than he probably should have looked. Definitely not as bad as those before-and-after shots of meth users she cycled through for her students every year. No skin pulled tightly against the skull. No welts or sores spotting the face. No teeth falling out of blackened gums.

He stopped in front of the table and gave her a bland, sheepish smile. "Smell got me up. What's going on?"

"It's my world-renowned breakfast," she said. "There's the extra-crispy bacon, the famous eggs. Perfect for getting up in the morning." And hangovers, she almost added.

He sat down. "Looks good."

"Enjoy it. I can eat a little, then I have to go to work."

He grabbed his fork. Immediately, he dug into the eggs, guzzled the coffee, devoured the bacon. Sarah was surprised, but she remembered herself and reached for a piece of bacon. It was like chalk in her mouth.

"You still have your appetite," she said, forcing the bacon down. Whatever else could be said about her brother, he was not a picky eater.

Sebastian paused between bites. "I was hungry. Didn't eat shit before the bus. I mean, not really. Just this bad cherry pie. Like rubber. You should've seen it."

Sarah was quiet. She prodded her own eggs. The longer she watched him eat, the more removed she felt, the more her optimism faded. Yes. This was how it was every time. She could imagine scripts in their hands, an audience across from them. Hands clapping for the fool, laughs stifled after each quip. Tomatoes thrown and peanuts pelted at the shrew. The tiny apartment a stage. Their lives rounded by a little sleep.

"Thinking about looking for work," Sebastian said. He wiped his mouth with his sleeve.

She turned her fork, studied her oblong reflection in the scratched silver. He was thinking about work. Sure. He was always thinking about work. What was next? Shelving a warehouse? Delivering food? When would the inevitable tantrum come around? When would he resume the disappearing act?

"Got any leads?" he asked.

"I'll ask around. See if anyone knows anything."

"Thanks." He pushed his chair out, burped. "I'm gonna take another shower. Still smell." He grabbed a bundle of clothes from his room and went into the restroom. Sarah waited, poked once more at her eggs, and then she moved. What was it this time? Heroin? Cocaine? Meth?

She went into his room and threw open the backpack. Just shirts, socks, and underwear. A pen. The sunglasses. No telltale plastic bags. No pills or capsules wrapped in glistening reds or greens. No syringes. Not even any cigarettes.

She put the backpack aside. The rest of the room was clean. Nothing? Not even a trace?

Wait. She lingered at the door. A smell. Rancid, like something dead. Maybe a rat under the floorboards or in the walls. God. This fucking place. This fucking dead place. She couldn't trust it. She couldn't trust him. Work, he said. Right. I'll work, Sarah. Everything's fine. You're so helpful. No, I swear I'm not using right now. I swear. I'm clean. Everything's good. Everything's gonna be different. Aren't you happy to see me? Aren't you glad I'm safe?

No, she thought, dumping the rest of the eggs and bacon in the garbage and piling the dishes in the sink. No. I'm not. Because now I have to do this again. Now I have to worry and stress and put up with all this again. Again and again and again and again and *again*. Because you don't give a shit. Because all you care about is the next hit, the next moment you inhale or inject or sniff or whatever the fuck you do to not face this. Face *me*. Goddamn you. Goddamn you to hell. You spineless loser. You weak-willed bastard.

She grabbed her purse and headed for the door, but her hand paused on the doorknob. She listened to the dull sound of the shower, the muffled groans of the piping. Tears prickled her eyes. Oh, Jesus. She was rotten. As rotten as the wood. As moldy as the drywall. You ungrateful bitch, he's alive. He's alive, and you have the gall to shame him. Shame on *you*. You should be thanking

God he's still here. You should be thanking Him every day.

In the parking lot, flattened by the glare, chilled by the wind, she mumbled a quick prayer. Hail Mary. Our Father. Protect him. Keep him safe. Keep *me* safe. But as always, she felt no better, no more relieved. Nothing had changed. Nothing would change. The spotlights would dim and then relight. The curtain would close and then reopen.

In her car, as she turned on the heater, a whiff of that dead smell reached her once more. She gagged. She thought she would puke. But fortunately, it passed, and only the burnt fumes of the heated air remained.

4.

Sebastian let the shower run while he sat on the toilet and waited. Five minutes. Ten minutes. Twenty. He poked his head out—Sarah was nowhere to be seen.

He took a moment to study the apartment. The dishes piled in the sink, crusty and stained. The essays stacked on the table, disheveled and unruly. The crosses on the wall, like an homage to their mother and everything he hated. Nothing had changed. The place was like a time capsule, Sarah's refuge from the world. She had wanted to downsize after their mother passed, but the apartment eerily resembled the old house nonetheless. The way the shadows in the corners seemed bigger, as though alive with intent and meaning. The way the walls crowded, as though simultaneously shrinking and expanding. The old house had always struck him as massive and mazelike. He hated the way its hallways twisted and turned, hated the way his father's yells and his mother's shrieks echoed down the long, dark stretches. As a child, he had scampered and shuffled towards Sarah's room, longing for escape, seeking a refuge of his own. But her door had always been locked. And when the door wasn't locked, she was never there, instead out in the night, spending as much time as she could away from the fight-ing and yelling. He had followed her example in the years afterwards, taking every excuse to stay on the street, whether that was getting drunk or getting high. Sarah became the one to stay in, like she was a prisoner chained to the warped floorboards and roped to the splintered doorways. In moving to the apartment, she had only swapped one prison for another.

He reached into one of the cupboards in the kitchen and dragged out the jar of cash Sarah kept hidden behind the cereal. She'd been adding to it. A ten here, a twenty there. Lots of change. He fished out his cab fare. He hadn't really been lying about a job—he was willing to give it a shot. He needed her off the scent for now, and that meant playing along with the ruse, making the most out of the script he'd been given. The most important thing was taking care of the manuscript. Keeping it hid-den. Keeping it safe. If that meant making sacrifices, well, there was no choice. He'd already given up most of the drugs—he could give up a few inches with Sarah if it came down to it.

He returned the jar to its secret place behind the ce-real boxes. She never kept count of her money. Whatever he took, she wouldn't miss it. She wouldn't even know it was gone.

The sun was high and shining by the time Sebastian got to the neighborhood he wanted. The glare blinded him even with his sunglasses. Sun out, and still Lorraine was nothing but blackened trees, shattered windows, and tagged brickwork. The town was more attractive at night when the lack of light concealed the rough edges. Maybe it was even dangerous, the dealers and deadbeats roaming around like zombies risen from fresh graves. In the morning sunlight, everything just seemed sedate and sad. The alleyways he passed swam with shadows. Hollow eyes followed him from the dark. Sneakers squeaked and squealed on the cement of a nearby basketball court. A car passed, followed by another. Still. Quiet. No clouds. No birds in the trees. Just the occasional, chilly gust of wind. Just the air wavering, shimmering.

He thought back to his exchange with Sarah that morning, the way she seemed friendly at first and then totally distant. Things were smooth with her so far, but he knew the crash was coming, probably faster than ever. Sooner or later, she'd want to talk, get lunch, nudge him some way, make him change. He would play along for the sake of the manuscript, but truthfully, the thought of this next act of their little play made him nauseated. He didn't want to get lunch, didn't want to talk, didn't want to listen to her stupid speeches because nothing ever changed. Go fetch, go catch, roll over, lick your ass, make sure it's clean, good, good, you're getting better, you'll be a respectable human being one of these days. Remember to cross your t's and dot your i's. Remember to brush your teeth and change your underwear. Remember to smile and pretend everything's okay, that you're not actually miserable. Sarah was the queen of pretending. Ever since she changed into that tired, dead-looking cartoon character, all she did was press her hands to her ears and shut her eyes to everything. The fact that she was still in that little apartment—the fact that she was still stuck on him, still stuck on what *should* be—was proof enough.

Finally, he got to the condo he was looking for, one of several in a cramped, congested neighborhood. They were two-story affairs, rooms on the top and garages on the bottom. The buildings leaned over as if old and tired, the paint chipping, the brick sagging, the shingles and doorways loose from years of rain and snow and heat. He went up to the second story and knocked on the door.

Someone hollered from inside. "*Esperame*! One second!"

A man opened the door. He was olive-skinned, doughy, with cropped hair and a thick mustache. A golden rosary hung around his trunk of a neck. He pulled out the cigarette he was smoking and gave Sebastian a long stare.

"Holy shit. Seb? That you?"

"Hey, Caesar. Long time, no see."

Caesar broke out into a huge grin. "Seb! Fuckin' Seb!" He pulled Sebastian into a hug. "Been worried sick about you! The hell you been doing? Where you been?"

"I was in Boston," Sebastian said. "With that bitch Billy Tripp."

"Billy? The fuck you with him for?"

"Thought I could get in on this dope he was selling. But it was a dumb idea. The guy didn't know what he was doing. It was a waste of time."

"I could've helped you if you needed money. You should've come to me."

"Yeah. More like I just had to get out of here. You know, my sister and all that."

"Well, next time, tell me when you're gonna take off. Fucking disappeared on me. One day you're here, next you're gone—what the fuck, man?"

"Yeah. Sorry about that."

"It's good. Long as you're safe. Come in, come in."

They went inside. "You thirsty?" Caesar asked. "Want a soda or something?"

"No. I'm good." Sebastian looked around—nothing had changed at Caesar's place, either. The same musty, beige carpet. The same old, brown sofa. The same busted television with the bunny ears. Weird how he never fixed it. Probably too busy fixing all the others that came in from around the neighborhood.

Caesar dragged from his cigarette and popped open a beer. "Was real worried about you, Seb. Real worried. But I'm happy you're okay. See your sis?"

"Yeah. She's the same. You? Business going good?"

"*Sí.* But it's a little different now. Things changed while you were gone."

Before he could say anything else, a teenaged boy walked out of the bedroom in the back, nothing but jeans on. He wiped some stray specks of powder from his mouth and nose. "You coming back, C?"

"Yeah. Just give me a sec. My friend Seb came by. Seb, this is Marcus. Been running him through the hoops.

Lots of guys been taking off. Hard to find anyone to get on the street anymore."

"I bet." Sebastian looked the kid over, saw the familiar dead-eyed stare. Another one of Caesar's pups. Sharp elbows. Ribs showing. Young and fresh, probably no older than sixteen. Nah, Caesar hadn't changed, either. Still had his same tastes. "Big Caesar," they called him around town. Still picking up strays and putting them to work. Still taking the ones he thought were pretty to his bed. Sebastian had been just like this kid after his stint in the psychiatric hospital. Lost and aimless, wandering the streets at night, looking for drugs or drinks. Caesar found him on the curb, took him back to the condo, threw blankets around him, fed him a reheated steak. Sebastian had been indebted after that. He dealt product for Caesar during lunch and after school, at the local bars, on the corners. Not a glamorous life, but a hell of a lot better than staying in that shitty old house with his mother and Sarah, and he'd made money. And for all the things Caesar did with the other boys, he never looked at Sebastian in that way. He was good to him. He'd never looked down on him, never treated him like he was a mess or a loser. He cut him deals, gave him flexible hours, always had something nice to say. Nothing was a mistake—not the wrong package, not even lost money. If something went wrong, it was just a lesson, a chance to make it right later. Hell, getting picked up by Caesar was probably the best thing that could happen to turned-out strays like him. No one else was gonna look after you the same way. Not your own mother. Not even your big sister.

"Listen, Caesar," Sebastian said, "that's what I wanna talk to you about. I didn't come back just to come back. I need help with something."

"Yeah. Marcus, just wait for me, okay? I'll be right back."

"Okay."

Marcus shambled back to the bedroom, the faded, shredded bottoms of his jeans dragging on the carpet. Caesar put out his cigarette and lit a fresh one. "What's that mean, help? You need money? Somewhere to stay?"

"Not exactly. I need a laptop. A computer. And maybe I do need money. But no handouts. I'll work just like always."

"A computer?"

"Yeah. Doesn't matter what. Just needs to go on the web, and I gotta write on it."

"What you need a computer for?"

"I'm working on something. A story."

"Like a book?"

"Yeah, sort of like that. Like a book."

Caesar nodded, let out a puff of smoke. Surprisingly, much to Sebastian's relief, he didn't pry more. "Okay. I can get you that. But the work, I don't know. Things changed, Seb."

"You just said you need more guys on the street."

"I know. Sit down."

Caesar took the nearby chair while Sebastian sat on the sofa. He couldn't help but wring his hands and tap his feet. This felt familiar, too, sitting and waiting impatiently for Big Caesar to regale with some story or reproach with a new lesson. Only this time Sebastian lacked the luxury to wait around. There was always this sense of doom in the back of his mind now—this sense that if he just didn't *finish* it, something was going to happen, something he couldn't control. Wheels were turning somewhere. Time was slipping away. He was chosen, but there were expectations, strings attached that, while he couldn't see them, he could certainly feel.

"I'm real glad you're back," Caesar said, "but it's not good to be here anymore."

"What are you talking about?"

"There's a new power in town. Name's Otto. Otto Jackson. Came outta nowhere a little bit after you left. Before you knew it, it was like he'd always been here. His people started coming by like it was nothing, started getting cuts off what we made. That was that. Some of the guys didn't want to play, but he made 'em. Now we got no choice but to go to him. He gives us everything to sell, and that means all the old connects, too. Got a club downtown that rakes in a lot of cash. He's everywhere. If I give you work, he'll hear about it."

"What, he the fucking godfather? Let me talk to him. It doesn't have to go through you."

"Seb. You ain't listening. You get in, it won't be easy to get out."

"I'll get out if I fucking want to get out. I don't care who he is. Don Otto or whoever the fuck. Look, Caesar, you don't gotta worry. I ain't staying long. I just need something while I work on this thing. Once it's done, I'm leaving."

Caesar sighed. He undid the rosary around his neck and studied it. He always did that. Whenever there was something he wasn't sure about it, something he couldn't decide on, he looked at the rosary and waited for some sort of answer. What answers he got, Sebastian didn't know. It was just a piece of metal, most likely from a market in some muddy Cuban village. A cheap knock-off that probably cost an American dollar or two. Just like the crosses his mother had, the ones Sarah kept on the wall. All different colors, all different sizes. All just pieces of metal and plastic and wood, never saying a word no matter how hard someone prayed or how miserably anyone cried.

Not like the manuscript. The words didn't just speak—they *sang*.

"Okay," said Caesar after a while. "We'll talk to him. But you keep your head down."

"There's another thing, too." Sebastian took a note from his pocket and gave it to Caesar. "I gotta find this guy."

Caesar squinted at the thin scribble. "Bryan Stevens? Who's he?"

"I said I was writing a story," Sebastian said, "but it's more like I'm finishing it. Thing is, I only got a part from the middle. This guy, Stevens? He has the rest. He sent me what I got."

"And you want me to look for him?"

"No. But maybe this Otto guy can find him. I can make a deal or something."

Caesar shook his head, the cigarette trembling in his hand. He got up and paced. This, too, was something he did often. Get nervous. Get fidgety. As if any disturbance threw his little world off its axis—his little world of dope and powder, corners and alleyways. Crazy to think Sebastian had thought of it as home once. Now, with his newfound bird's-eye view, he saw everything with clarity and maybe even a little contempt. For as much help as he had been before the manuscript, Caesar was as small and weak as Sarah. Both of them were trapped in tiny cages, four-by-six cells. Prisons of their own making with nothing to free them.

"I don't know," Caesar said. "I don't like the way this feels. This guy, Seb—you ain't seen what he does. You don't know him. Maybe you seen some shit before, maybe you did some with Billy, but this is different. Otto's not someone you want to deal with."

"Well, what the fuck am I supposed to do, Caesar?" Sebastian demanded. "I got no money. I know Sarah's gearing up to get on my ass. But this thing—this story— this is important. I wish I could tell you about it, but it's not something I can just talk about. Not till I finish it."

"You gotta give me more than that. How'd this all start? This something about what happened with Billy? Why you left?"

"It's when I was out there. I found it online. It's like I was meant to find it. And then when I started digging, I met that guy. Bryan. And when he sent it to me—when I read it—Jesus, C, it's like everything changed. You don't look at the world the same way after that. The sun, the clouds, the way the air feels—everything's different. Like it makes sense. And nothing ever made sense before. Nothing ever felt real."

"I don't get it," Caesar said. "That don't make sense."

"If you could read it—" Sebastian stopped himself, hesitated. "Look, it's like the Bible."

"You never read the Bible. How would you know?"

"It's just a fucking favor, Caesar," Sebastian said. "I just need help with this one thing. What's so hard about it?"

Caesar was on his third cigarette by now, burning through this one twice as quickly as the others. He sighed. "You serious about this?"

"I'm dead serious. Just let me talk to this Otto guy. It won't be on you, okay?"

Caesar put out his cigarette, then went to the fridge and grabbed another beer. As Caesar drank, Sebastian waited, flexing his fingers and tapping his toes. Finally, Caesar sat back down. With trembling hands, he lit a fourth cigarette.

"Okay. Fine. We'll talk to Otto. But you gotta promise me, Seb. You gotta promise me you'll play it cool. You'll follow my lead on this."

"Whatever you say, I'll do it. Just as long as he helps me find my guy."

"Otto does what Otto wants," Caesar said. "We just do what we're told."

He was silent after that. Sebastian twitched and held out his hand.

"All right. I'll take a cig now."

5

Sarah sat at her desk, picking absently at a salad. The barrenness of her classroom was especially evident without any students inside. The walls were hardly decorated save for a smattering of haphazardly arranged motivational posters and essay-writing diagrams. Torn, uneven butcher paper and loose, unstapled border exposed the blue musculature of the bulletin board on the far wall. Open textbooks lay at odd angles upon and underneath desks as if abandoned mid-reading. A miniature American flag bent over the blackboard, stars faded and stripes frayed.

She studied the tattered flag above her head, considered the most recent inked phallus to grace a desk. Sebastian. Every thought came back to Sebastian. Her entire day so far had been a waking dream, a blurry replay of the prior evening and morning. Sebastian, Sebastian, Sebastian. The same questions persisted as well. For how long would he stay? Why had he returned at all? Money, she kept telling herself. Food. Shelter. Everything a craven animal needed when it was smoked out of its cave. But those answers didn't seem good enough this time. There was something else, something on him that was nearly undetectable, hiding in the length of his shadow, roaming among the rips of his jacket and beneath the tears of his jeans.

A couple of students ran by in the hall, breaking her reverie. Their shouts drew attention to her worsening migraine. Their footfalls emphasized the crumbling leaves between her teeth, the taste of dirt on her tongue. She spat out her mouthful.

"Hey, babe. You look worse than me."

In the doorway, bulging belly in hand, was Louisa Oldman, a fellow English teacher. She looked on Sarah serenely, light eyes framed by butterscotch hair.

"Oh, Louisa," Sarah sighed. "What am I going to do when you're gone?"

"The same thing you always do: muscle through. And I'll try to cut the leave short this time." Louisa pulled up a chair beside the nearby desk. She smudged the ink of the phallus with her thumb. "Regular Picasso over here. You should get him to prepare a portfolio."

Sarah smiled. "Short leave? You're having twins. You'll have your hands full."

"But they'll be girls. Can't be any worse than the boys I already have—Jim included."

"I don't know about that," Sarah said. "You heard about the girl in Hugh's class? Almost punched out one of the security guards. I wasn't much better when I was a kid. Went home with a black eye more than a few times."

"A firm hand makes the difference. I ever talked back, I wasn't walking away without a slap across the face."

They laughed. Louisa leaned forward. "So, Sebastian's back?"

"Yeah. He came in last night like it was nothing. A whole year, Louisa."

"I tell you, you're a saint. I would have cut him off a long time ago. And I still think you should. A year, Sarah? There's helping family out, and then there's just plain abuse."

"I've thought about it," Sarah said. "But where's he going to go? I already try so hard not to scare him away. It's like I'm walking on eggshells all the time. One wrong move, and I have no idea if I'll ever see him again."

Louisa was quiet. "I had an uncle," she said at length. "Might've told you about him before. Just like your brother, except he was always drinking. Always a beer in his hand. My parents cut him loose. That was after rehab didn't work out. You ever put Sebastian in rehab?"

"No. I can't."

"After what happened with your dad?"

"Yeah. Sebastian wasn't the same after the hospital."

Sarah remembered. Her last spring break of college. Driving on the beach at nighttime, the wind whipping her hair, the salty spray filling her lungs. Her friends around her, beers raised high, singing along to Bon Jovi, Journey, Lynyrd Skynyrd. Dancing in clubs, singing karaoke, swimming in motel pools colored pink and purple while palms swayed and stars twinkled overhead. Standing on the shore, back to the bonfire, the arm of some guy around her waist. Watching the rosy sun dip beneath the waves. Feeling the sand between her toes.

But then there was the phone call. There was the rush back home, the police tape all over the house, her father in the casket. She didn't get to see Sebastian until the funeral was over, didn't get to see the skinny, shaking boy in white, his eyes hollow, his right hand trembling. How much time had she spent with him in that fucking room, trying to get him to talk, trying to make sense of the nightmare her life had become? She had screamed, pleaded, cried, been tempted to pound her fists into his head. She imagined doing it, imagined the way he would have curled up, all senseless and stupid. And then there was her mother. "Demon," she had called Sebastian over and over again. "Monster." Sarah imagined attacking her, too—slapping her, strangling her, pushing her thumbs through her eyes until she finally just *shut up*. It wasn't even about defending Sebastian, not after a point. She just wanted peace and quiet. She just wanted silence.

Louisa watched her. "You don't talk about him much. Your dad, I mean."

"What's there to say? He worked on cars. Drank more than he should've. Yelled at us. Called us names. He didn't touch me or Sebastian, but he hit my mother. I didn't help things. I was a real bitch. Even when he gave Sebastian a hard time, I was always 'busy.' I took every excuse not to be there."

"It's an awful thing," Louisa said, "a son killing his father."

Sarah was quiet, back in the motel that night listening to her mother scream and screech on the phone. He killed him! He put a knife in him, dear God! Your daddy's dead, Sarah! He's dead! He's dead, he's dead, he's dead he's dead he's dead he's dead—

Good, Sarah had thought immediately, feeling a primal relish like never before and never since, an ugly satisfaction she had only gotten close to feeling when she downed a few beers, took some asshole to bed, and finally got the peace and quiet she wanted, if only for a few measly minutes. Good. I hope he suffered. I hope he fucking felt it. And I hope you feel it, too, you dumb bitch, defending him like he was a saint, like he didn't do a fucking thing wrong. I hope you feel it, and I hope you die—I hope you fucking wither away and die—

And then, seconds later, the shame. The emptiness. She remembered sitting on the side of the bed, not saying a word, just shaking, feeling like something had changed in her, like something had been lost and she was never getting it back.

"IED." That's what the doctors called it. Intermittent explosive disorder. The doctors, the so-called specialists, who hadn't done a single thing for Sebastian. They blamed him, of course, for getting so mad that he occasionally hit the wall, hit himself. They blamed him, of course, for getting so mad that he grabbed a knife from the kitchen and stuck it in their father's back. They didn't take into account the daily yelling and screaming. They didn't consider the meanness or the cruelty. They didn't think about the literally stinking bitterness that hung on that fat bastard's clothes when he came home from the bar and started raging about the low pay and the lack of respect and the no-good family, the wife who cooked for shit, the cunt of a daughter with her loose lips, the bitch of a boy who couldn't look a man in the eye.

Those doctors—they didn't know a thing.

That afternoon, in the school parking lot, Sarah opened up her glove compartment, fished through the receipts and bills, found the pint bottle of whiskey hidden away. This was another ritual. She had other bottles: one under her bed, another behind the toilet paper, a third gathering dust in the closet. On occasion, maybe when she got sick, when she felt especially cold, they called to her. She would grab the nearest bottle, stare at it, tease the top with her fingertips, brush it against her lips. Same thing with cigarettes. Packs hidden everywhere, in the console of the car, under the seat, beneath the pillow. Keep your enemies close, right? If only that were the reason. Every time she felt the queasiness, the gnawing, she meant to take that drink, take that drag— but she never did.

How ironic that her vices were those of her father. Sometimes, at night, under the red glow from the window, she thought she smelt his reek, heard his laugh. Felt the quake of the old wood under his boots, the vibration of the walls as he slammed the front door upon coming home. Was he haunting her, lurking in those shadows she often thought were alive? Sebastian killed him, but he remained. He was a stain on their lives.

She put the whiskey bottle back into the glove compartment. She resisted because there was no choice to be had. Succeed or fail. Give up or keep going. That was the way of the world, and she saw it every day, on the news, in the obituaries, when a student stopped showing up to class. Her father had wanted the world to bend to him, a trait Sebastian had inherited. Sebastian. Sebastian, Sebastian, Sebastian. Always back to Sebastian. Like a brick tethered to her ankle. Like water filling her lungs. The surface with its light and quiet always out of reach.

She turned the car on and drove onto the street. No. Stop it. Stop thinking like that. It's not too late for him. It's not too late for you. As long as he's here, there's a chance. He can change. You can change. You can. You can. You can.

6.

"I got you a meet."

Caesar set down the television set he was working on, screwdriver in one hand, cigarette in the other. The garage reeked of oil and sweat despite the cold air blowing in from beneath the raised door. Sebastian leaned against the nearby van and regarded the scattered tools, the pieces of wire and fiberglass. Caesar had debriefed him here constantly, given him names and numbers, places and times. This garage, for all its grime and filth, was a safe place. Safer certainly than the church with its wooden pews and Christ on the cross—safer than his mother clutching his hand, forcing him to stare into that bleeding face, promising him an eternity of fire and brimstone if he didn't say his prayers and do right by his family. Safer than the old house with its stench of alcohol and pall of cigarette smoke. Safer than the lumbering, bearded devil that came in every night, trailed by discarded beer cans, shattered glasses, broken plates.

Sebastian focused on the garage, on the relatively happy memories of walking out with a bag of heroin in the back of his jeans and a wad of cash in the front. Caesar's strong hand would squeeze his shoulder, caress his neck. He bristled. Even he had been touched by Caesar in those little ways, though thankfully, he had never been taken to the bedroom, never slipped anything of which he was unaware. Respected, he always thought. Given more freedom and space than the other cubs. Or maybe Caesar just hadn't liked him enough to take that extra step.

"When's the meet?" he asked.

"Thursday night. At Otto's club."

"Thursday?"

"Don't tell me you can't. You're the one who wanted it."

"It's my sister. She wants to do dinner or something. She's been real pushy lately."

Caesar took a puff of his cigarette and poked at the television's wiring. "You gotta get her to lay off. Can't make a date with Otto and not show up. And Seb? You gotta keep it together when we see him. No fucking around. No back talk."

"What the fuck do you think I'm gonna do?"

"*No sé*, but ever since you been back, your head's someplace else."

"I'm all right. Jesus. You're starting to sound like Sarah."

"She's just looking out for you."

Caesar kept working, then looked up. "Oh, yeah. Almost forgot." He rummaged through the junk on the table behind him and held up a laptop. "Got this yesterday. Old, but they said it works. Good enough?"

"Long as I can write on it."

Sebastian surveyed the laptop. The screen was cracked, and some of the keys had been replaced. A cheap refurbish, if you could even call it that, probably snagged from some garage sale or pawn shop, but it was indeed good enough. He almost wished he hadn't sold his previous laptop for the bus ticket—so much time had been wasted just waiting around. Every night, he hardly slept, the pull of the pages like a super-powered magnet rattling under the floorboards. In a cold sweat, he would apologize to the darkness. I'm coming. Just be patient. I'm almost ready. I'll be there soon. I swear. I swear. Please. Just give me a little more time.

Time he didn't have. Time that was slipping away. And that feeling of something coming getting stronger by the second, getting so strong he now had a habit of looking over his shoulder. What was there? What would happen if the story wasn't finished?

He looked up from the laptop. "There a charger?"

"Ah, fuck. Let me check."

While Caesar rifled through the tools and scraps of metal on the table, a scrawny teen rode up on a bicycle, blank-eyed, dead-faced. Sebastian figured he must have been like that, too, when Caesar picked him up off the street. After his father died, the hospital was a blur in his mind, but he could remember vividly the hard blacktop of the streets and the cold bite of the nighttime air. Wandering as far from the house as he could, trying to escape the phantom of that goddamn monster. Even dead, his father had still been in the house, living in the walls and shadows, hanging over every moment his mother slunk away from Sebastian as though *he* were the monster. Him, just a scared kid, thick as a twig, barely able to remember a thing. Sarah had taken his hand, for the first time in her life speaking softly to him, thinking what she did mattered, that he gave a shit at all. You're fake, he wanted to tell her. You're fake, and nothing you say matters. She hates me. You hate me, too. So, just leave. Leave like you always do.

Sebastian admitted that he had been like these boys who worked for Caesar. Lost. Gone. But things had changed. The room of cloth found him, gave him back what had been taken. He wasn't a puppet, not for his father, Sarah, or even Caesar. He served something higher now. None of them would stand in his way anymore.

The kid came inside. "Got this morning's run, C." He held up a bundle of money.

"Supposed to be here two hours ago," Caesar said. He took the money, thumbed through the bills. "Everything good?"

"Hey, I got it."

"I know." Caesar grinned and stroked the boy's arm. "It's just I got routines. Can't be late on this stuff. Wish I could, but you seen what they do. We gotta be on top of things."

"Yeah. I'll be on time tomorrow."

"Good. Now, get outta here. And tell Roberto I'm waiting for what he owes me."

Caesar watched the kid ride off. "Can't be soft with 'em anymore. Not with Otto."

"This guy that much of a hard-ass?"

"He's got his rules."

"You think he'll help me find Stevens?"

"I don't know. Otto does what he wants. I just keep my head down."

He kept tinkering with the television. Sebastian wiped some sweat from his brow.

"He let you do your thing?"

Caesar plucked out his cigarette and stared at him. "What's that mean?"

"You know. That Marcus guy. This one. Otto let you do it? He know?"

"Know *what*, Seb?"

"Nothing. Forget about it."

Caesar grunted. He continued working, but his hands shook. His fingers twitched. "I ain't no saint. I don't pretend to be one. I help those kids. I helped you."

"Yeah. Just forget it already."

Caesar turned away, still trembling. "Oh, yeah," he said, picking up a bundled wire and throwing it to Sebastian. "There's your charger."

7 .

At first, Sebastian just chased rumors. So many threads about unresolved cases and strange sightings. Alien abductions. Ghost stories. Haunted houses. He didn't know what drove him to spend those long nights in front of the computer, red eyes lit up by the blue glow of the screen. Boredom? Curiosity? But the more forums he browsed, the more chatrooms he joined, the more videos he watched, the less he could help himself. Stories blurred together. There was talk of bodies found in bunkers, some in the desert, some in the mountains. Heads in freezers. Arms in attics. Legs in showers. Teeth and nails sold alongside drugs. Hair tied up in little bundles, advertized by age and color.

He would click the mouse.

Occasionally, there would be posts about some underpass, some row house, some lake. People would say they were going to investigate one of these places. They'd post pictures of the road trip, the rainy highway, the cheap hotel. They'd say they were getting closer. Then the messages would stop. E-mails would go unanswered. Threads would close. Sites would shut down. Servers would die. They say people go down there and don't come back. Really? Yeah, they just disappear. Poof. Gone. Funny thing is, they say you can still hear things. Sometimes they see her. She jumped off the bridge, supposedly. No, she didn't—she hung herself. You're both wrong. She drowned her kids, then herself. She drowned, but she didn't die.

He would click the mouse.

There were always ads. Ads for grass. Ads for salts. Ads for pills. Ads for guns. Ads for wives. Ads for husbands. Ads for kids. Ads for subjects. Ads for users. Come in. Tune out. Drop off. Join up. Watch. Read. Feeling down? Feeling blue? We'll pick you up. We'll help you. Change your name. Quit your job. Make a bomb. Put on a mask. Blow up. Shoot up. Find yourself. Find us. Find Him. He's with you. In you. He always has been.

He would click the mouse.

Car crashes caught on tape. Beheadings recorded on cell phones. Blinking lights, blaring horns, star-seeing eyes. Bloody arms, glistening entrails, mangled faces. Men and women tied to posts and burnt alive. Cats and dogs nailed to boards, dissected, heads smashed to bloody pulps, legs still kicking. Men in masks, in windowless rooms. Fires burning in dark forests. Women tied up, pig-tailed, French-braided, praying and pleading for their lives, choking on tears and snot. Families playing in parks, in their backyards, filmed from afar.

He would click the mouse.

Muffled interviews, pixelated, artifacted, the interviewees laughing or crying, he couldn't tell. Pipes and blades and knives and chains. Distorted voiceovers. Long shots of barren country and abandoned warehouses, of hotel hallways and empty railway platforms. Cartoons, the colors washed out, the sounds not quite right. People jumping off rooftops. Hanging themselves. Throwing themselves in front of subway cars. Blowing their brains out.

He would click the mouse.

Dead links. 404 pages. Content locked. Access denied. But if he dug, if he searched hard enough, if he followed the breadcrumbs, he could find traces. Stains left behind, forever marked onto the inky blackness.

That was how he found it. The story. The room of cloth.

No. How it found him.

If you read it, they say, you go insane. You go crazy.

don't be stupid. it's just a story. can't make you go crazy.

i don't like to mess with that shit theres some shit you don't mess with

watever wats it about??

yeh, whats it about!

Who knows no one's read it.

where is it can u find it?

No.

maybe

yEs

But it's not finished.
whut u mean?
It's never finished.
what
never
FINISHED
never finish

8 .

"Move dinner? Why?"

Sarah turned off the faucet, let the last of the plates soak in the soapy water of the sink. She dried her hands, rubbed the cracks across her palms, on her fingertips. She reached for the open trash bag and tied it up. The bag stunk of grape jelly and coffee grains.

"I'm going out Thursday night," Sebastian said. "Meeting up with a friend of mine."

"A friend."

"Yeah. What, you gonna start?"

She didn't spare him the look. Hardly home a week, and he was already disappearing whole days, already meeting up with "friends." It took everything in her not to slap him. That dumb, sheepish look. The puppy eyes. If she wanted a dog, she would have fucking bought one.

"Fine," she said. "So, when do we go instead? To-night?"

He seemed about to protest, but he kept his mouth shut. That was the thing. He couldn't bite the hand too often. If he wanted to stay with her, if he wanted to mooch, he had to play by her rules. That was her one consolation.

53

"Sure," he said quietly. "Tonight."

All throughout the day, at stoplights, at the front of her classroom, at the grocery store, Sarah thought about the upcoming dinner. She realized a long time ago that she could never really know her brother. Before the night he stabbed their father to death—since the day he was born, in fact—he had disgusted her. She remembered being six years old, standing by her mother's bedside and looking on, horrified, at the doughy, red *thing* in the pink blanket. A sci-fi mutant. A little monster. *That* had been curled up inside her mother all those months? *This* was the little brother she was supposed to love and take care of? That first night, as she listened to him crying in the next room, something even worse occurred to her: *she* had been just like that. She had grown inside her mother's belly. She had slid out, red and sticky. She had likely bawled and screamed. *Everyone* had.

She didn't sleep for days after that.

The crying didn't help. Day in, day out, all he did was cry. No matter how often their mother cradled him, cooed him, fed him, he wouldn't stop. After a while, Sarah just stood beside the crib and watched him. Finally, she figured it out. The warbling tongue, the pale gums, the dribbling drool—of course he was crying. No one would like being trapped in that tiny body. Trying to talk. Trying to see. Trying to get out. Confused by everything, and scared, terrified. Their father had been in the room once, watching Sebastian, sipping beer. "Little pussy," he growled, though Sarah didn't know what he meant at the time. Then he turned and put a hand on her head. "You didn't cry. Never heard a peep outta you." He grinned. "Still don't."

The noise didn't get any better as Sebastian got older. The noise only changed. At best, he was some annoying, whiny voice in her periphery, a little, big-eyed imp constantly in the way. How many times did he try getting into her things? To go with her when she went out? To talk to her? He haunted the halls of that godforsaken house. Waiting for her in the foyer when she got back from a late-night drive. Taking her CDs. Dropping her nail polish. Choking on her gum. Lighting her cigarettes. Finding the goddamn birth control pills. Jesus, he was everywhere. Always peeking around corners. Always following her like a shadow. Even if she didn't see him, she could hear the pitter-patter of his feet. A little rat scurrying in the dark. She kept her door locked at night. Kept headphones on to block out the screaming and shouting coming from the kitchen. Eventually, the yelling would stop. Eventually, his clawing would stop, too.

The house was empty while Sebastian was at the psychiatric hospital. Her mother was there, but she hardly counted. If she had been a wreck before her husband's death, a doll to be hit and snarled at, she wasn't much better afterwards. Shrill, fragile, like a parrot that wouldn't stop repeating the same thing. Sarah listened to her squawk and squawk and squawk day after day and night after night. What did it matter if Sebastian was gone and her father dead? The noise didn't go away. It just changed again. Sarah went back to being a prisoner. Only now she was the one who had to cook and clean instead of her mother. Only now she was the one who worried. That damn house just had its way. She couldn't get free of it, couldn't escape it. Funny how it was like her father never left. She could still hear his yells and his awful laugh as long as she was there. She could still smell his breath, full of the stink of beer and the reek of rotten teeth. She still locked the door to her room at night. She still put on the headphones.

Then Sebastian came home, and the joke got even funnier. She was the one doing the chasing now, trying to get him to stay put, to talk to her. She never went with him, and maybe that was her mistake. She knew of his world, sure. She grew up on its fringes. She watched the news, read the paper. She saw the missing persons reports, heard about the rising homicide count. The kids talked about it a lot during class. How things were changing. How they were getting worse. Even people she knew from school had turned up dead. One in a gutter. One in a bathroom. A few wound up in prison. Once in a while, pops went off in the night. No one wondered very much what they meant. They were just another reason to raise the volume. To clamp the headphones down tight.

Now, both their parents were gone. Now, the house was gone, or at least waiting to get torn down. It was condemned, part of that old section of the city that just got bigger and bigger every year. The place had been falling apart, anyway. Better that it be done away with.

Better that time just ate it up. "Things move on," Louisa told her once while they waited in the drive-thru for some hamburgers, with that faux philosophical air she adopted sometimes. "Things change, and people get left behind. That's how it is."

That was true. But then everything had a habit of coming back. People came back. Sebastian came back. She came back. She tried so hard for so long to run, to get away, but there wasn't any escaping. She deserved this. She let that little, big-eyed imp get lost in the dark. She left him out there, with all that screaming and shouting. That's why she had to try. Why she had to keep trying. Why she couldn't keep the door locked anymore. Why she hoped that sooner or later, he would crawl into bed with her, just like he always wanted to do. Wasn't that what regular brothers and sisters did? Wasn't that how they kept each other safe?

To Sebastian's credit, he was at the apartment when she got back that afternoon. He had on an old, white dress shirt—remarkable for Sebastian's standards. The shirt was too big, but better than some ratty long-sleeve or torn jacket. He had slapped water on his hair, combed it.

"You look good," she said. "Better than I expected."

"Yeah, sure. Can we just go already?"

The drive to the restaurant—a new, relatively classy seafood place, The Trident—was silent. The dead air between them felt worse tonight for some reason, festering the longer they were together. Every time Sarah looked over at Sebastian, his eyes were out the window, far away. His fingers drummed on the seat. His leg moved up and down irritably. Occasionally, he clawed at his cheek, cringed from some unknown pain. He could put on a shirt, try to fix his hair halfheartedly, but he wasn't *there*. He wasn't with her. How could she bring him around?

"So, what'd you do today?" she asked, trying to break the silence.

"Not much. Just hung around."

"You didn't go by the donut shop? I told you they were looking for somebody."

"Yeah. I forgot."

She fought hard to keep quiet.

Once they got to the restaurant, the hostess sat them down at a table in the back. The restaurant was markedly, pointedly red—red carpet, red drapes, red tablecloths. To Sarah, the red looked like caked, congealed blood in the dim light. A sea of blood, buoys sticking out, flashing their dull, orange lights in the fog. Fish floating on the surface, bones exposed, glassy eyes blank and even ruptured, a mist of flies hanging low over their bodies. The smell of the corpses was subtle at first, but increasingly pungent, like meat left in the sun to rot and attract scavengers. She thought the smell her imagination, but no, it permeated the restaurant. She had to pinch herself to recognize the dead fish weren't there. The sea of blood wasn't there. There were no flies, no buoys. Yet the smell remained. The same smell, she realized, that wafted through her apartment when she had a moment to sit and draw a breath. The same smell that followed her to the car every morning—every morning since Sebastian returned. What was it? Weed? Something else?

Sebastian stared at his menu, turned it over, pushed it away. "The fuck are scallops?" he asked. "Sound nasty. Like something from a porno."

"Keep it down," Sarah hissed, and then, with a sigh, "They're like clams. Oysters."

"Oysters? Shit. We couldn't get a burger or something?"

"This was important to me," Sarah said. "For finding out my brother was still alive, for wanting to make him feel at home, I felt fast food was just a little inappropriate. All right? Is that good enough for you?"

Sebastian laughed. "You're a real riot, Sarah, you know that? Who gives a shit? Like, seriously, *this* is your idea of going big? Look at this dump. Just a bunch of fakers."

"If you want my suggestion, go with the fried shrimp." She looked at the carpet again. Sharks in the red. Octopuses. Jellyfish. People. And the smell, more intense than ever.

"Whatever. Are they gonna get our drinks or not? I'm thirsty."

"Can you please just calm down?" Finally, Sarah looked at him, looked right at him, but she couldn't hold her gaze. All she saw was the empty-faced boy from the psychiatric hospital. The little, big-eyed imp creeping about the dark of the old house. The doughy, red thing in the pink blanket. A blank space. A hole cut out of her life.

"I'm sorry," she said. "We just can't have a normal conversation, can we?"

"You're the one that freaks out. I'll talk if you want."

"All right. You can answer some questions. Where've you been this whole time? What have you been doing?"

"You want the real story or a fake one?"

"I'd like to hear the truth."

"Okay. Don't say I didn't warn you. There was this guy I knew. Billy. He got a good connect and wanted to sell it. Said it was good dope, but it turned out to be shit. Said he'd split it with me. So, that's where I was, in fucking Boston dealing for that guy. Taking his shit, dealing with his problems while he screwed around."

Sarah closed her eyes and winced. With effort, she looked back at him. "So, you came back because it didn't work out."

"Dealing and shit," Sebastian said, "it ain't all it's cracked up to be. And now there's something else. There's something better—"

He stopped talking as the waiter came by and took their orders. After the waiter walked off, Sebastian shrugged. "That's the story. Happy now? Feel some peace of mind?"

Sarah sat quietly. Dealing drugs. Without guilt. Without remorse. She wanted to believe she could change things, fix him, and maybe she could, but where did one start? What did one do? Too much time had passed. There was too much distance between them.

Sebastian must have noticed her crestfallen expression because when he spoke next, the edge had worn off his voice, replaced by a surprising tenderness. "I was trying to tell you before, but things are gonna change, Sarah. I can't say a lot, but you gotta believe me. Something amazing's gonna happen. It's already happening."

"All right," said Sarah. The food arrived, and it was dull—her plate a grilled fillet that looked like cardboard, his plate some cold, plastic-like shrimp. Still, he swallowed each shrimp in single bites, downed mouthfuls of rice. He ate as though possessed. Sarah, meanwhile, could hardly muster an appetite. The day had drained her. And now that she was here, sitting across from him, actually engaged in some semblance of conversation, she only felt more lost.

On the ride back, she wanted to ask him what he did at night while locked in his room, the faint glow of the laptop coming from underneath the door crack. She wanted to ask if he smelt that terrible stench, if it wasn't just her imagination. But she didn't say a word. He said things were going to change, that they were already changing, but she didn't believe him. When she looked at him, all she saw was a black hole in the passenger seat, not even a person, just a hole in the air. Empty space.

No. Worse than that. Absolutely nothing at all.

9 .

Sebastian bolted up in his bed and nearly knocked over the laptop. "Fucking alarm," he snapped. He groped for the bedside clock and turned it off. The face of the clock was cracked, the once-shiny, gilded surface cloudy and chipped. A souvenir he snatched from Caesar's garage.

The time had come to meet the fabled Otto. He shut off the laptop and shoved the scattered manuscript pages back into their envelope. Another couple of hours wasted trying to write. Another good bag of coke wasted, too. He squashed the envelope and bag under the floorboard, but the floorboard didn't set right. He pushed and kicked fruitlessly. Finally, he just sighed and licked his teeth.

"Fuck it."

He threw a shirt over the space and left.

Sarah had been unusually quiet in the days since the dinner. Sebastian felt bad on some level—something about the dinner hadn't felt right, like something went wrong—but the less she was on his case, the better. Especially now that things were moving along. The problem was that it was taking longer to work on the story than he first thought. He wasn't a writer. He didn't know the first thing about it. Seemed so easy from the outside—just put words down, make shit up. Anybody could do that, right? But most of the time, he just stared at the screen like a dumbass, waiting for something to happen, something to click. Coming up with material was easier when he was high, but the drugs were running out, and it wasn't making much of a difference, anyway. He needed a solution, or the story was never going to get done. He needed Bryan Stevens.

When he wasn't writing, he was leeching off the neighbor's wireless, trying to get in touch with Stevens—or, as Sebastian knew him better, viper961. But viper had been missing online for weeks, not answering e-mails, not responding to chat invites, not hanging around his usual haunts. Other users said the same thing. He'd vanished.

Maybe he was dead?

That was the way it worked, supposedly. If you read the story, you died. Didn't matter if it was a page, a paragraph, a sentence, or even a single word. Didn't matter if you only heard the words being spoken. The story always took you. But the people who disappeared came back. They would send an e-mail weeks later, post a picture after months or even years. But the e-mails and pictures wouldn't be normal. The messages would be cryptic and broken. The pictures would be hazy, as if taken from a battered webcam or an old camcorder. Sometimes, a video would be posted, anywhere from seconds long to a few minutes. The footage was always of the same thing: a room covered in dull, beige fabric. No, not covered. Made of fabric. Made of cloth.

No doors. No windows. Just a padded cell. Often, the room was empty, but sometimes, there would be things inside. Mangled bodies with the spines twisted, the arms and legs torn off, bones jutting from the wounds. Blood oozing black down the walls, covering the floor. Rusted hooks hanging from the ceiling, clanking against one another. Hands pressing against the walls from inside, trying to get out. Faces screaming in silent agony. And the messages, if they weren't just random letters, numbers, or symbols: We're here. He's waiting. He's watching.

Underneath every message or video would be a hyperlink, which was supposed to lead to a text dump or a download page. An eternity of bliss, the users promised. Come on in. Join the fun. The more outrageous versions of the story had big, red letters pop out once you clicked on the link, saying you were going to be killed or haunted. Some even had chains shooting out of the screen, hooking into your flesh, dragging you literally into the fucking computer.

Those were Sebastian's favorites.

He used to think it was all bullshit. The stories were so crazy, they had to be untrue. But then he met viper961. Then he read a piece of the manuscript. And when he read it, he knew deep down in his core that the room of cloth was real, not a hoax, most certainly not a meme. Maybe the shit about chains and spooky e-mails wasn't real, but the story itself—the fucking *story*! That was real. The room of cloth was real. No one would believe, though, unless they read the writing themselves. Unless they saw with their own eyes the undeniable truth.

Now all that remained was one last e-mail from viper, not asking, but *telling* Sebastian to find him. His real name was allegedly Bryan Stevens, out of Hoboken, New Jersey. Only there could be countless guys with that name in Hoboken alone. That's why he needed help. He needed money, transportation. He needed addresses, jobs, phone numbers, anything to narrow down the search. This Otto guy could be the key to finding those things, to getting past all the other noise in the way.

Nonetheless, Sebastian couldn't deny there was fear. What if the stories about death and suicide were true? Would he be taken? Would he be among those phantom posts, those messages and videos from beyond the grave? But behind that fear and uncertainty was excitement, almost joy. To glimpse something transcendent—something actually, genuinely *real*, beyond the surface of appearances—was worth the risk of death. And honestly, what did he really stand to lose? What had this life given him?

"I'm going out," he said at the door to Sarah's bedroom. He waited, bracing for the inevitable speech, but all was quiet on the other side, and the door was locked. So, he just fastened his earbuds, donned his sunglasses, and left.

Caesar was waiting at his condo. "'Bout time," he said. "You ready?" His crisp shirt, tucked into a pair of starched jeans, took Sebastian by surprise. It was the first time he'd ever seen Caesar put any thought into how he looked.

"I know what you're thinking," Caesar said, "but we gotta sell ourselves right. Otto, he's gonna be looking at all that. You gotta show him you're professional."

"I'll do whatever, long as he helps me," said Sebastian. "I don't care about the rest."

"Seb, you gotta take this seriously. It ain't just you. It's me, too. You look bad, I look bad. I look bad, and shit comes down on me."

"Relax, okay? It'll be fine. Now, are we gonna go or keep moaning about it?"

They drove out of the garage in Caesar's van. By then, the sky was pitch black, but as they weaved deeper downtown, the horizon became lighter and started to pulsate red and violet. "There it is," Caesar said, sucking on a cigarette. "Otto's club. Rhapsody."

They drove up slowly. Cars clogged the streets around the building. A line of clubbers snaked from the entrance, bathed in hazy, purple light. Caesar parked in a nearby alleyway and turned off the van.

"All right," he said. "We play it cool, and maybe Otto'll help us out."

They got out and walked over to the club. "We'll go 'round back," said Caesar, the hip-hop coming from inside the club deafening. Sebastian followed him to a pair of double doors at the back of the building, where a bouncer waited.

"Otto's waiting for you in his office," the bouncer said.

Caesar nodded. "Thanks, Mike." They went in, and Sebastian recoiled instantly. The flashing lights, red then purple then blue, blinded him even with his sunglasses. The gyrating bodies on the dance floor were silhouetted against pinks and purples. The sweet smells of wine and liquor were thick in the air. There was howling, growling, screaming. Pills spilled across tabletops. Beer splashed on leather upholstery. He saw mannequins in the crowd, headless apparitions, fire-breathing, laughing mouths. There were chains, ball gags, riding crops. The lights burned. The walls bled. The shadows writhed and flailed.

Sebastian kept his head down. He was sweating hard and grinding his teeth. Reluctantly, he followed Caesar up a narrow stairway. Two sentries stopped them in front of a door. "He's in there," whispered Caesar. "Remember, I do the talking."

The sentries let them into a spacious office just as dark as the rest of the club. Streaks of red and blue light came in through a pair of windows overlooking the dance floor, and a haze of smoke hovered over the room. There were faint suggestions in the smoke: an enormous desk, a vault in the back, a man with dreadlocks in a dark suit, a woman off to the side, dress straps slipping off, mascara smeared. A violent splash of red lit up the office as though the room were on fire, flames coursing up the windows and lapping at the ceiling. The light revealed a third figure, a man behind the desk, arm propped up, a single silver ring shining on his forefinger. He looked at them—for a second, Sebastian thought his eyes blazed yellow.

"Caesar," the man said, rising. He was tall, black, broad-shouldered, built like a machine. His voice was heavy, maybe rehearsed. His white shirt and trousers were plain and simple. From appearances alone, there was nothing special about him, nothing extraordinary, but when he came around and leaned against the desk, like he owned it, like he *knew* he owned it—when he grinned and flashed teeth so white they might have been ceramic—Sebastian wanted to scream. All of a sudden, the heat inside the office was unbearable, the smoke suffocating. He felt around his collar and struggled to loosen his jacket.

Beside him, Caesar cleared his throat, fought his own shaking muscles and trembling lips. "Otto," he said, putting on a strained smile. "I brought the guy I was telling you about."

"Yeah, I see him." Otto smiled and watched. "You've noticed my right-hand man. Why don't you introduce yourself, Bless? Our friend here—Sebastian, right?—he's gonna know you soon enough."

The man with the dreadlocks came forward, slim and weaselly in a blue suit. When he smirked, one of his teeth glistened gold. "Nice to meet you, baby," he said. "Didn't know Caesar was going for white meat now."

The woman off to the side let out a sudden laugh. Sebastian looked at her and trembled, but Otto's eyes never left him. His easy smile widened.

"She's Candice. But don't worry about her. I don't want you nervous." His eyes flicked over to the woman. "Get out of here. I got business."

Her smile dropped. "But Otto—"

"Don't make me repeat myself."

She slunk out.

"Thinks she can impress me with her tits," Otto said, "like she's something special. But there are hundreds like her outside, all just waiting for a chance. I don't have time for them. It's why I keep my circle very small and very close. Know what I mean?"

Neither Sebastian nor Caesar said anything. Otto laughed.

"You're nervous," he said. "I get it. Caesar probably told you I was dangerous. But I'm also generous. Caesar's been good since I got here. He's been a good worker. Anyone he vouches for I'm willing to hear out."

"Really?" asked Sebastian, barely audible.

"Of course. You know, I can smell the fear. It might stink, but it's honest. It tells me more about you than anything you could say." He gestured to a couple of chairs. "Go on, sit. Relax. Want a drink?"

"Uh, no." Sebastian waited, watched Caesar sit down. He followed suit.

Otto returned to the back of his desk and poured himself a glass of whiskey. The whiskey fell in hard splashes.

"Caesar?" he asked.

Caesar shook his head. "Nah, I'm good. Thanks, Otto."

Otto said nothing, just grinned and downed the glass in one gulp. "So," he said, pouring himself another, "Caesar tells me you two go way back?"

Sebastian was quiet, still shaking. Caesar widened his eyes at him expectedly.

"Yeah," Sebastian choked out. "Way back."

"You used to work for Caesar?"

Sebastian looked over at Caesar, who started talking nervously. "Seb was, uh, the best I had. He sold for me—"

"Let him tell it," Otto said. Caesar shut up. Off to the side, Bless was still smiling. He lit a cigarette and started puffing on it.

"I worked for Caesar, yeah." Sebastian felt the eyes on him, the expectation. His stomach turned to jelly, his mouth to dust. "I sold a lot. Looked out on the street. Got money to people. Things like that."

Otto considered. "You ever use a gun?"

"No. Caesar didn't let us near that stuff."

"When I was starting out, that's all we knew," Otto said. "Bodies. Sometimes it was ugly. Guys beaten up, burned alive. Girls with eyes missing. One guy I knew had half his face sliding off like butter. You ever seen that?"

"Um, yeah. Sort of."

"Really? You seen a face come off like that?"

"No, I mean—"

He and Bless laughed. "Relax, *hermano*," Otto said. "Isn't that what Caesar would say? I'm fucking with you. I ain't seen that shit. Have you, Bless?"

"Might've dumped some acid on a guy's face," Bless said. "Can't remember."

"Acid, lead, it's all the same. Truth is, no one thinks about dying. Until you do. One day, you're alive. You're eating, you're sleeping, you're smelling, and then all of a sudden"—he snapped his fingers—"lights out."

Sebastian squirmed. Weird how he was so fucking scared, and not just him, either—Caesar clutched the arms of his chair with white knuckles. Caesar was always nervous, but this nervous? And the impression of being evaluated, toyed with—like floating in the ocean, surrounded by four or five great whites, their fucking fins circling and closing in little by little. What was it about this Otto guy? Big, yeah, a smooth talker, but also dangerous. Stories were stories, but Sebastian felt finally there was some truth to them. Him and this Bless guy were killers. Real, bona fide killers. They were like wolves waiting for the opportunity to strike.

"But enough of that," said Otto. "Caesar says it was off and on with you. Sometimes you would just take off. That true?"

"I wasn't always working for him," Sebastian said. "Sure, I left, but I always took care of my shit. It's hard for me to stick around one place, but I get things done."

"This last time, Caesar says you were in Boston. What about that?"

Sebastian took a breath, started talking. "There was this guy. Billy. He used to hang with us. He got a connect, said he was going to Boston to make his mark. His shit was good, so I went with him. I handled selling, and he took care of all the other stuff."

"And the whole time you were out there, you didn't get your hands dirty? Alone, no friends, a good product—that must have gotten attention."

"We kept it quiet. We made it work, at least for a while. Listen, that guy was an asshole. I fucked up going out there. But if you wanna know I'm good, I just told you. Give me a job, I'll do it. You need something done, I'll do it. We trade like that."

"Straight to the point. You made him sound like a flake, Caesar."

"He gets some balls once he warms up," Caesar said, chancing a smile.

Otto leaned back, looked up at the ceiling. Purple light flooded the room. "I can help you. Depending on what you need."

"I gotta find a guy," Sebastian said. "I have a name, a place, but that's it. I need to narrow it down. I won't get anywhere if I don't."

"Why?"

Sebastian was quiet. What little confidence he had developed dwindled in light of mentioning the manuscript, in light of revealing the room of cloth.

"It's complicated," he said.

Otto laughed. "That's funny. You want me to give you a job and find this guy for you—maybe threaten my own business—and you won't tell me why? That's a lot to ask."

"I'll do whatever you want," Sebastian said. "Anything. Just help me find him."

He waited for an answer. His right hand shook. His leg pumped up and down, running on energy he didn't have. He could feel himself closing the distance, scared as he was. Bryan Stevens. viper961. The rest of the manuscript. The room of cloth. The end of the story. Closer. Closer. *Closer.*

At last, Otto spoke, all smiles, all charm. "I'll get your info. But it doesn't come free. You have to do something for me first."

"Sure. Whatever you want."

"It's nothing too important. You can help Caesar do it. There's a friend of mine—a business partner, let's say. Name's Polo Arenaz. They call him Pollito."

"*Pollo,*" Caesar remarked. "Chicken."

"He collects money for me," Otto said, "like you used to do for Caesar. He's been good. We haven't had any problems until now. See, he tried to fool me. He got lazy, a little greedy. Thought he could rip me off a couple hundred. Just a little scrape off the top, you know. Not enough to be a big deal."

He reached for the whiskey again. "You could say it's just money, and you'd be right. I don't give a shit about money. A scrape off the top—hell, that could be a million, two million. It's not about that. It's about respect. Decency. Good business. And I want him to know good business. You hear that, Caesar?"

"I hear it," said Caesar lowly.

"Good. Take the kid with you. He might learn a thing or two." Otto drank down his glass, then looked at Sebastian. "You do this for me, and you'll have your guy. What's the name?"

The answer was instant. "Bryan Stevens. Hoboken, New Jersey."

"That is one generic fucking name," Otto said, "but I can do it. It'll take a few days. Enough time for you two to get this done."

"About that," said Sebastian. "This chicken guy— what are we doing to him?"

"Nothing too bad. You just follow Caesar's lead, all right? Make him hurt a little bit. Remind him how we conduct business in this city now."

Bless was behind them suddenly, his hands on their chairs. "That takes care of the powwow, sweeties," he said. "Time to jet."

"You'll have to excuse me," Otto said. "Bless and I have business to discuss. And I have to tend to the club. But we're settled for now, Mr. Creed. You help Caesar teach Mr. Arenaz some lessons in respect, and you'll have your information. An even trade, I think."

"Sure," said Sebastian. He stood up, eager to be outside. "We'll do it."

"Good. Be seeing you."

Bless ushered them out and shut the doors behind them. Sebastian shivered and wiped his brow. He had been sweating, but he didn't feel warm at all. He actually felt cold, like he'd been standing in snow totally naked for hours.

"Real big on that godfather shit, huh?" he asked, walking out of the club. "Thought we were gonna kiss his ring or something."

He looked to Caesar, hoping the bravado would ease the tension. But Caesar was silent, shaking badly, just barely able to light a cigarette and hold it to his mouth. He pinched his eyes shut and let the cigarette fall.

"Fuck it," he said. "I need a drink."

They went back to the van, then returned to Caesar's condo.

10.

No one knew exactly what the manuscript was about. Perhaps a doomsday manual, some suggested, a bible for the end of the world, depicting hell on earth. Lava running through streets, smothering buildings, engulfing crowds. Meteors hurtling through the sky, crashing into towns, cities, and oceans. Black, scaled beasts emerging from the earth. Tsunamis leveling mountains. Typhoons ripping through stone and cement. Hordes of locusts, wasps, and flies blotting out the sun. Mushroom clouds. Acid fogs. Whole population centers wiped out instantly. Hordes of bodies flying into the air like ragdolls. Entire continents sinking into the sea. Everyone—young or old, male or female—swallowed by the planet.

Others said the manuscript had to be something more psychological, more subliminal. The ramblings of someone insane. The diary of a serial killer. The chronicle of a slow descent into madness. Conversations that went nowhere. Discussions designed to infuriate. Rants about global warming, fashion, sports, music, diseases, video games, terrorism, big business, aliens, artificial intelligence. A spiral that went nowhere and everywhere.

And yet there was further disagreement. Deliberate madness can't be madness, one party argued. Insanity couldn't be by design, nor could insanity be smelt or heard or tasted or understood. They claimed the text had to be something more authentic—something that didn't seem crazy, but actually was. Just a normal novel, something one would find on a bookstore shelf—but *wrong*. Sentences without end. Periods in all the wrong places. Lines crossed out. Pages printed in different colors, in different languages, in made-up languages. Maybe deeper than that. Images baked into the pages themselves that could be seen only under certain lights, with only certain chemicals. Hidden messages encoded throughout the text. Passwords and keys funneled across chatrooms and forums. Only the chosen ones were able to crack the secret—and when they did, they found out something awful, something horrible. The truth about reality. The meaning of life. Or maybe the lack of meaning. The creator. The creation. The failed experiment. That would explain the disappearances, wouldn't it? After all, people don't just disappear. There has to be a good reason. Something really dramatic. Something really *scary*.

Some thought the story should be cursed. Just a normal book that some creepy guy nabbed from a library. He ripped off the cover, smeared the pages with goat blood, chanted some Latin or Theban, threw the book into a fire. But the book wouldn't burn. Something got inside. The would-be occultist tore the pages up, scattered them, went mad. But people found the pieces.

They spread the story. He told them to spread it. He? Yes. The occultist? No. Then who? He did. He who resides in the room of cloth.

The truth, Sebastian found as he read, was that the manuscript wasn't any of these things—not a doomsday manual, not a crazy journal, not a possessed pocketbook. Not even strictly a novel, nor a traditional story. Inside the text were many things, many people. The part given to him by Bryan Stevens started with a regular family in Minnesota, the Bretfords. And the Bretfords were dead.

11

The Bretfords were the quintessential American family. Dad Jim watched baseball and hockey, cooked out every Sunday, played ball with his son, worked as manager at a local retail store. Mom Pam cooked and cleaned, took care of the baby, watched soap operas in the evening. Big sister Kennedy listened to hard rock, wore black eyeliner, complained about how unfair her life was. Little brother Jim, Jr. played hockey, acted in the school theater, watched scary movies. Baby Liam cried and drank milk. Daisy the dog chased her tail.

Dinners ended occasionally with Kennedy storming off and shutting herself in her room. Jim pestered the others to turn off lights. Pam invited friends over on Tuesdays and worried about her weight. Jim, Jr. won trophies for both hockey and theater. Sometimes the family would visit the grandparents upstate. Kennedy hated those road trips. Jim, Jr. loved them. Pam had to air herself out every few hours or else she would lose her lunch over the dashboard.

Whenever the Bretfords came up in conversation around town, the subject was always about how success-ful Jim was, or how composed Pam was, or how Jim, Jr.

was such a star athlete, or how the baby was such a cutie pie. Few people talked about Kennedy—she was the ugly duck, the black sheep. "How'd such a nice family pop her out?" some would ask. "How could they go wrong?"

The family maintained a nice veneer, a pleasant picture, but things were unsteady beneath the surface. Some nights, Jim wouldn't come home for hours. When he finally did climb into bed, still dressed in his work clothes, he usually smelt of alcohol and was probably at least a few hundred dollars deeper in the red. Money wasn't the only issue. Jim hadn't found out about Pam's affair yet, but what would he do if he did? What if he was drunk? What if he hit her, like he had in the past? What would the kids do? Would they hate her? She thought about these things while watching television, washing clothes, feeding the baby, staring out at the dog in the backyard. She couldn't stop herself.

Kennedy was seeing someone older, a twenty-three-year-old guy named Chuck. She knew he was a loser, but he made her feel so good. He introduced her to more than just sex: drugs, alcohol, all sorts of concoctions one could use to get away. She didn't have to listen to the nighttime arguments when she was under the spell of some potion, didn't have to feel so immensely alone when another world was just a pill away. There was a more permanent solution, of course, but she couldn't stomach the thought of not waking up. Of not coming back.

Things were like that for a while, until one day Jim, Jr. came inside with a package. It was outside, he said. Like someone just left it there. A cardboard box, ruddy, a little damp. A few measly straps of tape kept the lid closed, and there weren't any notes or labels. Kennedy joked that there should be something ominous written across the front in black ink. Don't open it, she laughed. It's cursed!

Something about the box did feel off. Pam was struck with fear just by looking at it. She insisted they not open it, instead just throw it back outside, leave it somewhere far, far away. But Jim took one look at the box and was enthralled. He cut open the top, and out came this *smell*. It reminded Kennedy of blood. Pam thought of a meat locker, of her grandfather's old slaughterhouse. Dry, stinking slabs of meat hanging from hooks. Blood and grime flowing down a drain. She ran upstairs and puked.

Inside the box was a dog-eared spiral notebook. One-subject, wide-ruled, seventy pages. The front cover was blue, and, if held up to the light, the Bretfords could make out faint indentations, like the cover had been written on. The markings were difficult to determine—there were definitely letters, what looked like stick figures. Jim said later that for such a small notebook, it felt heavy. Not physically heavy, not like a rock or a weight, but *heavy*. He couldn't describe it any other way.

There was anticipation as he prepared to open it. The whole family sans Pam and the baby crowded around. But when he finally did open the notebook, there wasn't anything dramatic. No lights flickered. No sudden chill crept over them. There were just writings, drawings, equations. Every page, front and back, was covered in hard-to-read scribbles, hasty notations, and rough sketches. Jim just stared at it, just held it, and from that moment on, the notebook was with him wherever he went. He never left it out of his sight, never let anyone else even touch it. He read it in bed, flipped through it at work, even took it to the restroom. The notebook was always on his mind. When he made notes to himself, he found his pen sketching, drawing spirals, cubes, figures bound in chains. When he wrote e-mails at work, he would stop and realize he had typed whole paragraphs, entire pages, all from the notebook. Sometimes, he caught himself before he sent the messages out. Other times, he didn't.

He drank more, yelled more, cursed more. Pam stopped sleeping in their bedroom, complaining of that awful smell clogging the air. Like raw meat left out in the sun, she said. She slept with little Liam, took some comfort in knowing he was close to her. Kennedy asked Jim what was in the notebook, why it was such a big deal, but he would just stare at her. It's *mine*, he'd say. It belongs to *me*.

Jim started shedding pounds, started growing paler. Daisy, once the friendliest dog, barked at him, growled, kept her distance. He called in more sick days than usual, and he even stopped going out at night. But things just got worse. He hit Jim, Jr., screamed at Liam, very nearly strangled Pam when he found her about to grab the notebook from his bedside. He kept it locked in a personal safe after that, but it was still almost always with him. Next to him on the couch, on his lap when driving, under his arm while walking around. Pam made plans to leave and take the kids to her sister's. In secret, Kennedy arranged to run off with Chuck. They'd make it work somehow, he promised her, and she believed him. She *had* to believe him. Anything was better than staying in that house.

Finally, the night came. She snuck out, backpack over her shoulder, suitcase in hand. Chuck was waiting outside, and they sped off. Kennedy had no idea that within the same hour, Jim came out of his room with his hunting rifle. She had no idea he went outside first and blew Daisy's head off. She had no idea he climbed up the stairs to her brother's room and did the same to him. She had no idea her mother tried to protect the baby and had her stomach blown through in the process. She had no idea Jim pointed the barrel of the gun at Liam's crying face and pulled the trigger.

Something gnawed at her, made her want to turn the car around. Chuck was hesitant, but finally, he did as she told him. They crept back inside, her hiding behind him, him shaking with the cheap gun he'd brought along. They went room by room through the house, found the bodies, saw the blood. Kennedy screamed, clutched her dead brother in her arms, went hysterical at the sight of her mother and the baby. But the master bedroom was the worst. Chuck turned on the lights and almost vomited on the spot. The walls were covered in blood and guts, painted entirely red. Jim lay eagle-spread on the bed, one of his hands and both of his feet sawed off. The hacksaw was still tight in his other fist. He had been dead for at least fifteen minutes, but his eyes were wide, and his mouth was open in a big laugh.

Kennedy had never seen him so happy.

12.

The night after meeting with Otto, Sebastian and Caesar sat in the van on a barren street. A block away was a worn-down tenement building booming with muffled rap, the windows of its top floor flashing red, green, and blue.

"Pollito" was in there.

The plan was simple: stake him out, beat him, maybe wait for a crowd to make the message stronger. Sebastian thought he would be scared, but he was actually excited, thrilled. And the real reward was still waiting: Bryan Stevens and the rest of the manuscript. He could finally make sense of the thing. He could figure out how to finish it.

For four hours, they had been parked underneath a shattered streetlight, swathed in shadows. The only light came from another streetlight in front of the building, an orange halo that would make Pollito easy to see once he came out. Caesar said that spotting him wouldn't be a problem since he had a red mohawk. "Get it," he said, "like a chicken?"

Sebastian slouched in the passenger seat, hood up, sunglasses on, crumbs speckled across his lap. He burped and reached for another bag of chips on the dashboard.

Caesar was in a parka of his own, all black. He alternated between swigs from a flask and puffs from a blunt, his bloodshot eyes never leaving the halo of light that marked the building's entrance. Crumpled beer cans littered the floor around his seat. The thick, weighty smell of alcohol only intensified with every hour. Mixed in with that stench was the strong odor of weed—they passed the blunt between themselves, lighting new ones as time went on.

"The fuck was I saying," Caesar said, sniffling. "Oh, yeah. Fuckin' Maury. Had no game. He was shy. Shyer than you, Seb."

"I'm not fucking shy."

"Yeah, you are. You shrink up, get all tiny. I ain't never even seen you with a girl, man."

"Whatever. What about Maury? What's the deal with him?"

"Maury, yeah—fuckin' Maury. We were helping this friend of ours move. It was a shitty weekend, just things going bad the whole time. I was getting looks from everybody. But it wasn't just our skin, wasn't just our fucking accents. If you're not from a place, it don't matter what you do, what you say—you're kept on the outside. You could be the nicest motherfucker around, and they still look at you the same way. And you *are* on the outside, that's the thing. But you're still a fucking human being, you know that? We're all the same under God, but these guys, Seb, these fucking *putos*, they just hate you, they hate you so much. And I don't want to be the same way, but sometimes, you just get so angry, so fucking *angry*—"

"*Maury*," Sebastian said. "What the fuck about Maury?"

"Shit. Maury, right." Caesar raised the flask to his lips again. He drank messily, spilled some liquor on his chin. "Maury," he said, wiping it away, laughing. "Maury, right, right! This guy, Seb, you shoulda seen him. We went out to this bar, you know, just having a good time. We wanted to help him out, right? It was like, for the first time in his life, Maury was gonna get some fucking pussy, whether he liked it or not. And you gotta remember, Seb, this guy, he was like a puppy. A little puppy. He'd get so nervous he'd piss himself. He didn't have no control, man, no fucking control. He'd just piss himself. So, anyway, there's this girl at the bar, with just the biggest fucking tits you ever seen in your life. Even I had to admit this girl was fine. Now, Maury, he was just staring at her the whole night, just staring, and we kept making fun of him, kept blasting him, you know, saying all this shit, egging him on. Well, Maury was so wasted, so fucking out of it, he just got up and went over to that chick, and he just fucking grabbed her tits—didn't say a fucking thing, just grabbed 'em, and the next thing we know, he's on the ground, you know, some guy's beating the shit out of him—"

"He just grabbed 'em?" Sebastian laughed. "Holy shit!"

Caesar laughed, too. "You shoulda seen it, man. You shoulda fucking seen it. We were draggin' him out of there, running away from these guys. And the way that chick screamed! All of a sudden, shit was just out of control, like a movie."

He paused. His eyes grew distant. "Later on, we asked him, you know, what the fuck were you doing, Maury? The hell were you thinking? And he just laughed. He just wanted to do something, just wanted to not be the way he was. For that one second, he wanted to be somebody else. He wanted to change."

His words floated up, mingled in the air with the smoke Sebastian exhaled from the blunt.

"You think somebody can change?" Caesar asked.

"I don't know. I don't think about shit like that."

Caesar grabbed the blunt back, took a drag. "What's this book, Seb? Why's it special?"

Sebastian sat silent, thinking. He wanted to say, but he wasn't sure if he even could. Ever since reading that excerpt, something had triggered inside him, some hungry desire. The room of cloth, what was within the room of cloth, was waiting for him. Finally, he was needed. Finally, he belonged. But it wasn't for just anyone. He had been chosen. Hand-picked. To give it away—he couldn't do that. What if he violated his privilege? What if he lost what little access he had?

He geared up his weed-addled brain to formulate the right response. "It's like you said," he explained slowly, "about being outside. Working on this story, the same way all these other people did—that's being inside, man. That's being part of something. I never felt that before."

He cracked open a beer and paused briefly. "There's one time, I guess. When I was real little. I can't even really remember it. It's more like a feeling. Being on the couch with my mom before she got sick. She's got her hand in my hair, and we're just sitting there, watching TV. That's all I can remember, but that's it. The same feeling. That's the closest thing I can think of."

Caesar smiled. "That's nice, man. My mom, my *abuela*—I remember that, too."

They sat in silence after that, smoking and drinking, basking in the warmth of their reminiscing. Sebastian fixated on the memory of his mother, how he felt cuddled up against her side, her fingers stroking his hair and caressing his scalp. There was a smell, too—the cinnamon candies she liked to eat. But again and again, another image intruded: his mother shriveled like a prune, wired to machines, smelling of shit. Sarah forced him to stand at the bedside, forced him to take that mummy's limp, icy hand in his own. Sarah looked on unflinchingly, breathing hard despite the godawful smell, almost as if she were getting off on their own mother dying. "We have to be here for her," she said. Sebastian just laughed. "Why? She was never there for me."

He shoved another handful of chips into his mouth. "Yeah. Fuck that bitch. Couldn't even take a punch."

"What's that?" Caesar's eyes were trained on the streetlight ahead of them.

"My mom," Sebastian said. "My dad would hit her, and she'd go down—"

"Stay here," Caesar said quickly. He finished what was left of his flask in one gulp and then crossed himself.

"The fuck you—" Then Sebastian saw the slim figure heading out of the building, his red mohawk glowing briefly under the streetlight. "Oh, shit! Do we follow him or—"

Sebastian stopped. He saw finally the black gloves Caesar was wearing. He saw the silenced pistol come out from under the seat, saw the safety click off. Then Caesar was out of the van and walking up the street, hood drawn, gun swinging at his side. Sebastian followed reluctantly. Caesar called out.

"Hey, Pollito!"

Pollito turned. He barely made it a couple of steps before the back of his head blew open. Sebastian flew back and hid behind the broken streetlight. No flash, no loud boom. Just a pop, like a quick jet of steam. Just dark, meaty chunks flying into the air.

Caesar walked up to the body, stared down at the twitching fingers, the shattered skull. He raised the gun. Pop, pop, pop. There went the face, the head, the jaw. Pop, pop. Wet, pink flesh. Thick, ruby blood. Bits of gray and bone. He left the mohawk intact. It told the story.

Caesar went straight back to the van. He grabbed the flask, put it to his lips, realized it was empty. Sebastian came back in, dumbstruck.

"Holy shit," he said. "Fuck."

They peeled out from beneath the streetlight and drove away.

13

Sarah was at her desk, once again trying to grade papers and once again unable to focus. Since the dinner with Sebastian, she had been anxious. She knew depression, but this was different. The void in her felt larger, the ache more painful. Reforming her brother had always been a dream, but now the dream seemed hopeless. The gulf between them was larger than she thought.

He was gone, physically sleeping just a few feet away, across a tiny, cramped apartment, but mentally separated by miles, by continents. At night, she would wake up and peek into the hall, and the blue light coming from his room would tell her he was still awake, working on that busted laptop he'd brought in the other day. What was he doing on that thing? Where did he go during the day? Was he selling drugs like he did in Boston? Seeing junkies and dealers? What was that name he mentioned once? Big C? God, the idea made her sick—

"Miss Creed?"

She looked up. A girl stood in the doorway. "Janette," said Sarah. "How are you? Do you need something?"

Janette was one of her sophomores, one of her best. If the girl was absent, it was almost always because of something at home—a mother working two jobs, a baby sister to take care of, a father in jail. Sarah could relate. In her case, she hadn't been a particularly good student, at least not until she realized she would need scholarships to get out of Lorraine, and a lot of them. Good grades hadn't been the best way of getting back at an overbearing mother and a waste of a father. She had turned to the bottle for that, to drugs and boys. Janette was at least smart enough to avoid all that. Hopefully, that wouldn't change.

"I'm okay," said Janette. "Just thought I'd visit. Missed you the past couple of days."

"Yeah, I'm sorry about that. I didn't feel well."

"You're better now?"

"I think so." Sarah sighed, leaned back. "It's my brother. He came back after a long time away. It's been making me nervous."

"I didn't know you had a brother."

"Yes. He has a habit of getting into trouble."

"Sounds like Paul," Janette said. "You know he got home last week? Dumbass got caught—" She blushed. "Sorry."

"It's okay. I heard about it. He stole from a store?"

"Yeah. He's so stupid! Took some candies and bolted. Took it during the day when people could see him, too. He thinks he's this big-shot gangster, but all he takes is some chocolate, and then he comes home and eats our food, doesn't even do his own laundry."

"Paul was one of mine," Sarah said. "He was good."

"Well, not anymore. I'm not gonna be like him. I'm getting out of here, Miss Creed. And when I make enough money, I'm buying my mom and Tina a big house. They won't have to worry about anything after that."

Sarah listened, half-amused, half-pitying. Her own fantasy of escape had been less selfless. A dream of sailing from port to port, an actress here, a singer there. Touring cabaret clubs, stalking runways. Reinventing herself completely. Expunging the memory of the old house. Expelling the little, big-eyed imp who haunted its halls. Never looking back, never conceding. Had Sebastian never taken the knife from the kitchen, never struck their father down, she might never have returned. She would have disappeared like Faulkner's Caddy, a postcard for a hapless third cousin to find among sepia-tinted photo-graphs and dust-laden ledgers. But no. Sebastian had indeed taken the knife. He had indeed struck their father down. And the gravity of this place brought her back, mocking her all the while. No runway for you. No sea-side cottage. The only plane ride had been a one-way ticket back to Maryland. The only reinvention had been that of the rebel girl into the frail woman who lay awake every night, who jumped at the shadows of her own home, who lived in fear of the big-eyed imp—no, now more like a goblin, a troll—forever shackled to her ankle.

Afterwards, before she left the school, she lingered at the door to Louisa's classroom down the hall. The door was locked, the room dark. The twins had been born without any problems, but Louisa would be gone for maternity leave. Sarah placed her left hand on the window, felt the cool of the glass.

Her fingers shook.

When she got back to the apartment, her first impulse was to grab the nearest carton of cigarettes. She paced back and forth in the kitchenette, waiting for the emptiness to ebb, the loneliness to fade, all the while looking at the walls, the ceiling, the floor. Throughout middle school, high school, college, her fantasy included living somewhere the complete opposite of this—maybe a villa by the coast or a cabin in the woods. Somewhere fresh and cold, the air clean, the streets not covered in trash. The goal had always been to *get out*, to disappear into the night and never come back. Even before college, running away would not have been that hard. A suitcase packed with some essentials, her favorite CDs, cash from the jar her mother kept in the kitchen. The funny thing? Sarah kept a jar just like it. And just as she pilfered from her mother's jar, so did Sebastian take from hers.

She opened the door to his room. What was she looking for in here? Some sort of sign? An indication of retribution or penance? You abandoned your family, she thought. You deserve this punishment. Whatever he is, whatever you find, it's your fault. You've only yourself to blame. But there was no sign or indication to be had. Everything was the same. Everything was empty. Shirts and socks scattered over the floor. Posters of metal bands stuck to the walls. The toy robot standing atop the desk.

Everything vacant, everything empty space, like an oil-painted canvas to be ripped away, a prop-ridden sound-stage to be wheeled off. An ocean of absence. A room of dull, off-white walls and nondescript, gray floor underneath the facade.

She brushed aside a sock and sat down on the bed. There was his laptop, half-open. She held up the computer. Cumbersome and heavy, most of the letters on the keys smudged out, the screen cracked in one corner. Still, the laptop worked. She powered it on.

Sebastian always liked computers. Sarah remembered him playing on the old PC they had when they were younger. A big, blocky thing, ancient compared to modern models, but at the time, enough to distract him. Bullies, bad grades, bad dreams—he mentioned many things to her, many things she ignored. And what had her callousness awarded her? What was her "freedom" now that their parents were gone? Long, sleepless nights. An old, rundown apartment. One hundred kids a day staring at her, most of them doomed to live in halfway homes or waste away in cells if they didn't die in an alleyway first. And she couldn't change a single thing. She was a twig in a torrent, a piece of paper in a raging storm.

The laptop's screen lit up, demanded a password. Her fingers froze on the keys. She tried vainly their mother's name, their father's, but she knew those were long shots. She even tried drugs, every possible slang term she could think of. The more attempts she made, the more absurd and desperate they became, the more she realized she was just guessing based on appearances. Her brother was an illusion, a mirage. He faded in and out, there one day, gone the next. Addict. Loner. Junkie. Dropout. Demon. Monster. Son. Brother. They were just labels. *Who* was he? Who was Sebastian Creed?

She set the laptop down, her hands shaking badly—no, just her left hand. She clutched it to her chest, felt tears push inexplicably from her eyes. This black mass inside of her, this sad lump, never struck her so strongly before. She wanted to curl up into a ball and cry, cry her eyes out, but she was stronger than that. No. No crying. No faltering. So, take a break instead, the cigarettes beckoned from back in the kitchenette. Take a tiny puff.

"No," she breathed, steeling her nerves, tightening her muscles. "No, I won't. I won't. I won't, I won't, I won't." One of her mantras. Not very elegant, but effective. A moment later, she was fine, back in control. She stood up.

And then she smelt it.

The same rancid, dead smell from the restaurant, so strong she almost fell back. How could she have missed such a stench when she walked in? The reek was everywhere, so thick she could almost take it into her hands. Grimy, festering, all over her, all over the laptop and the bed and even the sock she pushed aside. Compulsively, she wiped at her sleeves, her skirt, her calves, but the filth stuck to her fingers, to her palms. Dirty, soiled. Like dried sweat. Like caked blood.

So stupid, she thought. So fucking stupid. I've been smelling it. *I've been smelling it.* Sebastian, whenever he came inside, whenever he walked past her, yes, even that night he came back, that burnt smell, that lingering stench of decay followed him. She had passed the smell off as her imagination, maybe the weed she figured he was smoking, but this was definitely not weed. This was something dead. And there was no denying he had brought it with him, no denying it clung to him and his clothing like a funeral shroud.

She looked around the room frantically, fighting against her tears to follow the smell, to find its source. But it was no use, it was everywhere, it clung to everything, it—

In stumbling around, her foot caught one of the shirts on the floor, revealing a loose floorboard underneath. She stared, hand over mouth, the nausea almost too hard to contain. There. Under there. Get it out. *Get it out.* She took hold of the floorboard, pulled, got hit by a fresh, potent wave of the stink. Jesus! She imagined a big, fat rat in the space, more maggot than meat, half its head gone, the eyes eaten out. Oh, God, she thought, her hands practically glued to the floorboard, her skin about ready to peel off, her eyes clouded with sweat.

Another tug, a grunt, and the floorboard came loose. No rat underneath, but a bag of cocaine and a squashed, stained mailroom envelope. She flung the bag aside with a shiver, but the envelope she took into her hands with a little more care, with something almost like tenderness.

She held the envelope up, surprised by its weight, its texture, her curiosity almost making her forget about the horrid smell and the gross, sticky feeling on her hands and arms and legs. All coming from this. From inside.

She undid the string, raised the flap. The smell was in her mouth, on her tongue, heavy and metallic, as if she swallowed a rusty coin or drank a pitcher of blood. If she wanted to vomit before, now that feeling was back tenfold, yet she reached into the envelope, regardless. She pulled out the stack of pages, saw the words on the topmost page, read them aloud.

"Room of Cloth."

14.

When Sebastian got back that night, he found the apartment dark and empty, Sarah's door locked. "Hey, Sarah?" he called. "You good?" When she didn't respond, he just shrugged, grabbed the peanut butter from the pantry along with a spoon, and went to his room. He sat against the bed, breathed in deep that glorious scent of cinnamon, and brought out the manuscript. He didn't notice the shirt was in a different place or that the floorboard was slightly skewed. Not even the cocaine got his attention, nor the weed he brought from Caesar's. The second he laid his eyes on the three words on the title page, he was gone.

It felt like only minutes later, the sun creeping over the horizon, when Sebastian got Caesar's text. Apparently, Otto was ready to keep his end of the bargain. Barring the initial shock of Pollito's murder, Sebastian was surprisingly okay with it. What had he thought, they *weren't* going to kill him? You don't steal from big-shit drug dealers and live to tell about it. Sebastian wasn't about to feel sorry for some asshole trying to play the game.

Besides, there were more important matters. He was making slow progress on the story, adding to a fresh file he was going to print and bundle with the rest. If everything went as planned, Bryan Stevens would hand over the parts he was missing—or, more to the point, the parts Stevens hadn't sent him in the first place. Sebastian understood the manuscript was sensitive, but the goose chase was wearing on him. He knew one thing for certain: he would get the rest of the manuscript no matter what, Stevens or no Stevens.

Sarah still didn't answer when he came to her door. He considered vaguely if something was wrong with her—more wrong than usual, at least—but he quashed the idea quickly. He wasn't her keeper, and besides, he was already thinking of new places to crash once he got the rest of the story. Maybe Caesar's place for a while. Still, staying with Sarah had its advantages—like the jar of cash, for example. He dragged out the jar, pocketed a few tens, and headed out, turning up his music as he went.

When he arrived at Caesar's condo, the door was ajar. He hesitated. He nudged the door open, when suddenly, he was pulled inside and thrown onto the sofa beside a nervous, clammy Caesar. "What the fuck?" he demanded. "Jesus!"

"Relax," said the man who grabbed him, the one who had been in Otto's office at the club. Bless. When he smiled, very relaxed, very easygoing, his golden tooth glinted. "Been waiting for you, sunshine. Otto! The kid's here!"

There were two other suited men standing in front of the hallway. They moved when Otto emerged from the back room, tall and imposing in a white suit. "Nice to see you again," he said. "Sorry about this. I'm in a rush this morning."

Sebastian didn't say anything. Next to him, Caesar trembled.

Otto sat down across from them. "We heard about what happened to Polo. Real shame."

"You're the one that fucking wanted him dead," Sebastian said, trying to muscle out his fear. "Doesn't look like you've been crying."

"Seb!" hissed Caesar, but Otto only laughed.

"It's true. I did want him dead. That little bitch thought he could get away with stealing from me. Thought he could make a fucking fool out of me—out of *me*." He lit a cigarette. "Now, I don't have to see his fucking face anymore. Now, the people got another re-minder that I rule this town. It's mine."

He stared at Sebastian, Caesar, then laughed again. "But enough of that. You did what I asked. You didn't pussy out. I respect that." He held out his hand. "Bless?"

Bless passed him a folded piece of paper. "This is a list of all the guys named Bryan Stevens living in Hoboken," Otto said. "You got lucky—not too many of them. You got addresses, account numbers, birthdays. Nothing you probably couldn't find on your own, but you paid for convenience." He held out the list. Sebastian exchanged a glance with Caesar before accepting the paper. Otto stood and flashed another smile.

"Take Caesar with you," he said.

Caesar looked up. "You sure about that, Otto?"

"Yes. Think of it like a vacation. You've done good work, Caesar. I appreciate good work. We'll get someone to cover for you in the meantime."

He whistled, and the other men joined up at the door. "Like I told you, busy day."

"Wait," Sebastian said. "Why help me? What's in it for you?"

"It's an investment," Otto said. "I'm taking stock. Planting seeds."

He left with the others. Sebastian looked over the list. Everything was there, just like Otto said. The sight of the names alone made his heartbeat double. "I'm a little closer, C," he said softly. "I'm a little fucking closer."

"That's great," said Caesar. He rose from the sofa and took a long breath. "That's real fucking great, Seb. You know that was the first time I ever had anything like that happen? Guys busting in here like that? All these years I been doing this shit, that ain't never happened. Never."

"They didn't do anything. We're fine."

"Didn't do anything? They broke into my fucking house! They just came in here like they own the place—fuck, they *do* own the place! Now we gotta go to Jersey. Fuck, Seb, whatever you're doing, whatever shit you brought back from Boston, you got his attention now.

You get that? You got his attention. You're fucking stuck!"

"Hey, we took care of that chicken guy. I did my part. I don't owe that asshole anything."

"That's what I mean," Caesar said. "Otto, man, he don't care about what you *think* you owe. You owe what he *wants* you to owe. You think we got a choice about going to Jersey? He's gonna be watching us! You, me, everything we do! We piss him off, you can bet he'll be coming through your door next."

"Fuck Otto," said Sebastian. "Here's what's gonna happen, Caesar—we go to New Jersey, I find the guy, I get the rest of the book. Then we get the hell out, and if I need to go, I go. It's not on you."

"I vouched for you, Seb. It *is* on me."

"Just don't worry about it, okay? First things first. We gotta go."

"Fuck." Caesar sighed. "We can leave today. Might take us a day or two to find the guy."

"I just gotta get some extra clothes. Then I'll be right back."

"Fuck," said Caesar, eyes wide, lips quivering. "Oh, fuck."

On the ride back to Sarah's apartment, although Sebastian knew he should have been scared, even terrified, his excitement was overwhelming. It didn't matter that Otto had all but thrown threats in his face. He imagined how the complete manuscript would feel in his hands, freshly printed, warm to the touch. He could smell the ink, sense the weight. He salivated, barely able to stay in his seat. It was coming. The promised time was coming. Hell, it was already here! He just needed to take one more step to make it over the threshold. Just one more tiny step.

At Sarah's apartment, he fumbled with the key, ran straight for his room, stuffed his backpack with shirts and pairs of underwear, the laptop and the envelope. A whiff of cinnamon reached him from the backpack, and he laughed. He was shaking.

Halfway back to the kitchenette, he nearly walked right into Sarah.

The look in her eyes took him aback, kept him from going around her. For the first time, there wasn't a single hint of accusation in her stare. There wasn't resentment or indignation. There wasn't disappointment. She didn't even seem like she pitied him—in fact, he pitied her in that moment, how messy her hair was, how dark her eyes, how pale her skin. Some of the buttons on her blouse were undone, her bracelets crooked. Even at her worst, her most exhausted and self-righteous, Sarah still kept herself up, kept herself prim and proper. Was this even his sister standing in front of him? What was wrong with her?

Like a bad high, he thought absently, unconsciously. Like when that acid knocked him on his ass. Like when some dickhead laced the weed and didn't say anything. But Sarah never touched shit. She didn't even drink beer. She was clean. Always clean.

"Where are you going?" she asked.

He searched for the right thing to say. He couldn't muster an insult with her looking like this, couldn't even come up with an excuse. The truth stumbled out of him. "I'm going out of town for a couple of days. To New Jersey."

"To do what?" she said. "Buy more drugs? Leave again?"

"No. This isn't even about that."

"Then what is it about?" She stared at him, laughed weakly. "Why do I even bother? Every time you come back, I think it'll be different. I start imagining things. You cleaned up. The two of us getting out of here. Just anything else. Just not *this*."

"Sarah—"

"No. No more lies. I should have put you away years ago. I thought I was sparing you pain, but I was really just letting you do whatever you want. And this is what you are now. So, go ahead. Go. Just give me your key. I don't want you back. I don't want this anymore."

Reluctantly, he gave her the key. Neither of them said anything. The shock of seeing her like this was wearing off, though. Sebastian remembered his purpose. His mission.

He went for the door.

"It doesn't have to be this way," Sarah said suddenly. "Whatever you're doing, Sebastian, you don't have to do it. You have a choice."

"What?" He turned around, surprised by how different she looked now. Her eyes were bright, her face aglow. Her shoulders trembled. Her jaw shook. Her whole body was different, more alive, more energetic. When she spoke, her voice came out stronger, stronger than he ever heard it before. Even stronger than when she had been her old self, the fierce rebel of his youth, the one who looked their father in the eye and told him to go to hell. The one he'd always chased in the shadowy maze that was the old house. The one who kept her door locked.

"You have a choice," she said. "No more drugs. No more running away. You stay here with me, and everything I just said, we do it. You won't be by yourself. I'll take care of you. That's my job. I'm your sister, and that's my job."

She took his hand, the mere touch of her skin alien to him. Threatening. "I know I've been a shitty sister. I wasn't there for you when you needed me. I kept thinking about myself, about what *I* wanted. I never thought what it must have been like for you, living with them. God, I hated them, you have no idea. There were times when I honestly wished they'd die. My own parents, Sebastian. *Our* parents."

Her grip tightened. "And they did die. They did die. But that's in the past. What I wanted's in the past. Now we're here. Together. They turned you into this, into what you are. I know they did. I know because they did the same thing to me. But whatever you did, Sebastian, whatever you're doing, whatever they did to you, it doesn't matter. You're not them. You're *you*. You're you, and I know you're good."

"Let go of me, Sarah," he said quietly, unable to withstand her touch, unwilling to listen to her increasingly shrill voice, her almost manic pleas. "I'm leaving, okay? I'm going to New Jersey. I gotta go—"

"You don't have to. You can stop this. You don't have to fight me. You *shouldn't* fight me. I'm your sister. I'm your sister, and I'm trying to help you!"

"Let go, Sarah. Seriously. Let go right now."

"No. You just have to stay. You stay, and we leave. We get out of here. We fix it. We start again. We make it right. We can do it, Sebastian. I know we can do it. We can fix it."

"I'm not staying," he said. "I'm leaving. I'm leaving right now, and you can't stop me."

"No, just listen to me, this isn't you, it's them, it's not your fault—"

"—leaving, I'm leaving, I'm leaving, *I'm leaving*—"

"—not you, Sebastian! You can change, I'll help you, you can be better, you can—"

"I'm fucking leaving!" he roared. He shoved her away. "What the fuck is wrong with you? Jesus! I'm the one that's crazy? *You're* crazy! You are fucked up! You are a motherfucking crazy psycho bitch! Do you get that? Does it get through? You're crazy! You are a crazy fucking bitch and I am *leaving*! I'm leaving and I'm never coming back!"

Sarah didn't say anything, just stood there with her face falling apart, ready to burst into a million tears. Holy shit he couldn't even look at her. For the first time, with the light coming through the window, with the chilly air around her head, he saw just how absolutely pathetic she really was. How *old* she was. Christ, those wrinkles. The cheekbones. The messy hair. What a mess. What a crazy, fucking mess. He couldn't even feel bad for her. No, right then, all he felt for her was disgust. Sickening, quaking disgust.

And the worst part? Blaming it on their fucking parents. When it was all her. When it was all fucking her and her annoying, stupid shit.

He couldn't stand it. He turned to the door, grabbed the knob, twisted it—

"I read it."

He froze. Slowly, very slowly, he turned around.

"What'd you say?"

"I read it," she said, barely above a whisper. "I found it under the floor, and I read it. What is it, Sebastian? My God, what *is* it?"

He screamed loudly, ferociously, and slammed his fist onto the countertop. "No no no *no*! You weren't supposed to read it! *No one's* supposed to read it!"

Sarah backed away, watched as he clutched at his head and moaned and twisted and writhed. "Goddamn it! Goddamn it, it's not yours, it's *mine*! It belongs to *me*!" He punched the countertop again and again and again, each time harder than the last, his fist coming away redder and bloodier with every blow. "It's mine! It's mine, it's mine, it's mine, it's mine, it's mine, it's mine, *it's mine*! It picked me! It didn't pick you! It didn't fucking pick you!"

"Sebastian, please. Please calm down—"

He knocked over plates, shattered glasses, threw knives and forks and fruit to the floor. "You didn't find it!" he screamed. "You don't understand it! It's not for you! It never was!"

"Sebastian, what are you talking about? What is it? What in God's name is it—"

A vase flew by her head. She didn't even register it until the shatter, until the force of its breaking buffeted against the back of her head.

"Shut up! Only I can know! Only I can fucking know! Only *me*! And you spoiled it, goddamn it! You fucking spoiled it! You spoiled *everything*!"

He hit the countertop one last time, uttered one last, vicious yell. Then the violent energy in his eyes was abruptly gone. His heaving breaths slowed down. Gently, he cradled his bloody hand against his chest. He grabbed a napkin from the floor and wrapped it around his knuckles. He didn't even look at Sarah—just walked out silently.

Sarah didn't do anything for a while. Eventually, she grabbed her carton of cigarettes and curled up on a chair, at any moment ready to light a cigarette, the entire time aware only of the overbearing, putrid stench of death that surrounded her, that blanketed her, that leached through her skin and into her bones.

15.

The drive to Hoboken was long and rainy. Clogged highways, slick roads, bad reception. Sebastian kept quiet for most of the trip, slouched in his seat, hidden in his parka. Caesar didn't say anything about the bruised hand. It wasn't the first time he had seen Sebastian hurt himself.

The hand twitched throughout the drive, but Sebastian kept it hidden in his pocket. The rage had a way of festering. It wouldn't go away—instead, it would simmer, harden, attach itself like a tumor. He didn't want to think about what happened, didn't even want to picture Sarah's fucking face, but she appeared to him again and again, crying and moping hysterically, a fucking banshee, a goddamn ghost. He wanted nothing more than to lock himself in a room and *work*. All these people around him, all these vultures and rats, they didn't deserve it. Even Caesar didn't deserve it. Sebastian had found the manuscript. He had stayed up all those nights reading the excerpt and continuing the story. The room of cloth had spoken to *him*. There had been others, like Bryan Stevens, but it was Sebastian's turn now, his opportunity to join their ranks. The countless followers of the room of cloth, connected only by plastic and optical fiber, known only by cryptic usernames and obscure profile pictures. They were shadows, voices in the dark, together more than human, collectively more than flesh and blood. They didn't have to hide behind masks. They didn't have to live up to expectations. They existed however they liked, however they really were, free-flowing, formless. Sebastian had found a special, secret, quiet place among them. The outside, full of noise, full of lies and bullshit, didn't matter. Didn't even need to exist. And no pathetic, screaming sister would ruin that for him.

They stopped at a burger joint along the way. Sebastian stayed in the van while Caesar went to get their food. Rain pelted the windows. Thunder boomed far off in the distance. Trying the radio was pointless—there had been only static and the occasional garbled bits of music so far. Sebastian tried it again, aimlessly, but heard only the same white noise. Wait. There was something else behind the static. Voices. Laughter. Screams? He turned up the volume, leaned in close. Words came through to him.

—waiting—

—waiting for you—

He's waiting for you—

Sebastian shut off the radio. Maybe he was losing it. He hadn't been sleeping enough, hadn't been eating very much. But he just had to hold out a little longer. Then he could rest. Then he could take all the time he needed.

He had sent one last e-mail to Bryan Stevens telling him he was on his way to New Jersey. Otto worked fast—there would already be a place ready for them when they arrived. Sebastian had included that address in the e-mail, too. In the event they were unable to find Stevens, maybe he would find them instead. But Sebastian knew that wouldn't be the case. He would find Stevens. He would find the manuscript. There was no other option.

Caesar came back in with the food. As they ate, the smells of bread, meat, and ketchup filled the van. Rain still fell hard.

"I'm not gonna ask about this book thing," Caesar said, "but you been pretty quiet. More than normal. And your hand—want to talk about it?"

"Not really." Sebastian bit into his hamburger. "I got into it with my sister. That's all."

"I always wanted a brother or sister," Caesar said. "Cousins don't make up for it, 'specially when they treat you like shit. You start looking for things to fill it up, and you pick the wrong things. The wrong people."

Sebastian scoffed. "Sarah didn't give a shit about me when we were kids. She acts like there's something be-tween us, but there's nothing. She's not really guilty, either. She just gets off on being the victim." He glanced at Caesar. "Honestly, C, you're the closest thing I have to family. You're like my brother. You looked out for me. Sarah, my parents—what'd they do?"

Caesar didn't say anything. In truth, he'd just picked up a kid back then. Just been driving, looking, surveying the streets. Checking who could make him a quick buck, who could be good for a little something extra. He'd done the ritual so many times before, so many times since, that it was old hat. The lost boys were his world. Drugs weren't even necessary sometimes. He just had to give them something to do, give them a reason for existing. They were on-board after that, and they rarely protested. He'd taken a liking to Sebastian, sure, trusted him with more, but what did that really matter? Caesar scouted him like any other.

The apartment set up for them was sparse and spacious, with a monochromatic interior of black sofas and white beds. A few abstract paintings adorned the walls, either cosmic swirls of reds and purples or astral landscapes of blues and greens. The windows provided a clear view of the waterfront. Through the sheets of rain, the city and river appeared gray and desolate, like a sodden wreckage long left for ruin.

Sebastian idled in the den, admired the flat-screen television and robust sound system. "Snazzy," he said. "Otto's hooked up."

"Don't get too comfy. Word'll get back if we leave a mess."

"I'll make sure not to get the fucking couch dirty. So, we gonna go now or not?"

Caesar finished his cigarette, his sixth since they started the trip. "Yeah, might as well."

They went from address to address. First a house, next an apartment, then another house. Sebastian would shamble up to the door, ask for Bryan Stevens, introduce himself as his username LostOmen, then get shooed off quickly, sometimes politely, sometimes not. For hours, they repeated this, driving around town, scratching entries off the list. Sebastian felt his eagerness turn to desperation, almost outright horror. *Someone* sent him the manuscript. *Someone* told him to come. So, where the hell was he? Why was he just *gone*?

By the time they drove up to one of the last addresses, the sky was a deep blue, the streetlamps orange in the downpour. Caesar stared past the windshield wipers at the row house across the street. "We been at this all day, Seb," he said. "After this one, we pick up tomorrow."

Sebastian approached the house. He stood in the rain, shivering, and looked up at the dark windows, the silent bricks. A sign next to the stoop said the building was for sale. No one even lived there.

Fucker, he thought, walking back to the van. Piece of shit. And then, surprising himself: I'll kill him. I'll kill him for this. That fucking snake. He stewed on the ride back, hand twitching again, teeth clattering. Why? Why was this happening? Did he fuck up? Sarah read it, and now this was his punishment? Was that it? Let in the club for a split second, then spat out? No, he almost said. I can fix it. I just need another chance. But he knew, sinking into the seat, that there would be no second chance. There would be no escape.

He pulled up his hood, made sure his sunglasses were firmly set. The last thing he needed was Caesar seeing him fucking crying.

They returned to the apartment complex. The rain had let up at last, leaving the parking lot covered in puddles that reflected the dark indigo of the sky. They trudged up the stairs. A young woman leaned against the railing, smoking a cigarette. A couple came out of a room on the other side of the tier. Traffic went by. A distant boom of thunder foretold more rain.

"I'm gonna grab a candy or something," Sebastian said.

Caesar opened the door. "Fine. I'm gonna shower."

He handed over the keys, and Sebastian headed to the convenience store across the street. He grabbed some cookies, a few bags of candies. Disappointed as he was, he took some solace in the fact that within fifteen minutes, he would be working on the manuscript again. It was his comfort zone, his place to hide away from the noise. Maybe he had failed—maybe not. The pages would speak to him as they always did. The words would sing their song. The room of cloth seemed to exist outside all this, but also inside—far away, but also deep within. It was its own special space, independent and removed. It didn't play by the same rules, didn't have to accommodate those who failed to understand it. It simply was and would be.

He had to believe there was still a way inside. That there was still a spot for him.

The bell over the door jingled. He grabbed a soda from one of the coolers. Sarah's face appeared to him again despite his resistance. Her exhausted eyes. Her frayed hair. The halo of cold light around her head. In the past, ignoring her had been easy, but he felt the vaguest sense of responsibility creeping up on him. Had the room of cloth done that to her? Had he?

"Omen."

He looked up. Leaning against the adjacent cooler was the young woman who had been smoking before. She was petite, wearing a ratty pullover, a black skirt, a pair of worn leggings. A magenta streak cut through her dark hair.

Sebastian stared at her, unsure of what to say, and then she raised her hand, pulled lazily at her hair. Tattooed on her inner wrist was a purple cobra.

His breath caught in his throat.

"viper961."

She smiled. "Been waiting for you. Out on the town?"

"Yeah. Looking for Bryan Stevens."

"I can explain that, but not here." She fished out a cigarette. "Can you lose the Mexican?"

"He's Cuban," said Sebastian, "and, yeah, I can."

"Good. There's a cyber lounge called The Hollow Deck that's close by. I'll be there at midnight with something to show you. Then we can talk."

"How do I know you'll show?"

"Come on," she said. "I had to see if you really wanted it. And I think you do."

She left. Sebastian paid for his snacks and went back to the room.

16.

He tried to sleep in the few hours he had before meeting the girl, but when not writhing restlessly on the sofa, his sleep was plagued by nightmares. Dead forests, all of the trees gray and withered. Mass graves filled with emaciated bodies, the arms and legs twisted, the faces contorted in agony. Oceans reddening, turning black, chunks of meat rising to the surface. Empty houses. Abandoned cities. Dogs prowling and rummaging through trash-flooded streets. Spiders and roaches and maggots crawling over the ground for miles. Dark rooms in which people sat before bright monitors, their bodies held in place by chains and hooks. Whispers in his ear telling him to hurry, to come soon. They were all waiting for him.

Awake, he thought about Sarah again. He admired her once, as hard as that was for him to believe. She seemed so strong when he was a kid, so full of rebellious spirit. That had been before their father died. Sebastian knew in a mechanical, objective sense that he had killed him. He knew he had an "episode," triggered by something his father did or said. But he couldn't remember the night—couldn't remember the hospital, at least not clearly. There were flashes of a bright room, snatches of patients playing board games or watching television. Orderlies. Doctors. Lush, green trees outside the window. Blue skies. You can change, Sarah had told him. It's not your fault. But that's what he didn't understand. What had he done wrong?

She's jealous, he told himself. Jealous that I'm free. Jealous that I was picked. But try as he might, the anger wouldn't turn to hatred, nor the pity to disgust. He could recall any one of her lectures, could make her voice that much louder and shriller in his mind, could focus on that scrunched-up, wrinkled face until his brow hurt— and still the image of that old, young Sarah broke through, shining like a star in the vast dark, radiating a warmth and glow he couldn't understand or explain.

At 11:30, the phone Caesar lent him vibrated softly and spilt blue light into the pitch-black living room. He sat up. Caesar snored in one of the bedrooms, buried beneath pillows and sheets. Sebastian grabbed some of the cash they brought, flipped on his hood, and left.

He got a cab. Cabs and buses had become his trademark. They were just easier, more convenient, even if they were usually filthy. You just slipped away, an anonymous non-entity among others. Outside, the streets were always the same. Dark. Empty. Violent. It didn't make sense, how lifeless everything could feel one moment, and then the next, there would be gunshots, stabbings, muggings. Blood splattering against brick, screams echoing through alleyways, boots crunching on asphalt. Pollito was just one more notch on the big wall.

Another body to clutter the gutters. Another worm-ridden corpse to fill an unmarked grave.

Fifteen minutes later, he was at The Hollow Deck. A thick darkness hung over the lounge, punctuated by swells of muted electronic music. Faces were colored silver by their respective computers. Underneath each desk, a light alternated between blue and green, occasionally burning red. When the lights changed, so did the faces. No. No, stop. Nothing changed. Get it together. Sebastian took off his sunglasses, rubbed his eyes. viper961 was in the back.

She didn't look up when he sat down next to her. Only smiled. "You came."

"The rest of the story. Where is it?"

"Don't rush so much," she said. "The beauty's in the details. Check out the video on your desktop. I set it up for you already."

He turned to the monitor in front of him. There was a video file near the bottom of the screen, something called "room 1." He hovered the mouse over the icon, but hesitated. He could feel her gaze on him.

"Put the headphones on," she said. "You'll want to hear it."

He put them on and clicked on the file. The media player window buffered. More than once, the screen stuttered. Sebastian steeled himself for the wave of nausea he knew was coming. His legs trembled. His arms shook. His right hand twitched. Finally, the video started to play.

His eyes widened at the sight. A bare room, as large as a cell, covered in a beige fabric. Covered in cloth. No—made of cloth. No door. No windows. For five straight minutes, the video was just running footage of the room. Heart drumming, mouth dry, Sebastian turned to the girl.

"Keep watching," she said.

He looked back. Something had changed. Red droplets—blood, had to be blood—started to hit the center of the floor. One after another, coming down faster. The splats were loud through the headphones, followed by— what was that? Whispers? Moans? He tried to make out the words, but there was too much static. All the while, more blood came down until it was a steady stream. And then something jutted into view from the top of the screen. He squinted his eyes, made out what must have been toes. Broken, ashen, bloody toes, and then feet, two feet bound together at the ankles by rusted, iron fetters. Sebastian shook uncontrollably now, watching as something descended from higher above. Hairless, gray legs. A ragged, bloody hole where the genitals should have been. Hands shackled over a naked chest, the fingers and thumbs mangled and broken. Chains wrapped around the torso, around the arms. Hooks buried in the flesh of the back, the chest, the arms and legs. The body twitching erratically. Sebastian tried to close the window, but there was only the dull thud of a useless command. Dun. Dun. Dun, dun dun dun dun dun dundundundundun. The video distorted, colors inverting, artifacts appearing, the whispers and moans now screams, howls, cries. A glimpse of a muzzle—

The window closed. Sebastian was one gag away from puking, one shock away from convulsing. With effort, he calmed down.

"Your first time seeing him?" the girl asked. "You did a good job. A lot of people go straight for the razor. At least that's what I've heard."

"What the fuck was that?"

"Someone recorded themselves reading," she said. "I don't know how much—a few paragraphs, a chapter. Enough of it, I guess. They read it very slowly, made sure to get every sound right. Then they put it through a converter, and that's what came out. A video. Unbelievable, right? And you know what else? Anyone else in here watched it, it would have just been static. Maybe a couple of shapes, some of the voices, but just static. You saw it because it was already in your head. Believe me, you'd seen him before. Just not with your eyes."

"Why'd you show it to me?"

"I had to be sure. But you're good. He picked you." She smiled again, showed her teeth. "He reveals himself only to the chosen. The manacled man. Waiting in the room of cloth."

"Jesus. That's him. He's real."

"Yeah. Everything you read, everything you heard— it's all true. I mean, in a sense. There's truth *in* the lies, is maybe a better way to put it. All the stories start somewhere."

"You read it?"

"I read part of it, just like you. Bryan read some of it, too. We read it together."

"Bryan's real?"

"*Was* real," she said. "Killed himself. I found him in the bathroom." She stared at her screen for a moment. "He couldn't take it. The pressure was too much. But he wanted it finished just like I do. And that's where you come in. I've been keeping track of your e-mails. That's how I knew where you were staying. It wasn't meant to be a trick, cutting you off, going silent, but I had to know you would go the extra mile. That you wouldn't end up like him."

Sebastian looked into the darkness of the lounge, watched the faces of the other occupants, all of them isolated, suspended in their own virtual bubbles. Sounds coming in from their headphones. Monitors filling up their vision. He processed what she said, made sense of it. For as heavy as it all was, he didn't feel especially nervous—the furious anxiety that had struck him as he watched the video had already faded. Instead, there was calmness, tranquility. He finally had answers, or at least a better view of the big picture. The holes in the story were filling up. It wasn't just aimless wandering in the dark anymore, wasn't just random stabs at ideas or speculations. It was real, concrete, right next to him. The girl was a portal, a gateway that led deeper into this world he so desperately desired.

And to think he'd been nervous. Afraid he'd lost his chance. On the contrary, he'd been initiated. This was his welcome party. This was crossing the threshold.

"And who are you?" he asked. "Bryan's girlfriend?"

"Girlfriend? Are you twelve? No. But we were together. Sometimes. We had a common interest. That can do a lot to bring people close." She grinned. "My name's Miranda. What about you, Omen? Who are you supposed to be?"

"Sebastian."

"Well, Sebastian, you passed the test. I guess it's time for your reward." She reached under her chair and pulled up a duffle bag. It's in there, Sebastian thought excitedly. The truth. The world. Everything he was seeking. Everything he had lost.

"Take it with you," she said. "When you get back to Maryland, send me another e-mail."

"You gonna come?"

"You know how it is."

"Yeah," he said. "You can't stay away from it. From him."

"That's right." The lights flared red again. "I can't."

When Sebastian returned to the apartment, he lay down on the sofa, the duffle bag hugged to his chest. When he closed his eyes, no cataclysmic disasters came, and no images of his sister dispelled them. A deep, serene sleep overtook him, and he did not wake until morning.

17 .

Terry Stewart was a freelance website designer who lived in Montana. He graduated in the top ten of his senior class in high school, and he graduated *magna cum laude* from college. He got his degree in computer science. His mother was a schoolteacher, his father the manager of a hardware store. Thanks to some lucrative clients, Terry had been able to migrate to a small apartment in the big city. He quite liked urban life—there was activity in his building, in the next one over, all across the city. He did not miss the silence of the rural town where he grew up. No life. No activity. Animals rustling in the underbrush, maybe. The whistle of the wind at night, the creak of wood and leather.

Terry had a girlfriend named Amanda who was studying postcolonial literature in California. They talked for at least thirty minutes every two days via videoconference. This was mainly Amanda's rule. Because she was so busy with her doctoral work and teaching, Terry was the one who usually went out to visit. Despite expenses, he arranged trips whenever possible. Those were very long, very busy Saturday nights, he'd joke to friends.

His favorite hobby was watching movies and television. Every night, he would look up obscure old films or more contemporary series. He did enjoy the occasional night out with the guys. Cracking open beers around the television. Playing basketball on the weekends. Listening to bands play at gigs.

Overall, he was happy. His was a tame, almost muted life, but one he enjoyed. He didn't have any specific ambitions, didn't anticipate any great windfall or change of fortune, didn't consider living for any particular purpose or cause. He just lived.

Until, that is, he found the disc.

Nothing about the box itself had stuck out as remarkable. The package was from a client out of Wisconsin, a woman opening up a restaurant. Inside were reference materials: photographs, menus, mock-ups. Less convenient than a simple e-mail, but he never questioned his clients. Opening the box let out this inexplicable *smell*. He thought of stale meat, specifically the dead coyotes he came across as a boy when hunting with his father. He rummaged around, and then he found the source of the stench, a CD under the stack of menus. Lightly scratched, in a dusty, frayed sleeve. Even stranger was how sticky the disc felt, how weirdly heavy. The smell persisted, and every time he touched it, he felt compelled to wash his hands.

He called the client about the CD, but she had no idea what he was talking about, and he was inclined to believe her. Did someone open and reseal the package?

He couldn't work without glancing at the disc, couldn't sleep without thinking about it. He got hold of a disc drive from a friend and reviewed the contents.

There were two files, one a video and the other a text document. The video was short, roughly ten seconds in length, depicting heavily compressed, black-and-white footage of passing countryside, shot from car or train. There was no sound, the visuals barely comprehensible. He watched the video over and over again, trying to retrieve meaning or motive. The text document was stranger. A single, unformatted page, entirely in French. He processed a sample through an online translator, and what came back were random words, nonsensical sentences. Names. Robert Thomas, Kristen Wertz, Shijima Hiroshi. Many more.

Weeks passed, and Terry was beset by an awful depression. He just felt so inexplicably *crushed*. Amanda asked him what was wrong, but he shrugged his shoulders and shook his head. I don't know. It's like the color's gone. He thought about telling her of the CD, showing her the video, sending her the text file, but he didn't want to. It was his, he thought with sudden, fierce possessiveness. It was *his*. It belonged to *him*.

Watching movies, going to bars, nothing was the same. He couldn't focus, couldn't work. He always came back to the text and its nonsense. Even after translating all of it, nothing made sense. But the *words*. There was something about them, some inherent power and intelligent design under the insane surface. The words compelled him, possessed him. He saw them every-where—on billboards, in commercials, in magazines and newspapers. He'd be reading an article, perusing a web-site, and suddenly, the words would change. In his dreams, he was the one riding that car or train. He was the one filming that countryside.

As time went on, Terry felt weaker, lazier. He stopped eating much. He fell behind on his work. He didn't go out as often. He slept more. When he did man-age to sit down and start working, he would start writing the same sort of gibberish from the CD amid his code. His fingers would move on their own, typing out strings and sentences that made no sense, words he was positive he had never even seen before. His dreams became more violent and bizarre. Gutted animals lying on roadsides. Statues dissolving under acid rain. Arms and legs and torsos tumbling into chasms amid waterfalls of blood. The countryside from the video, slowly becoming dark. Slowly becoming dead. Thousands, millions of dead fish lying on shorelines, in bays. Birds falling out of the sky in droves. A room of cloth in which the walls moved, in which the walls moaned, in which the walls bled. A man waiting within, suspended by chains.

Eventually, Terry stopped eating altogether. He stopped going out. He simply sat in the dark, watching the video on loop. He let his mind wander, let the inspi-ration flow—he wrote pages upon pages, and when he was done, he read them aloud, he recorded them. He filled up entire hard drives with his narrations, and then he uploaded them. Now it was his to share. Now it was his to finish. And to finish meant getting help. He linked to his narrations. He streamed them. He mailed out the hard drives, left them under benches, in mailboxes, atop cars. Then he went back to his apartment and never came out.

He didn't return calls, didn't reply to e-mails. It was typical for him to go some time without speaking to his parents, even to his friends, but Amanda? She booked a flight as soon as possible. The last time she had spoken to Terry, he had been pale, sluggish, and distant. He had hardly looked at her. His usually bright eyes had been dead.

When she got to his apartment, she had the landlord open the door. The air spilt out hot and heavy and dirty, and she had to close her eyes, pinch her nose, shut her mouth. Terry? Her voice cracked. Terry? Sweetie? Terry oh God. Oh my God my God oh my *God*—

Terry hung nude and bloody from hooks slung through his arms and chest and back. Amanda screamed—not because of the loss, not because of the death, but because of the look on his face. Mouth open and laughing. Eyes wide and gone.

She had never seen him so happy.

18.

Sarah stood in a clean, white lobby, through which flitted nurses and orderlies. Vibrant, green trees swayed in
the breeze outside the windows. A dream, but nonetheless so real. So accurate.

She went down one white hall, and then a second, a
third. Hall after hall after hall. Windows in each, out of
which she saw the same lush trees, the same swaying
branches. The halls grew dimmer and more dilapidated
with time. The white walls became a sickly yellow.
Cracks spread throughout the tiled floor. Screams and
yells came from the rooms, the cells.

At last, she arrived at a familiar door. Covered in rust,
virtually bleeding, but his all the same. The door opened
slowly, and she waited, watched with dread. On the other
side was a room of cloth, with no windows, no lights. She
wanted to scream, wanted to run, but her voice didn't
cooperate, her legs didn't listen.

A boy sat in the room, facing away from her, thin
and brittle, crying and trembling. His right hand shook
the worst. The moaning voice, the slumped shoulders,
the bowed head. She had seen him like this so many
times. What had they done to him? What had he done to

himself? Why was this happening? Why did it keep happening?

She reached out. It's okay, Sebastian. It's okay. I'm here. It's Sarah. See? It's me. Remember? Sarah? Your sister? Sebastian? You have to remember. You have to say something. Sebastian. Sebastian, look at me. Look at me, please. Sebastian, please. *Please.* Sebastian! Just look at me! *Look at me!*

And then he did look—

She shot up in bed, drenched in sweat, skin like a stove. Even the fan on full blast couldn't keep her cool. She got up and poured herself a glass of water. She had dreamt about Sebastian in the past, had dreamt about the psychiatric hospital, but never like this. And yet night after night, ever since reading those horrible pages, nightmares assaulted her. They weren't always about Sebastian. Sometimes, they were just images she didn't understand. Buildings in black and white, the windows bleeding. Hollow-eyed people walking around offices and subway platforms, their voices like static. Things roaming in the dark of woods and the shadows of tunnels. And almost always, there was that room. The people within mangled and tortured, chains tearing their flesh, spilling their blood. Screaming and crying. Grinning. Dancing. Laughing. Above them all, lurking in the endless darkness, the man in chains. Always watching her, always following her. She couldn't escape his eyes. However far she ran, wherever she turned, she saw them.

Those red fucking eyes, furious and hateful. Always getting closer.

Things weren't any better when she was awake. Anxiety was her constant companion now, and so was the feeling that someone—or some*thing*—was watching her. Logic dictated it was paranoia, stress, but how many times had she turned and sworn she saw something in her periphery, just out of focus? How many times had she been sitting at her desk, grading papers or filling out forms, only to look down and find dark swirls, random words, sketches of figures without hands or feet? Constantly, she would turn her head and catch a whiff of that awful smell, like rotten meat or rusted metal. And sooner or later, she always thought about what she had read. The words hadn't made any sense, but they stuck like glue, held fast like cement. The more she tried to ignore them, the more they intruded and invaded her thoughts. Trying not to think about what was on those pages was mental quicksand—suppressing the words only made their influence worse, only made them more powerful.

Slowly, painfully, Sarah feared she was losing her mind. Shamefully, guiltily, she wondered if maybe she and her brother weren't so different after all.

Sebastian had read the words, too—had even contributed to them if the chicken-scratch marginalia and cross-hatch commentary were any indication. If she felt half-mad after only a few days, what was happening to him? How long had he been immersed in whatever this thing was? The way he acted when he stormed out—was that the manuscript, or was that him? When he had been at the psychiatric hospital, the doctors told her about his sudden, violent episodes, but whenever she visited him, he had been unresponsive. When he came back home, he was the same as she remembered him: aloof and distant, not gentle, not even friendly, but certainly not violent. All these years, she had struggled to understand how that quiet, docile boy did what he did to their father, but now she knew. There was something inside of him— something that maybe, possibly, she helped grow.

There were voices in her head. Drink, they commanded. Taste. Revel. Enjoy. Sweet-sounding, but also raucous. The cold stillness of her apartment, so isolating, so stifling, gave way to a festival heady with the smells of wine and sweat, laden with heat, heat from the torches, heat from the many bodies steaming, twisting, and convulsing under the night sky. Teeth rent skin. Hands groped breasts. Legs trembled and trickled come. Sarah was carried on that wave, smiling, laughing, her exposed breasts and crotch surprising her. She hadn't felt them like this in so long, how sensitive they were, how delicate. Yes, she thought. Drink! Taste! Revel! Enjoy! *Enjoy*! It's all for you! For us! For him!

Among the moans and laughter, she heard screams. Past the crackle of the flames and the crunch of the grass, people screaming as their stomachs were slit open, their necks cut. The torches moving, wriggling. Bodies struggling to break free as flames consumed them and blades struck them. Ropes slithered around necks, around arms and legs, around *her* neck, around *her* arms and legs. And that red light in the sky grew, blossomed, heralded by the chanting and singing as she was brought to position in the middle of the clearing. That comet, that fire, that fallen angel. Blood pelting her, drenching her. Chains descending. Froth dripping from behind the muzzle. She couldn't even scream, she was so terrified, so exhausted. He's here for you, they said. You're here for him. For all of us. And she knew it was over, staring into those hellish red eyes as they got closer, closer, too close. She knew he had come—

She dropped her glass and screamed. Not water spreading over the floor and around the glass pieces, but whiskey. She had opened the bottle without realizing it, had nearly taken the first of many sips. That bacchanal vision a distraction. That orgiastic nightmare a trap.

"I won't," she said, clenching her fist, fighting the tremors away. "You won't make me. You hear me? I won't let it happen. I'll bring him back."

She emptied the other bottles into the sink. She threw away the many packs of cigarettes. No more maybes. No more temptations. Her little life. Her little world. If you wiped Sarah Creed off the face of the earth, if you deleted her name from a database, if you scratched out her face, it wouldn't matter. She wasn't a part of anything, not connected to anyone. She was alone. Separate. Free. For better and worse, just like she always wanted. But it couldn't be like that anymore. Not with the wraiths lurking in the shadows. Not with the manacled man coming down from his throne on high. Not with her brother in the sights of those red eyes.

19

See, at first it had just been another creepy myth, another scary story. Read this thing, yeah? This book. I read it. Yeah, bullshit. You'd be dead. Hey, maybe you don't die. Maybe some people just can't take it. But what if it chooses you? What if there's a test, and if you don't pass it, you die? What if you die, but come back? Or what if you don't come back?

Taken? By who? It's a book.

It's not just a book. It's more than a book.

Books have authors. Someone wrote it.

This one doesn't. No one wrote it.

Then how'd it get made?

It wasn't made. It just is. Maybe at first it was just words, what people whispered to one other in the dark. And then they wrote the words down. Maybe they painted pictures. Maybe if you go to some of those really old cave paintings, you'll see it.

See what?

It. See *it*. Whatever it is. You see it, and it stays with you, and you take it out of the cave, and you take it back to the rest of the world. Sooner or later, you open your mouth, and it comes out. No one keeps secrets. Especially not anymore. Now everyone knows where you are all the time. They know what you're eating, what you're drinking, what you're watching, what you're buying, what you're selling, who you're dating—

Words don't just happen. Pictures don't just happen. They're symbols. They're symbols for sounds, and the sounds represent actual things. Phonemes and morphemes. Signifiers and signified. They're pixels and ink and little dots of lead. People make them.

Yeah, but people are just vehicles. For other things. For their feelings. Our brains register sensations. That feels good. That feels bad. That's pleasurable. That's painful. I don't like that. I like that. That sounds nice. That doesn't sound nice. They're feelings, and we start to put them together, we start to express them. We use words and pictures. *I like this.* Now you know what I like. Now you know what I feel.

But it's more than that. It's more than feelings. All animals feel something. Maybe plants do, too. We do more than that. We *think* about our feelings. We study them. We give them names and try to explain them. We try to control them—and then we fail. And when we fail, bad things happen. Sometimes it gets worse.

What gets worse?

Something. Something gets worse. When people go crazy, maybe that's when it happens. They start breaking. Like machines, like gears and bolts popping out. You start to rust. No, that's when you get old. That's when everything starts to go.

But thoughts and feelings don't hurt people. They don't kill them.

They *don't* hurt people? They *don't* kill them? LOL Are you stupid?! Are you fucking retarded?! They always hurt people! They always kill people! They're the most dangerous fucking thing we use to hurt each other! You don't just go and shoot someone, you *feel* it and then you *think* it. Right now I'm making you feel like a retarded dumbass because that's what you are, and it makes you feel like shit! These are my words, see? I'm just a goddamn fucking box of text on a screen made of glass and plastic and who the fuck knows! I'm fucking pixels! I'm nothing! I don't have a face, I DON'T EVEN HAVE A FACE and you hate me! You want me to slit my wrists and go fuck myself! *You* are that something wrong! When people jump off bridges and hang themselves and kill their parents it's because of YOU. It's always because of YOU. YOU ARE WHATS WRONG

Christ.

wtf

what crawled up his ass? lmao

i dunno. Anyway yeah

troll

dont delete it yet

Yeah someone get a pic? love it when these snowflakes blow up

it's all over my feed lmao

The story

oh yeah

So it's a room right?
yeah it is. if you read it you see it
have u seen it?
nah. I did hear about it though. a guys in the room
a guy?
He's not wrong. It's a guy. Has chains on. Dick cut
off. Some serious SM shit.
eww gross. who is he?
No one knows. They just call him the manacled man
and
hes
always
watchinnnnnnnnnnnnnnnnnnnnnnngggggggggggggg

20.

The evening sky of Lorraine was a light peach when Sebastian walked out of the convenience store. The air smelt like candy, like ice cream. The street was empty, but as the dark fell, things would change. Fiends would crawl out of their gutters and trash heaps. Whores would walk along in tatters and threads. Sirens would go off. Demons would come out.

A few days had passed since he got back from New Jersey. Caesar had pressed him about the manuscript, about the woman, but Sebastian kept mum. Truth was, he didn't know what the fuck to think of her. viper961. Miranda. The manuscript had been *his*—or at least that's what he thought. But this girl knew so much more. She let him into the circle, started his initiation. She even showed him that video. He hated her for tricking him, for acting so fucking smug, for being so much closer than he was. He wanted that connection badly, but he also wanted her. He wanted to be the one in control. He knew lust, but this was more than just getting his dick wet. It was a fucking communion! It was coming face to face with a new god, a new meaning. The girl was the gateway to all that, and he hated her and wanted her because of it.

Just the thought of her face, the dark hair, that streak of pink, made him hard. It had to wait, though—first, he had to find a place to work. He had been crashing at Caesar's place, but that couldn't last for much longer. The whole manuscript was right there, waiting for him, sitting in that bag, and he couldn't do a goddamn thing with it! He couldn't risk Caesar seeing, couldn't let any of the others passing through get even a little curious. He already screwed up with Sarah. Even if he couldn't stay mad at her, he wanted to keep all of that out: the history, the past, the blood. Besides, blood didn't make family. Blood didn't make anything.

Another thought gnawed at him. She tried so hard to be "good" all the time, to be the way everyone else wanted her to be, and it was ruining her. Maybe he had to share the manuscript, after all. Maybe that was the key, the only way to actually finish the story. There needed to be a plan, a logic that made sure the message came through as clearly as possible. Much as he hated to admit it, he needed help with that. Maybe Sarah could be that help. Maybe he could let her in eventually like Miranda did for him. He could show Sarah what was *really* true. He could show her how everything else, all this noise, was just bullshit. And maybe, *maybe,* they could stop pretending to be a family and actually *be* a family—

No. Who was he kidding. Sarah was gone, worlds away, no, entire fucking *universes* away. She wasn't ready or able to understand the truth. She could never accept it. And, worse, she didn't deserve it. The manacled man didn't choose her. The room of cloth didn't call to her. The only reason she had even read it was because he had been just the tiniest bit careless. Who cared if she disappeared, if she wasted away under all the bullshit and lies and propaganda? Good riddance. One less conformist, two-faced, conniving, arrogant, egotistical bitch.

He was halfway up the block, musing on these things, drinking a soda, when a black van pulled up alongside him. The window rolled down. "Hey, sweetie!" called the driver. "Sebastian, right? Ain't that your name?"

The driver was Otto's right-hand man, Bless. "I know you're not deaf!" he laughed. "Listen, man. Otto wants to talk."

"No, thanks," said Sebastian. The soda churned in his stomach.

"That's too bad. Maybe we could talk to that sister of yours instead? The blonde one, yeah? The teacher?" Bless whistled. "I seen her around. A little skinny, but sometimes I like that. Nice change of pace!"

Sebastian stopped. So did the van. He stared at Bless for a long time, then looked down at his trembling right hand, at the purple knuckles beneath the gauze. He didn't know what to say, what to do, so he just stared, just waited for something to happen.

Bless jerked a thumb to the backseat. "Stop fucking around, man. Get in."

Sebastian did as told. The van started moving again. Otto sat in the back, eyes on the street, hand under his chin. Sebastian kept his gaze down.

"You know about my sister?"

"Of course. I know all about you." Otto smiled. "How about that little stint at St. Mary's for instance? You didn't say anything about that."

"I don't remember it."

"No need to be nervous. I don't mind that you killed your father. I'd have done the same to mine if the bottle hadn't gotten to him first. Honestly, I'm impressed. What takes more balls than swearing off your family?"

"I told you. I don't remember it."

"That doesn't change the fact you did it, does it? Deep down, you made the choice."

Sebastian didn't reply.

"Maybe you don't want to admit it," Otto said. "It's hard at first, the idea that you're not good, that you're just as bad as the rest. The ones on the inside, they look at us, and they see trash. We're the ones they blame for living in this shit. But we're not really to blame. We get our hands dirty because sooner or later, we admit to ourselves we're just not scared. And I know you're not scared, either. I see it in you. You want the same things I do."

"What things?" asked Sebastian through his teeth.

"Power," said Otto. "Respect. Something that's mine. Something I can call my own. And I want them to know it's mine, all of those on the inside. I want them to know they're just too weak to get it. They'll hate me for it, but so what? What can sheep do to a lion?"

Sebastian faced him despite his shaking, despite the plummeting feeling in his gut. "Enough with the bullshit. The fuck do you want with me?"

"I just want to give you what you want," Otto said.

"Fuck off. I helped kill Polo. I did what you wanted. Our deal's done."

"But you *didn't* do what I wanted. Caesar did. He always does what I ask, no questions, but he doesn't like doing it. You? I see something different in you." He waved a hand. "Listen, I don't give a shit about your sister. She's safe as long as we understand each other."

Sebastian looked away. Otto went on.

"I'm gonna give you a choice. I want to see that book you were talking about. The one you brought back from Jersey. Must be a real piece of work for all that trouble."

Sebastian bristled at this. Otto chuckled. "I thought you'd feel that way. Something special, isn't it? You know that just makes me want to see it more. But I'm willing to wait. So, that was your first choice. The second is that you do something for me."

"Do something?"

"Yeah. Like before. Only no Caesar to hold your hand."

The soda went up, lapped at the back of Sebastian's throat.

"I have an old friend in Baltimore," Otto said. "She knows things about me, things that can't be known anymore. I don't want it this way, but it's time to make the call."

"Who is she?" Sebastian asked.

"She goes by 'Angel.' Every month, I send a package to her, my best product at a discount. Bless sees to it personally. Only this month, we're gonna be early. Tomorrow night, in fact. At seven o'clock, Bless is gonna stop at Caesar's place. Either you give him the book, or you go with him to Baltimore. That's your choice.

"Now, if you don't make that choice, when Bless comes back, he's gonna head over to your sister's place. Maybe you can't tell, but Bless has particular tastes. And his stamina is something else. He can go on for hours. I don't know where he gets the energy."

He grinned at Sebastian's pale face. "I know what you're thinking. But it doesn't matter what leverage you think you have. I know the book's at Caesar's. I know where your sister is. I know where you are. I'll get what I want sooner or later. If I'm good at anything, it's waiting."

Otto finally stopped talking, and the ensuing silence in the van was crushing, horrific. He studied the small, shaking figure beside him. "Tomorrow night. Don't forget."

The van came to a stop. Bless got out and opened Sebastian's door, but Sebastian didn't move. He just sat there and shuddered. As Bless reached for him, Otto held up a hand. "Hold on. He's gonna say something."

"If I do it," said Sebastian slowly, "you gotta give me something in return. A place. Doesn't have to be nice, but I need something private. Somewhere I'll be protected."

Otto nodded. "Sure. You can have your pick."

Sebastian slid out of the van. Once Otto and Bless drove off, he went up to Caesar's condo and puked.

21.

He waited outside the next night, and just like Otto said, the same black van drove up right at seven o' clock. The day prior had been spent agonizing over impossible choices. Run away, they go after Sarah. Give up the book, still probably get muscled around, if not killed. Not to mention that surrendering the book meant forsaking the very thing he was fighting so hard to protect. The manacled man had chosen him for a reason—because he was brave, because he had put aside everything else for this one goal. Why not just run away, make sure no one unworthy got his or her hands on the manuscript?

But Sarah. Sarah, Sarah, Sarah. Why couldn't he give up Sarah?

A quiet voice urged him from within. Run. Get away from it all. Give her up. Let her die. And yet another voice prodded him to go in the opposite direction. Let go of the restraints, it said. Let go of the weakness. Kill the woman. Do this for Otto and benefit from the perks. Do this for the room of cloth, for the manacled man, and get your ticket inside.

He had to kill Angel. How else could he both protect Sarah and protect the book? Anyway, giving Otto the manuscript was out of the question. There was no fucking way, not after he had finally got a hold of the whole thing. Even if the skies opened up and the oceans rose and giant, fuck-all meteors came crashing down, he still wouldn't give that son of a bitch the manuscript. He wouldn't give *anyone* the manuscript. It was too sacred, too holy. Only the worthy could read it—no, not just read it, fucking *partake* in it. Was Otto worthy? Was some scumbag, piece-of-shit, murderous fucking asshole worthy? No way. If it was give up the manuscript or watch the world burn, he'd watch the world burn. He'd kill as many people as he had to if it meant keeping the story in safe hands. In the right hands.

Yet he couldn't sacrifice Sarah? He could let the whole world burn, but not her? What the fuck? Was the choice less about Otto and more about her? Goddamn it. Goddamn it! She just couldn't stay out of his fucking shit. Reading the manuscript, getting used as a pawn— always in the fucking way. And he couldn't reach out to Caesar for help, either. Even if it stung, keeping Caesar in the dark was for the best. Provided Otto kept his word, Sebastian would get his own place, somewhere he could work alone, without distraction. Nothing mattered anymore but the book, and he knew this was a step he needed to take. A demonstration of his worthiness.

He got into the van. Bless sat in the driver's seat, grinning like usual, his golden tooth visible in the blue light of the console. "You didn't pussy out," he said. "No book, neither. So we're clear—"

"I'll do it," said Sebastian. "Just get me over there, and I'll do it."

"You got some balls, man. My first time, the whole time we were waiting, I was shitting my pants. You touched my face, it was like a sprinkler went off. Think I threw up my lunch like five times. But you? You're cool as ice."

"Let's just go. Before I throw up, too."

Bless laughed, and then they drove. Soon, they were on the highway, the black speeding by, the headlights of the van revealing only more and more asphalt, a never-ending plummet into the cold night.

After a while, Bless spoke. "What I said about your sister—sorry 'bout that. It's just talk. You know how it is. Gotta scare you."

Sebastian kept quiet. Bless laughed.

"Shit, man, I have sisters. Drive me crazy, but they're my blood. I'd take a bullet for 'em. Back when, guys would try and impress 'em, puff up their chests, do all that dumb shit. Some were just dumbasses, but there were a couple of real shitheads. Tried to take advantage, went around, made it like they were the ones that got wronged." His eyes lit up as if he were reliving the memory. "Yeah, I remember 'em real well. Tony, I think was the name of one of 'em. Tony and Bob. I followed 'em, I waited, and when they were fucking some other girl, when they were coming outta some bar, I was on 'em."

He flexed out his hand. "I had these gold knuckles. Not real gold, you know, just painted that way. I loved those fucking things. Fit like they were made for me. Shit, maybe they were. Don't remember. Anyway, I had them on, and I was just pounding into those guys, their cheeks coming off, their eyes all red and bloody."

He cackled. "Shoulda seen good ol' Bob after that. One-eyed, pirate Bob! All he needed was a goddamn bird, a big green one, and one of those fucking wooden legs! Yeah! He'd have gotten all the pussy he wanted after that. Fuck, I shoulda taken a leg, too! Put a plunger on it."

He burst into more laughter. Sebastian waited for this most recent volley to subside.

"So, who's Angel?" he asked.

"Curiosity killed the cat, baby!" Bless exclaimed. "You sure you wanna know?"

"Can you just tell me?"

"Sure, sure." Bless grinned, drummed his fingers. "She's an old friend of Otto's. Was with him back in the day, when he was just a pup. She knew him before I did."

"And you're not scared? That he'll do the same thing to you one day?"

"No way, man. Shit's different between us. Me and Otto are tight. Not blood, but we could be—fucking should be. I been with him a long time now. Angel? She's like a ghost. One of those that ain't with you anymore."

"But what if it *does* happen to you? What'll you do?"

"It won't," said Bless. "Shit, I'll be dead soon, anyways. That's what happens."

They were in Baltimore. The roads were slick. The air in the van stung. Sebastian tried swallowing, but his mouth was dry. Now he *really* had to do it. If he didn't, they would know. They would absolutely know. And then it would be over—not just for him, but for Sarah, too.

They parked in front of a tall, run-down apartment building. Bless reached underneath his seat and raised a package wrapped in brown wax paper. "Good coke in here," he said offhandedly, then gave the package to Sebastian. "Fourth floor, the room with the horseshoe over the door. Say I couldn't make it, but that I think you're the best one for the job."

"Okay, but what about—"

"Oh, yeah! Why didn't you say somethin' sooner?" Bless reached under the seat again and this time withdrew a plastic bag with a pistol inside, the silencer already attached. "All you gotta do is point and squeeze, sweetie pie. Like they do in the movies. Bang bang!"

Sebastian took out the gun, felt the cold steel in his clammy hand.

"You'll know who she is," Bless said. "Easy to tell. Might be some other bitches in there, but who cares. They won't do anything. When you get in there, she'll want to weigh the coke, so just give it to her. It'll pass, and then she'll give it back. She'll probably say to go put it in the kitchen. Do that, take out your piece, and then come back out and take the shot. Bring back the gun and coke after."

"What if someone hears?"

"No one's gonna hear. Just come back down. I'm gonna wait for you. Then we go back, like nothing ever happened. Just a bad dream, right?" Bless smiled and patted him on the cheek. "Now get going. Don't got all night."

Sebastian climbed out of the van. The apartment building loomed over him like an enormous grave. With every breath, the dank, metallic stench of blood filled his nostrils. He tasted blood on his tongue, felt it slide down the back of his throat. Rotting meat. Buzzing flies.

He idled in the lobby, winced at the lights shining off cracked tile and from behind broken fixtures. Even with his sunglasses on, everything was too bright. Up the stairs. One floor, and then another. He saw colors. The red of Otto's club. The blue and green of the Hollow Deck. The pink streak in Miranda's hair. The gray of Polo's smashed skull. Pop, pop, pop. The shattered mirror. The dark red oozing from his slashed palm. The frosty black rolling outside the van. The crisp blue light hovering upon Bless's face. The same blue light from the computer screen, from their old television in the den. The mustard yellow of the carpet where his father had fallen. The milky green bile dribbling down his chin as he reached the fourth floor.

It wasn't that killing was hard or gruesome or anything like that, just that it was so *final*. You killed someone, they didn't come back. There weren't any more thoughts. There weren't any more feelings. All those years somebody lived, building relationships, experiencing things, going places, loving and hating, all of it just gone, done, a waste. That was the scary thing. That's what was so fucking depressing. People weren't like bugs or even cats or dogs. They didn't live maybe ten, twelve years and then just give out. They didn't just eat and play and fuck. They *knew* they were going to die. They thought it, they felt it. They understood it. They stayed up at night, lying in bed, staring up at the ceiling, counting the seconds, the minutes, the hours, knowing it was all just trickling away until it wasn't. Until there was nothing left.

It was a waste to live. Pointless. He didn't know what was worse—dying young or dying old. On the one hand, you didn't live, you didn't even get that much. On the other, you lived so much, and you lost so much, too. Jesus, would he just wake up and all this crap go away? Could he fast-forward and get past all this shit?

He was stalling, leaning against the wall of the fourth-floor landing, his legs buckling so much someone might have thought he was going to piss himself. Fucking pussy, he thought. Just get up there. Do it. It's just some dead bitch at the end of the day. Bless said it himself: she's a ghost. She doesn't exist. She's not real. None of this is happening. Okay? It's not fucking happening. So, just go and do it. Do it! Or do you want to crawl back to Sarah, tail between your legs? You want to roll over and be her little bitch for the rest of your life? You're no one's bitch. You're one of the chosen—you're a fucking *god*. No one can touch you. No one can hurt you.

There was her look again, full of contempt and judgment and disgust. Like she was any better. She was the disgusting one. She was the crazy one. She could stay in that tiny, shithole apartment for all he cared. She could shrivel up and die like their mother. Get cancer and turn into a zombie. Get punched around by some drunk asshole. Who cared if she was losing her mind? He wasn't responsible for her. She brought it on herself. She brought it on herself. She brought it on herself. Crazy fucking psycho bitch. You brought it all on yourself.

Finally, his legs moved, and just like Bless said, there was a horseshoe above the door. Sebastian gathered himself and knocked. There were sounds within—dishes being piled, music swelling from a television. The door opened. A girl stood on the other side, no older than fourteen, hair styled in braids, face covered in acne.

"Yeah?" she asked. "What do you want?"

Sebastian wavered. "I got Otto's package."

"Oh, yeah? Who are you?"

"I'm new."

"Where's Bless?"

"Bless couldn't make it. He said I was the best one for the job."

"He said that?"

"Yeah. The best one."

The girl hesitated, then called into the apartment. "Aunt Kendra, there's a guy here with Otto's package! I let him in? Bless says he's the best one for the job!"

"Let him in," came the tired voice of a woman. "I'll look at him."

Sebastian walked inside. The walls of the apartment were a dark, chipped salmon. The carpet was a spot-stained beige. In the living room, a woman sat in front of an old, vintage television. Her face was wrinkled and cut and tired. Long black hair, patched with gray, curled down her neck. She picked at a bowl of popcorn in her lap, the glow of the television falling on her, the sounds of an old Western reaching Sebastian—the loud pop of gunshots, the dramatic boom of brass horns. The woman didn't look away from the television when she spoke.

"It's okay, Tisha. Go to your room."

The girl frowned, but departed dutifully through a nearby door. Sebastian just stood there, eyes stung by sweat, breath caught in his throat. He squinted, and the pink walls were suddenly red with blood, guts, fat, and muscle. He felt another wave of bile wash into his mouth.

"Well, come here," said the woman. "Let me look at you."

He walked forward. Lazily, the woman slid popcorn into her mouth. "Take off the hood and glasses," she said. "I want to see your face."

He did as asked. The walls moved. Clumps of skin trailed behind bits of glistening fat.

"You're nervous," the woman said. "Why?" She looked straight at him now. "You look like you seen a ghost."

He swallowed the bile down. "Are you Angel?"

She smiled. "I stopped being Angel a long time ago." She turned over her limp arms, revealed the faded black ink of an angel wing on each wrist. "See them? Twenty years ago, I got these. They don't go away no matter how hard I scrub."

She seemed to lose herself, seemed to drift away, but then she focused on him again. "What about you? Bless says you're the best one for the job?"

"Yeah. He couldn't make it."

She clicked her tongue, studied him with those sad, tired eyes. "So young," she said. "Just a little child, and they got you doing this." She ate more popcorn, then held out her hand. "Let me have it."

He gave her the package. She tested its weight with one hand before returning it to him. "Good. Leave it in the kitchen. Then you can leave."

He stared at the package dumbly before heading into the small kitchen. The air smelt heavily of lemon, orange, some salsa. Dirty dishes were stacked underneath a rusted faucet. Magazines and old cookbooks cluttered the countertops alongside mason jars filled with cherries, pickles, and peaches. Down below, far below, dogs barked and growled in an empty lot. Their howls came back to him like pained, tortured cries.

"And you?" Angel asked as he came back. "What do they call you?"

"My name's Sebastian."

She chuckled. "You religious, Sebastian? You like that poor saint they named you after?"

"No," he said. "My mom was, but me and my sister, we aren't. I mean, she pretends to be, but I don't think she is." He couldn't face the woman. Those eyes moving in that limp, lifeless face. Those eyes studying him. Seeing straight through him.

"You have a sister," she said. "I had one. Her name was Nadine."

"Had one? Is that girl her kid?"

"Oh, no. Nadine didn't have children. Tisha there belongs to a friend. I look after her when her mother's working. She helps me a little on the side." She turned back to the television. "And your sister—what's her name?"

"Sarah," he replied softly.

"Sarah. Your momma really loves her Bible. And where's Sarah right now?"

"I don't know. At home. Where she always is."

"Shouldn't you be with her? You're family, after all."

"That doesn't matter," he said. "We're not the same. She doesn't get it. She doesn't get me. Blood doesn't change that."

"She lost?"

He nodded, and she laughed. "Then you two *are* the same," she said. "You're lost, too. That's why you're here. Go on. Show it to me. I want to see it."

The knowing look made him relent. He drew the gun.

She gazed upon the weapon. "I knew it was coming. For a long time, I knew it was coming. And now you're here to do it. You made a deal with him, didn't you?"

"What?"

"A deal. He's offering you something. Something too good to pass up."

Sebastian's grip on the gun wavered. "I need his help," he said, straightening his back out, trying to make himself bigger than he was. "The thing I'm working on, it needs to get finished. Once it is, I'm done with him. I'm done with all of them."

"You're never gonna be done," she said. "Never. Even if you get away from him—and you won't—you're never gonna be done. It's gonna find you. Just like it found me."

"Look, I'm sorry, but I gotta do this. I have to."

"You *have* to?" she asked. "No one *has* to. Question is about what you *want*. You're here right now because you think you don't have a choice, but you do."

"Then what the fuck am I supposed to do? Just walk out?"

"You can. Or you can point that thing at my head and do it. Doesn't matter to me. I died before. I'll die again." She stared at the television, eyes glassy, frail hand sifting through the popcorn. "I guess the thing you have to wonder about is you. That sister of yours. What Tisha's gonna think when she comes in and sees me."

"I'll be gone."

"Not your shadow," she said. "Not that smell you dragged in here. Smells like rotten meat. Like roadkill. You brought that in here, Sebastian. You're already carrying it with you."

"I'm on a mission," he said. "I'm not wrong."

"You're just a child. That's why he picked you. You don't know."

"Don't know what?" He raised the gun. "You just keep talking like you know everything, like you got all the answers. You don't know shit, lady. You think I'm lost? *You're* lost. It isn't your way—it's *my* way. That's why he picked me. Why he *chose* me."

"Oh, yeah?"

"Yeah. I got a purpose. You and Sarah—you think you know better, but you don't. You're the ones scared because you've been left behind." The gun shook in his hand, but he struggled, aimed the barrel at her head. "I do this, and I'll have everything I need."

"You don't think you got a choice," she said, "but you keep stalling. He make threats? Say he gonna do something to that sister you're trying so hard to hate?"

"Shut up. You don't know anything about me. Or her."

She smiled, but it was waxy, just the bottom half of her face moving while the rest stayed the same. "And you know?" she asked. "You got it all figured out?"

When he didn't answer, she scoffed. "You say you got a purpose? If so, you better stick to it. You can't be wishy-washy like this. Do it or don't." She turned back to the television, heavy eyes drooping. "Do it, or let me finish watching my movie."

He stared at her, now focused fully on her saggy, wrinkled face, her exhausted eyes, her patched, frizzled hair. He didn't know. Who he wanted to be, what he wanted to do—he didn't know. He never thought about it. Slowly, the gun fell to his side. He felt different suddenly. He saw it again, that safe, hallow place. Clearer than ever before. Leaning against his mother on the couch. Watching some old movie. Golden light coming in through the window, the smell of the cinnamon candies so strong, so potent. He wanted to be that boy again. He wanted to feel his mother's touch, back before she hated him, before he became a monster in her eyes. Back when he was still just a pure, smiling, little boy, a lovable thing, a doll. Back when, for the briefest of times, even Sarah smiled at him and teased him, before he became real. He wanted all of that again, but there was no way to get it back. At least not here. Not in this place.

But in another place—

"I want to be a kid again," he said, "but I want this more. I want to know what's in the room of cloth."

He raised the gun and shot her. Pop. A quick hiss, muffled by the cracks of gunfire from the television, the thud of hooves. Her head snapped back. The hole between her eyes trickled blood. As though she were daydreaming, slipping away, imagining a better place, a better life.

When Sebastian returned to the van, Bless didn't say anything. He just grinned and winked, and they drove off.

2 2 .

Sarah rang the doorbell of the row house. The early af-ternoon sky was a clear blue, the few clouds puffy and picturesque. She zipped up her sweater as the wind swept by. Cars passed. A group of kids walked down the block. As tired as she was from the lack of sleep, she felt clear-headed. It's the air, she thought. Good to get out of the apartment.

The door opened. "Miss Creed?"

"Hey, Janette. Sorry for the wait."

"That's okay. Come in."

Sarah entered. The foyer was cramped, lined with photos of the three children: Janette, her brother Paul, and their baby sister. "Mom wanted to be here," said Janette, leading her into the kitchen, "but she had to go to work last-minute." She placed upright an overturned cereal box, wiped some stray crumbs off the table. "He can't even clean up after himself. I gotta pick up all his dirty clothes he leaves around, too."

As she spoke, Sarah thought of her own brother and the messes he used to leave behind. Clothes scattered over the floor, unfinished food left on the table, even the occasional syringe out in the open—all were regular occurrences, aggravating if not devastating on the worst of days. Trash just seemed to accumulate around him, growing and growing and growing as though he were a walking broken window. Yet she would have gladly taken the strewn clothes and half-eaten food and even the used syringes over what was happening now. Haunted, paranoid, tormented, filled with dread, without reprieve. Watching always for some impending, inevitable doom. Waiting always for the ground to open up beneath her, the pits of Hell to reveal themselves in searing flame and biblical anguish. When she closed her eyes, there were scenes of blood, of torn flesh and broken bone, death and decay. Voices called to her. Cooed to her. Sang to her. Come, they said. Join us. Join *him*.

"Your brother," she said, shivering, coming out of her thoughts. "Paul. He's here?"

"Yeah, just like you wanted." Janette pointed to the door leading to the living room. "He's in there goofing off, watching TV. You want me there when you talk to him? I already told him not to try anything."

"It's okay. It's probably better I talk to him alone."

"You sure? I—" A baby's sudden cry interrupted her. "That's Tina," she sighed. "Probably gotta change her diaper. Just call if you need anything, okay?"

"I will, Janette. Thanks."

The girl went upstairs, and Sarah walked into the living room. Gaudy floral wallpaper greeted her. An old sofa took up space in front of a large, blocky television.

Sunken into the sofa was Paul, in a black t-shirt and shorts. He was lanky, taller than she remembered.

"Hello, Paul," said Sarah. "It's good to see you."

He looked up at her, a flash in his eyes betraying recognition and maybe even pleasant surprise. But then he turned back to the television, eyes hard, face tight and cool, no doubt the way he had practiced many times in front of the mirror and on the street.

"Miss Creed," he said. "Didn't think you'd show."

Years ago, Paul had been a bright spot in her classroom. Shirt always tucked in and hair neatly combed. Turned in work without issue. Never missed a day. He even shared with her some of the poems he wrote. "None of that gangster stuff," he said at the time. "This is real, Miss Creed. What's happening." A spoken-word prophet—that had been his dream. Diagnosing the ills of society. Lambasting the crooked corporations and corrupt government that oppressed the common man and kept everyone in chains.

God, was she really so cynical? Had she actually looked that boy in the eyes, told him his work was good, his goals true, without believing a single word of it? She peddled the same story to Janette, to her other students, to Sebastian, to herself. Be good. Choose. Resist. But she was afraid, the chains rattling in the back of her mind, the invisible blood caking her skin, that her beliefs were only futile hope and desperate delusion.

She was fractured, fleeting, made up of unbound wisps and air caught in a loose net. A hole in a life no longer her own. Kept together by sheer force of will, by the gravity of exhaustion, by anchors and weights digging deeper and deeper into the material. But they're coming, she thought, rubbing her wrists, feeling the raw skin where the ropes had been fastened tight. Coming to take her apart. To free her. To release all that energy into the sky, into the stars.

No.

Get a grip.

Focus.

Here.

Now.

"It must be strange," she said, sitting down in a chair. "I'm probably the last person you were expecting to see again. How have you been?"

He didn't answer.

"How about your poetry? Are you still writing?"

"Cut the shit," he said, looking at her at last. "You ain't my teacher anymore, and I know you're not here for charity. Why don't you just say what you need to say?"

"You're right. You're right." She tried to say more, but the television distracted her. There was a music video playing: dancers wrapped in bandages, mist spreading around them. Strobe lights flashing red. Arms and legs bound by leather. Chains slinking into view. Rap that sounded more like chanting. Like screaming.

"Can you turn that down first? In fact, can you just turn it off?"

He glanced at her, eyes narrowed, but picked up the remote and obliged.

"Thank you." She took a moment. "You're right that I didn't come here for you. I came for my brother. He's in trouble."

"Oh, yeah?" asked Paul. "What's that have to do with me?"

"He's into something bad," she said. "It's hard to explain, but I don't know where he is, and if I don't find him, I'm afraid something terrible might happen. You know this town better than I ever could, so that's why I'm here. You know how I can find him."

He scoffed. "You don't know what you're doing, Miss Creed. You don't got the slightest clue what it's like out there."

"Paul, please. I just need some information. A few days ago, my brother went to New Jersey, and he hasn't been back since. But there has to be someone who knows where he is. My brother knew someone. He hung out with him a lot, talked about him a few times. A 'Big C.'"

"Big C." Paul spat the name out with disgust. "Wasn't expecting that."

"You know who he is?"

"Yeah, of course. Cuban guy. Sells a lot of good stuff. Everybody knows him. Knows what he does, too. He makes young guys work, then he does shit with 'em. Some of them are just a little older than Janette. Me and the guys, we don't go around that part of town. I've never seen him in person."

"What does he do?" asked Sarah quietly.

"You know what I'm talking about. Once they're hooked on the drugs, they don't fight him. They work for him, too. They do whatever he wants. Like his whores."

She shuddered. "So, my brother—"

"Probably."

"My God." Sarah rubbed her eyes, suddenly even more exhausted. Some pedophile drug dealer on top of everything else. She didn't even want to imagine.

"He's bad news, Miss Creed," Paul said. "Ain't my business, but you should leave it. If your brother's working for him, he's as good as gone. Especially now. You can't even go out at night anymore. Not with Otto's guys around."

"Otto. I've heard that name before, from the kids."

"All the dealers in town are working for him. If they're not, they're dead. So, if your brother's working for Caesar, he's working for Otto." Paul clicked his tongue. "My advice? Forget about it. It's not worth dying over."

Sarah heard his warning, processed the message, yet it made no difference. Once, the mere mention of these phantoms may have inspired fear, but however awful these men were, they didn't compare to the biggest phantom of all. The manacled man hung overhead, with those red eyes, that frothing muzzle. His influence was everywhere, and Sebastian, if he read those pages, if he was carrying them around, was tangled in that demon's web.

"Paul," Sarah said, smiling softly, "I get what you're saying, but look at my face. Do you think it matters how dangerous it is? What would you do if it were your sisters?"

"It *wouldn't* be my sisters," Paul said. Something in his eyes changed. In his face. "Don't screw with me, Miss Creed. My sisters. Fuck. Like my sisters would be caught dead in that shit. But it figures, coming from someone like you. Looking at me like that. Pitying me."

"I don't understand," Sarah said.

Paul was no longer lounging back, uninvolved. He was upright and heated, his voice louder, its passion reminding her of the way he used to speak as her student. "You got it backwards," he said. "You come in here thinking I'm a victim, that someone let me down. My parents or the government. Maybe you even think it was you. You feel bad, you feel guilty. You look at me like I went wrong. But I didn't. No one let me down. I didn't have to steal from that store, but I wanted to. I wanted to do it. Your brother's the same way. We wanted it, so we got it. It's not because we're poor or stupid. It's because we wanted it."

Sarah said nothing. Paul was smiling—had he been waiting for this? Anticipating the moment she would walk in, so he could throw this at her? Was it her fault? Had she earned this? Or was Paul just licking his wounds, finding the most convenient scapegoat?

"You want to meet Caesar?" he asked. "Go ahead. I know the place even if I ain't been there. But don't be surprised when you don't like what you see."

"I didn't mean to insult you," she said. "Whatever I did, I didn't mean it. I just want to help my brother—"

"Shut up." He grabbed a piece of paper and scribbled down the address. He handed the paper to her without looking at her face. "You come when it's convenient. And then you feel bad afterwards, like you could've done something. Like it was your responsibility to begin with."

She stood up, holding the piece of paper in her trembling left hand.

"Thank you, Paul."

He didn't reply, just sat back down and turned on the television. Sarah returned to the kitchen, where Janette waited.

"Everything go okay?" she asked. "You talk to him already?"

"Yeah. He gave me what I needed."

"Miss Creed?" Janette looked into her desolate eyes. "He say something to you? What—" She paused. Sarah watched, apathetic, as Janette sniffed the air. "What is that *smell*?" she asked. "Where's it coming from? It wasn't here before."

"Thanks for having me, Janette." Sarah went to the door. "I better get going."

"Miss Creed, wait. Whatever Paul said, forget about it. He's an idiot."

"No," said Sarah. "Your brother's smart, Janette. Maybe too smart. He always has been."

Outside, she looked at the note Paul gave her. He had been a bright, earnest student once, his heart on his sleeve. Her? As a teenager, she slept away days, partied through nights, clouded her mind, ravaged her body. No ambition. No aspiration. Only that desperate want to escape, to be free. Almost as if she were hunted. Hunted then, and hunted now.

"I'm sorry, Paul," she said under her breath, closing her eyes, breathing hard. However refreshing the breeze had been before, now it was humid, clogged with that awful smell that followed her. Did it want her to sleep, this bug in her head? Was it looking to exhaust her? Sooner or later, she knew she wouldn't be able to fight it anymore. She would need to sleep, and the nightmares would begin again. Nightmares, she thought, that maybe Paul shared on the days when everything seemed at its worst.

"Here it is, baby," said Bless. "All cleaned up and new just for you."

Sebastian surveyed the apartment. White walls. Gray floor. Kitchenette with refrigerator and stove. No furniture in any of the rooms. Windows without blinds or drapes. He looked down from one of the windows and saw the alley below dripping wet from rain, cluttered with overfilled, rusted dumpsters and overturned, dented trash cans. A brown, mangy dog sauntered through, tongue hanging, tail wagging. The dog sniffed around some trash, then was gone.

"I'm gonna need something," Sebastian said. "For the windows."

"No problem, sweetie. You want your privacy. We'll hook you up. Whatever you want." Bless clapped his hands and put on his typical grin. "Tell you what. Make me a list, and I'll get my guys to get you anything you want. Like a genie in a bottle!"

"Well, I could use a bed."

"Yeah, yeah, everyone needs a bed, babe. Gotta get that shut-eye! Gotta count those sheep! Anything else? Food? Drinks?"

"I don't know. I'll think about it."

"Yeah, of course. Take your time. Oh, yeah. We'll have some guys in here tomorrow to set up that computer you wanted. Real high-speed shit. We'll rig it right up! Can't say Otto doesn't take care of his people, can you?"

"He's putting down a lot of money," Sebastian said.

"It's an investment. You did good work, mama-san. Otto respects that. *I* respect it. We're just paying you back. Deal's a deal, right?"

"If you say so."

When Bless left a few minutes later, Sebastian went to work. For the first time since coming back from New Jersey, he took out the bound manuscript from the duffle bag Miranda had given him. It wasn't very thick, but it still felt heavy in his hands, like a pair of bricks. Just holding it sent spasms up his arms and through his body. He was shaking, he realized, just holding it away from himself, admiring it from afar. His lips quivered. His arms and legs trembled. Everything that had consumed his thoughts for the last few months, all that had swallowed his nights, it was right here, right in his hands. Printed on the front page were three stark, bold words in all capitals: ROOM OF CLOTH. He wondered briefly who had compiled it, who had spent the time and effort necessary to find the vignettes, the rumors, the stories, and knit them together, weave them into a whole. Had it been Miranda? Bryan Stevens? Or had it been someone else, maybe others, maybe many, *many* others? Over how many years?

He laid it down, barely resisting the enormous temptation to flip it open and devour its secrets. Not yet. *Not yet.* He stood up, fetched the dirty, splotched manila folder where he kept the rest. There was a heaviness in the room, a weight he couldn't explain. As he laid the folder beside the bound volume, the heaviness grew, became almost physical. Sebastian felt the pressure around him, felt it drag him down like great weights on his arms and legs. He could almost reach out and touch the magnetism, feel it, caress it. It was an embrace, he thought, a welcoming, a gratefulness. Two halves rejoined, reunited—a spark of life, an overflow of magic, beautiful, wondrous magic. A cold, dead heart heating back up, becoming hot, beating slowly at first, then more vigorously. Blood pumping. Bones creaking. Muscles contracting. Flesh reanimating. Yes, this was everything he had dreamt of. Everything he had fantasized about.

Miraculously, gratefully, Sebastian felt safe. He felt at home. Surrounded by this presence, smothered by its hot weight, coated in its sweet smell of cinnamon, he thought himself nestled against his mother once again. But this was not his mother, not that old, sick bitch in the hospital bed. It wasn't Sarah, either. It was his new family, his new father. His real father. Finally, his initiation was complete. The bullshit games were over.

He reached out, eager to begin, when his cell phone buzzed. It took everything in him to look away from the manuscript and pick up the phone. Caesar wanted to see him. Sebastian deliberated. His first impulse was to go back to the book, but he knew that was a mistake. He would cut ties eventually, but for now, Caesar would just get more suspicious. He would just ask more questions. The best thing to do was humor him.

Caesar waited for him in the meantime. He sat in his dim, dirty living room, a glass of whiskey in his hand. He had been anxious the past few days. He kept thinking about Sebastian, this kid who had wandered right into the belly of the beast. Caesar hadn't wanted him involved with Otto—*he* didn't want to be involved with Otto—but it was impossible to get around. One day, the man appeared like some sort of ghost. Him and his goons. Without missing a beat, he started recruiting workers, started issuing threats, started taking everything and everyone into his web. The ones who didn't play along, they vanished. Here one day, gone the next. Thought you were tough shit? Thought you had some power? You didn't. Not next to this guy.

Caesar downed the whiskey. He had never fucked around with Otto. He saw what happened to guys he knew, to guys who thought they could play the game better. But you can't win when the guy in charge knows all the cards you have, when he's making the plays before you even think of 'em. That was Otto. *El Coco. El diablo.* A dark man. A phantom. And his lackeys were just as bad, maybe even worse. Like that fucker Bless. Drags some poor asshole into an alleyway, behind a dumpster, out to a ditch, and blows his brains out. Beats him to death—or doesn't, stops right before the last breath, then maybe cuts off a finger, takes the scalp, leaves a mark so that everyone knows. The regular folk, Otto would say, they don't know business. They don't know loyalty. They work their asses off, take care of tons of kids, never sleep, and that's all they know. Nothing higher. Nothing better. You have to teach them, he'd say. You have to tattoo on the fear, beat in the respect, carve out the loyalty. Relay the message in a language they'll understand: blood and bone, knives and bullets, muscles and guts. Everyone knows it. They've known it since the cave. They've done it to one another for a long, long time.

But Caesar, shit. Did he have a right to complain? Was he any better? Polo was the fourth guy he'd done for Otto. And they were all the same. Scared shitless. Praying to God. Begging not to die. Please, please, *please*, don't kill me. I wanna live. I wanna fucking *live*.

I wanna live, too, is what Caesar always thought. I don't wanna die. I don't wanna get dragged into that alley. Because it won't be quick, not like this. This shit right here, this gun-to-your-head, one-pull-and-it's-done shit? That's *mercy*. Those other guys, for them, it's sport. For them, it's like playing with their food. We never took off the nails before, right? Oh, shit, we have. What about the eyes? Fuck, man, think bigger—what about the eye-*lids*?

It didn't matter, though. Not in the end. Dead was dead. And now Caesar had given Sebastian up, had wrapped him in gold paper with a little red bow. And for what? A *book*? To keep himself out of trouble? The fuck did it matter? Wasn't he supposed to take care of the kid? Wasn't he his friend? His brother?

Maybe it might have been better if he never found Sebastian back then. If he hadn't thought the frail thing sitting on the sidewalk hadn't looked so fucking *gone*. If he hadn't felt pity instead of lust. Maybe the end would have come sooner for the kid. Maybe that would have been better. He hated himself for thinking that. Like he needed more reason to hate himself.

Someone knocked at the door. It was Sebastian.

"Hey, Seb," said Caesar quietly. "Come in."

"No company?"

Caesar felt the sting of the question, but he kept his smile on. "Nah. Just me." He refilled his glass. "Little drunk. Sorry about that."

"What'd you want, C? I'm busy."

"Just wanted to talk. Maybe drive a little. You been avoiding me the past couple days."

"I've been busy."

"Yeah, sure." Caesar turned to the door. "Come on."

They got into Caesar's van and started cruising. Sebastian saw that Caesar was indeed drunk—even while inching slowly down the dark, wet streets, he took hits from his flask, his eyes unfocused, his hands shaky. Much like the night they staked out Polo's party. But there was little point in thinking about any of that. Polo was dead. Angel was dead. Dead was dead.

They passed slummy houses and saggy apartments. Passed homeless in trailing rags and tattered jackets. Passed prostitutes in frayed furs and high heels. Passed dogs. Passed *the* dog, the same dog from earlier, its skin raw and exposed, its fur falling off in tufts. Passed shambling children chained together, their eyes missing. Passed old men with skin like leather. Passed old women with cobwebs for hair. Passed angels with their wings shredded and mouths bloody. Passed demons with their tails clipped and horns broken. Passed torsos without limbs, arms without hands, bones without meat. A procession marching from one darkness into another, deeper darkness, one blood-red and black. They stared at him, those eyeless children and legless men and armless women. Come, they whispered, burdened by their chains, bled dry by their hooks. Join us. Be one with us.

Together.

With us.

Together.

Where you belong.

Together.

With *him*.

Caesar stopped the van. The procession was gone. Only the early night remained with its fresh, cold veil of darkness. The van's headlights were fixed on a street corner. "What are we doing here?" asked Sebastian. "What's going on?"

"You don't remember?" Caesar pointed his flask at the sidewalk. "This is where I picked you up, Seb. The very first time."

"Why are we here, C?"

"When I saw you," Caesar said, "I thought, shit, he looks so fucking sad. *Pobrecito*. That's what my *abuela* would say. Poor baby. Poor kid. I just felt so bad, like I found some broken toy. That's why I picked you up, 'cause I felt I had to. I had to fix you."

Sebastian stared blankly at the spot in the headlights. To be honest, he couldn't even remember the first time he met Caesar. So much of that time after the hospital was still a blur, a wash of images and sounds that came together only occasionally to form coherent memory. But apparently, this little patch of cement was some big fucking deal, like a Mars rover had found alien life here. Only in this case, Sebastian figured, he was the alien life. Always the alien life.

Caesar was still going on. "I had to fix you," he said. "I had to fix you, but why you? Why not the other kids, you know? Why not all of 'em? But then I think, fuck, it ain't any different. Fix you, fuck them—it's still the same. It's still using you, and it's wrong, 'cause you're a *person*, Seb, you're a person. But I still felt like I had to do something. Like I had to help you. You get me, right? You get what I'm saying?"

"Caesar, what the fuck are you talking about?"

"I'm saying it's me!" Caesar cried. "I'm responsible for you! I know you been with Bless, with Otto—I know they got you to do something, and I hope it's not what I fucking think it is. You gotta tell me, Seb. You gotta tell me I'm wrong. You gotta tell me you didn't do it!"

"Just stop talking, Caesar. Take us back."

"Seb, you gotta listen to me. They ain't good. I shouldn't have set up that meet. Fuck, I was scared! Scared that he'd find out, that you'd go to him, anyway. Fuck!" He threw his flask against the dashboard. "That *pinche cabrón*! Thinks he owns us, that he can do whatever the fuck he wants! Don't you get it, Seb? The longer you stay, the more he won't let you leave! That's why you gotta go! You can't end up like me!"

"That cunt doesn't own me," Sebastian said. "Don't fucking say that. No one owns me."

"You don't know," said Caesar. "This guy, what he does—you don't know. And it's my fault. You hear me? It's my fault."

"Christ," Sebastian muttered, trying to contain his laughter. Another meltdown. Another fucking joke. What the hell was going on? What was happening to all these people around him? "I can't believe I'm hearing this shit."

"I'm trying to help you!" Caesar said. "I'm trying to fucking help you!"

"You're just helping yourself!" Sebastian hit the window with his twitching fist. "You fucking people. You keep thinking you can tell me what to do. You keep thinking you can use me. You keep thinking you can fucking use me!"

He hit the window again. And again. And again and again and again. "I'm tired of being treated like I'm fucking stupid! I'm tired of being looked at like that! I'm tired of being some problem everyone needs to fucking fix!"

"Seb," said Caesar, "Seb, calm down. I'm not saying that—"

"You *are* fucking saying that! You are, you are, *you are*!" He snarled, teeth bared, eyes bulging. "Fuck this shit! Fuck you and fuck Otto and fuck Sarah! I don't need any of you!"

He threw open the door and stormed out. Caesar called after him. "Seb! Seb, wait!"

But Sebastian wasn't listening. Even Caesar. Even fucking *Caesar*. They were all cunts. They were all fake. If it wasn't Sarah pulling him in one direction, it was Caesar, thinking they knew the way to be. Was there really no one to whom he could turn? Maybe not a person, he thought. Maybe people were all the same, all on the outside, all ignorant. But there was a place, wasn't there? A place where all of this didn't matter anymore. A place where everyone was on the inside, together. Where everyone was welcome. Where everyone belonged.

He smiled, walking into the night, the many phantoms around him resuming their eternal march. Eyeless, limbless, they watched him. They waited for him.

2 4 .

want to see something cool? Here, take a look!

What is that?

o shit

its the room

room of cloth?

No fucking way. That shit isnt real

Don't feed the troll guys its just bait

wait who says it isnt real

Yeah, who says?

i think ive seen OPs name around

Common sense says. It's a book, it's not real, it's just words.

Just words, lol. lmao :)

o wait that guy?

yeh, TC posted here a long time ago

Isn't this off-topic? (What's the link, btw?)

my cousin's friend said she read it. havent talked to her since tho

I'm flagging this topic FYI. Enjoy your moderation.

is this the saem guy in this pic?

what the fuck

what is that

That has to be edited, what the hell!!

Don't click on it

The link's dead.

people r posting on other sites... anyon seen this?

Stop

Wait, the guy who posted the second pic. His account isnt even active?

someone close the topic already!!

u just bumped it bro!

Why hasn't this been modded yet??!!

That guy in the pic . . . that was my brother.

what?

Yeah, right

No look. This is his graduation pic. He was 17.

holy shit

oh god

That's him but his eyes

hey

hey

How old's that pic? Looks kinda old

heh heh eh

heh

heyheyhey

heres the pic when they found him

....

....

HES HAVING LOTS OF FUN WITH US :)))))

[Message deleted.]

Is that guy gone now?

He hasn't posted in weeks.

smart to bump this topic?

I don't see why not. All of this was probably just a hoax.

Like those guys were in on it together?

Yeah, has to be.

I dunno

The links are down, right?

Yeah.

no not for me

Huh?

Says the image has been removed.

no i can see it

but theres no guy i saw my mom

Yeah, I saw my girlfriend!!!

shes smiling

Everyone's smiling.

look at that smile

hahahhahahahahhahahahhahahahhahhhaaaha

she looked so pretty in that dress

LOOK AT THAT SMILE HES SO HAPPY

:):):):)

HAHAHAHAHAHAHAHAHAHAHAHAHA

HAHAHAHAHAHAHAHA

HAHAHAHAHAHAHAHAHAHAHAHAHA

HAHAHAHAHAHAHAHA

HAHAHAHAHAHAHAHAHAHAHAHAHA

HAHAHAHAHAHAHAHA

its the same dress

[Message deleted.]

HES THE HAPPIEST PERSON ALIVEEEEE

[Message deleted.]

[Message deleted.]

the same dress from her funeral

[Message deleted.]

him i saw him i saw him i saw HIM I SAW HIM I SAW HIM

[Message deleted.]

[Message deleted.]

HAPPPPPPPPPYYYYYYYYYYYYYYYYY

[Message deleted.]

:)))

a!434lsjdgljashdgiuy**wiuen/||vYYYkajsdf######45{

JUST WORDS. These are just words. You're just words.

The room of cloth exists. It exists in the mind of anyone who knows about it. Then it becomes real. They make it real. They don't even think about it. It just happens. It's happening right now. Oh, sure, you can't get up and drive there. Or maybe you can. Maybe the next time you open the door to the bathroom in the middle of the night, or the closet, or whatever, it's not the room you thought it'd be, but a different one. You go outside, and you're there. And then you can't get out. You're stuck with him.

So it's like a thought?

Yeah, and that thought becomes reality. It's in your head, but it's real. And sometimes it comes out of your head. It builds itself when you're not looking. Where you're not looking.

That's crazy.

No. No.

You're crazy.

It's because you haven't seen it. You don't believe in it.

I don't believe in stories. They're fiction. Reality's here, it's real.

Everything's fiction. Everything is distorted. The TRUTH is outside, not in.

Apparently there was a group of people somewhere in Arizona. Some basement, not sure, OP didn't specify. Anyway, police go down there and find like thirty people all dead, adults and kids, had been like that a few days. They're all in these white gowns, like hospital gowns. They have masks on. Everyone took pills. The smell was really bad.

I call BS. No way that happened.

I'm just passing it on. And on their wrists and ankles, you know what was there? Chains. Drawn with markers. Even on their necks, all around. The kids, too. Everyone had them.

And?

And there was a door right in the middle of the room. Just a door. It was open, but it didn't go anywhere.

Why a door?

Well, they're a cult. They got to be praying to something.

They're praying to a door?

No, not the door. Where the door *goes*.

Oh, shit. You don't think it really goes there, do you?

Yeah, I do. It has to. The chains, man.

They all killed themselves? The kids, too?

Yeah. Everyone.

Nah. That didn't happen.

Maybe it did. Maybe it didn't. Where's that guy that was talking about fact and fiction?

Don't know. Hasn't posted in weeks.

I still don't believe it. That's just part of the whole story. You got to make it sound real to make it scary. It's fake. All this shit is fake. I still haven't even found the stupid book.

Fact is, it's easier to say it's not real. Lets you sleep at night. Don't have to think about if that door went any-where. But you're gonna think about it anyway, in bed, when you're alone. You're gonna think about it. And then it won't matter. Yeah, maybe that door was just a door. Maybe it didn't go anywhere.

Or maybe it did.

Miranda arrived a few days after Sebastian abandoned Caesar on that street corner.

He had been sitting in the living room of the bare apartment when he got the message, the only light coming from the screen of the new laptop, the nearby modem flashing green and orange, a slew of cables running to the wall. The manuscript pages were spread over the floor for easy access. Empty yogurt cups, soda bottles, and meal trays lay scattered about. He put some garbage bags over the windows for privacy, but otherwise, he had not bothered with furniture. All his time had been devoted to working on the story, and he preferred staying inside, anyway. The light outside was getting to be too much, and so were the noises, the colors. He swore he saw things, too. Ashen faces watching him from crowds, from windows. Young kids. Old women. Black pools where their eyes should have been.

Caesar left voicemail after voicemail and message after message. He didn't know where the apartment was, and Bless wasn't telling him, so good. Sebastian didn't need Caesar anymore. Not him and definitely not Sarah. They were slaves to their systems, stuck in their self-righteous bubbles. But Sebastian was free in the swirling, collective darkness, connected to millions of people, their network undivided by party, race, or creed. They were bound by a shared wish, a common want. A place without judgment or hypocrisy. A place where they could feel safe and loved. A place of thought and feeling and instinct outside the superficial guise of "real life."

He couldn't deny the excitement he felt when he saw Miranda's message. He had e-mailed her after getting the apartment, but she hadn't responded for days. He had started losing hope. Without her, his chances of success were slim. She knew more, understood more. Together, they had a chance. He didn't want to think about just how long the story had existed, just how long the manuscript had changed and evolved. The stories of insanity and suicide drove him to sudden bouts of panic. But he kept telling himself he was strong enough, that he wouldn't end up that way. He was chosen after all. He had seen the manacled man. The others before him had been weak, but they had paved the way. Now, he was responsible for finishing the job, laying down the last brick, uniting the countless corpses that had mounted to reach this zenith. Yes, he stood atop a summit, the sun rising like a torch, the night sky fading away like smoke. This was it. The moment. The revelation.

Of course, there was the other reason he wanted to see Miranda again. He could picture perfectly her little mouth, her tongue. That streak of pink in her hair.

They arranged to meet outside a local bowling alley. Bless loaned Sebastian a car. "Have fun!" he cackled. "Anyone gives you shit, call me. Otto always gets the last word." Cars, guns, money—nothing seemed out of reach for them. They could snap their fingers, and there would be all the money you could ever want, all the food, clothes, women. Anything and everything.

At the bowling alley, Sebastian waited in the car. The sky was overcast once again, dense and desolate. A family of four left the bowling alley, the father carrying a cake, the daughter pulling along a cluster of red and blue balloons. Sebastian looked away from them and studied his hand. Healing well, although looking at the pink and purple knuckles made him queasy. There was Sarah. There was Caesar. Even his mother and father appeared to him. No. No more. Fuck them. Fuck them all.

Someone knocked on the passenger door window, and his heart leapt. Miranda smiled at him from outside. The streak in her hair was now navy blue.

She climbed inside with her bag. "Well, nice to see you again," she said. Then, with that little smirk, "Omen."

"Yeah. Nice to see you, too."

She rolled a lollipop in her mouth, threw an arm over the headrest. "Never been to Lorraine before. Not as much of a dump as I thought it'd be."

"How'd you get here?" Sebastian asked.

"A little money and tits go a long way." She laughed. "The difference between men and women is that all men are boys, and all girls are women. One's born stupid, and the other's born smart. Guys are wired for the short term. All they want to do is fuck. Women? For years and years, they have to make sure the little thing in their belly stays alive. That's why they think about the long term. Which all means I'm pretty smart."

She giggled at his noticeable unease. "Hey, chin up. Don't get all gloomy about it. You didn't choose what you are. Me, neither."

"I'm not stupid," he said.

"Fair enough." She leaned back and propped a dirty tennis shoe on the console. "Listen, I am *starving*. Think we could get a bite?"

They stopped for hamburgers nearby. Sebastian didn't eat anything. He just watched as Miranda devoured one burger and then another. Occasionally, his eyes swept over the assortment of wristbands, the curve of her neckline, the shape of her breasts.

"You got a nice car," she said. "Really nice. No offense, but I didn't think you could even afford a scooter." She laughed and dipped a fry into her milkshake. "Anyway, you got a place?"

"Yeah. It's big enough for both of us."

"Cool. A nice car, a little apartment. You've certainly got it made. If you don't mind me asking, how'd you get it? Or do I even want to know?"

"You have money," Sebastian said. "I'm not asking where you get yours."

"I do what I have to do. Whatever and whenever." She finished the milkshake, sucked noisily on the straw. "Let's see this place of yours."

They drove back. Miranda talked, but Sebastian caught only a selection of her snide comments on the weather and the city. He kept his eyes ahead, kept his shaking hands from drawing attention. She made him nervous. Something about the way she looked at him set him on edge. He didn't like the way she toyed with him, the way she used her knowledge as a dangling carrot. But that carrot was more than tantalizing. Here was someone connected to the great dark. He wanted to be part of it, too. Part of her.

When they arrived at the apartment, Miranda shook her head in disappointment. "Look at this," she said, glancing at the bare walls, the bland tile. "Or maybe *don't* look because there's nothing here. Wow, Omen. You got any personality at all?"

He shrugged.

"Exactly. This place is so *boring*. But it'll do, I guess. Nothing a little paint can't fix." She walked in, dropped her bag, removed her jacket. "A nice red would work. Very moody. Very stern. Or maybe beige. Some burnt orange. We make our tribute to the manacled man."

She paused. She shuddered. "I can feel him here with us. I can smell him."

Sebastian smelt him, too. The cinnamon and sugar, like a musk, filled the room. The weight was there again, the pressure. Better than any high he ever had. Becoming part of the dark, part of that web of electric lights. What hovered between people, within them, heavy and wet, unspoken and suppressed. And it was time for those things to spill out. To flood the world.

"Let's get to work," Miranda said, her eyes bright. "After all, he's waiting for us."

26.

Sarah snapped awake.

The hammer of rain on the windshield. The crash of thunder in the distance. No chanting, thankfully. No smell of sulfur. No beating drums or booming trumpets. She rubbed her eyes and looked down at the half-eaten burger in her lap, the long-soggy fries. Ridiculous, she thought, unable to keep from laughing. Falling asleep while eating a fucking hamburger.

She started the car and drove out of the parking lot.

Rain again. Seemed like it was always raining now. How badly she wanted to feel the warmth of the sun soak through her skin and boil her blood. But she had almost given up on that possibility, settling instead for the cool mist of the rain, the chilly wetness of discomfort and dread. Sleep was a luxury now that the anxiety attacks and nightmares were getting worse. She would lie paralyzed in bed, seized with fear of shapes and figures moving in the shadows. She swore she heard whispers when she sat alone: eager, excited voices promising pleasure, promising love. The fits had so increased in frequency and severity that she called in sick for the week, and maybe even longer. The worst moments were those when the unease pushed her out of bed and into the restroom. She would stand there, trying to breathe, trying to calm down, but her arms would shake, her legs buckle. Her left hand would twitch and jerk. Through the darkened mirror, she would see a red room, the walls like skin, the floor a bloody mire.

She knew what he was doing, that bastard in the chains. But he wouldn't win. At a stoplight, she cracked open another energy drink. She would make it. First to this Caesar person, and then to Sebastian. She would make it. A prayer to keep her awake. Keep going. Keep going. Fight. Resist. Burn me out, you son of a bitch. Burn me out. I dare you.

The neighborhoods got worse the farther she drove. The houses became shabbier, the streets narrower. The old house was out here, waiting to be torn down, biding its time like the rest of the town. Sebastian had been more at home on these streets than in that house, and she honestly couldn't blame him. That labyrinthine, shadowy place, still reeking of their father's drunken rage, still reverberating with their mother's petty anger, deserved to burn, and maybe so did the rest of this spread of decay where "Big C" made his lair.

Thanks to Paul's note, she found that lair at last. She stared at the condominium across the street, fought down another bout of sudden shaking. No. Not now. She couldn't be afraid. She couldn't be weak. She was about to confront the man likely responsible for exploiting her brother, for manipulating him, for leading him deeper and deeper into the abyss until he was so deep, he couldn't see the way out. She couldn't be weak in the face of that, and she especially couldn't be weak with these monstrous, awful words ready to burst from her body.

She got out of the car. The words she wrote with her shaking, possessed hand were always there, always spilling out some way or another. But she didn't let them get far. Every page she wrote, every image she scrawled, every line she scribbled—she destroyed them all. Ripped up the pages. Burnt them. Stomped on them. The words were vomit, spillover, mounting with each minute, forcing their way outside. Writing them down gave her some relief, but the words always came back. Destroying them caused her pain, too. The process was like tearing herself apart piece by piece. Peeling herself strip by strip.

How many more times could she do it?

She walked up to the condo door. The possibility remained that she would go inside and not come out, that this Caesar would wrap a hand around her thin neck and snap it like a twig. But she had to go into the abyss. She had to drag Sebastian out even if he hated her for doing so.

She knocked.

Caesar sat inside, flask at his lips. He was tired, but he couldn't sleep. He was sad, but he couldn't cry. Sex had done nothing for him the past few days, and no amount of booze or drugs did the trick, either. It wasn't even about Sebastian. The outburst rattled him for sure, but what the outburst revealed was even worse. Strip away all the bullshit, he thought, and there's the truth: he wasn't any better than Sebastian. He was blindly stumbling around, groping for direction, looking for anything that could make all this easier. He ended up in Otto's web in the same way—he had closed his eyes and covered his ears and shut his mouth. And it made sense. When you hate yourself, you don't want time to think. You don't want to remember. Because then you end up like this. Sitting here, getting drunk, making a pitiful, pathetic fool of yourself.

Someone was at the door, but he didn't feel like getting up. Maybe it was Otto's guys here to take him away in a garbage bag at long last. Maybe it was some kid willing to trade a blowjob for extra dope. That's right. He was a businessman. The village doctor. The fucking shaman. Here's your medicine. Take two in the morning, two at lunch, four at night, take as many as you fucking want. Pray to your gods. Respect the earth. Dig in the dirt and stay there where it's safe. Outside's too dangerous. It's everything scary. Everything true. And that's what frightened Caesar most of all: truth, staring him in the face, getting under his skin, sleeping with him, waiting to strangle him. Always waiting. Checking its nails. Licking its teeth.

The knocking continued. "It's open!" he yelled. Just go away, he wanted to scream, but the words wouldn't come out. The energy wasn't there. He wanted to stay in that chair, sitting like a stone, unmoving, unthinking, sinking into the fabric. He downed the rest of the flask and waited, watched as the door opened.

He and Sarah saw each other. He blinked, squinted, but couldn't process her at first. Not Otto, not one of the boys, but a woman. A skinny, blonde white girl, worn out and ragged. Almost like Sebastian, actually. Almost exactly like Sebastian.

She had trouble seeing him, too. He wasn't some towering demon with horns and massive muscles whose footsteps wilted flowers and whose breath dropped butterflies. He was just a man, just a guy with a potbelly and a receding hairline and a big mustache. He looked so small, actually, just sitting there, limp and round, eyes hazy. So small, as though ready to die.

Still, she couldn't underestimate him. She breathed in deep, straightened her back, summoned her strength.

"Are you Big Caesar?"

He laughed. Big Caesar. Big fucking Caesar. He hated that name. But names stuck, didn't they? They were like wads of gum you couldn't scrape off, like ticks hanging from your arms, getting fatter and fatter, eating up more myth than truth. He was Big Caesar to them on the outside, but, really, he was just Caesar. Just another homeboy. Not big at all, but small. Small Caesar. Little Caesar! As small as any wad of gum or tick. Fucking tiny and worthless.

Sarah stared at him, unnerved, irritated. "That's fucking good," Caesar said. "Yeah, I'm Big Caesar. In the flesh. Who're you? Never seen you before, lady."

Sarah walked up to him, the light of the lamp washing over her. As Caesar's mystique faded with each second, she felt stronger, more confident. She stood tall over him. "My name is Sarah Creed," she said. "You don't know me, but you know my brother. You know who he is, and you know where he is."

Caesar stopped laughing. "What'd you say?"

"My brother. Sebastian. Where is he? What did you do to him?"

"You're Seb's sister?" Now that he looked more closely, he saw the resemblance with clarity. The same hair. The same eyes. The same look. The same fucking *look*. The same look when Sebastian was angry, when he was distant. He was in there. Sebastian was in there, hiding behind this woman's face, judging him, condemning him. Fucking tiny Caesar. Worthless little Caesar. Can't help me. Can't help anyone. Can't help yourself.

"Oh, shit. Oh, fuck." Caesar turned away. "You really shouldn't be here, lady."

"Just tell me what I want to know. My brother's out there right now, and I need to find him. I think he's in real trouble."

Caesar didn't say anything. Sebastian *was* in real trouble. If he was involved with Otto, sooner or later, something would happen. And Sebastian had never been able to take care of himself. He couldn't stick to anything for very long. That wouldn't fly with Otto. If you were lazy, unmotivated, greedy, Otto came down on you fast. It was only a matter of time.

"Look at me," Sarah said, her voice rising. "I know you're the same guy he always went to. I know he came to you this time. I need to know why. I need to know what he's doing."

"I don't know where he is," Caesar said. "And you shouldn't go after him. The guys he's with are bad. They're the guys that pay me, the same ones that run this town. You get in their way, they dump you in a bag. That's it. No coming back."

"It's not them I'm worried about." Sarah shuddered. "He brought something back with him from Boston. Something bad. A lot worse than any guy with a gun."

The words cut through Caesar's buzz. He understood immediately.

"The book. The thing he got in Jersey."

"You know about it?"

"Yeah. He didn't shut up about it. Some story he had to finish. Was a guy in Jersey that had the rest, but we never found him. Went around the whole day, and nothing. Then the next morning, there's Seb with this bag, and he says we're done. He got it. Some girl gave it to him. That's all he said. But the way he looked when he talked about it, it was like he was someplace else. Like he wasn't here no more."

"That book," Sarah said. "It's real. I read it. Not a lot, just a few pages, but that was enough. And it's not good. It's not right. Maybe that doesn't make sense—maybe it sounds crazy—but it does something to you. It puts something in your head, and it doesn't leave."

She felt the tremors in her hand again. "It put something into Sebastian's head, and it's been there for a lot longer than mine. Whatever it's doing to him, I know it's getting worse. And if you know my brother, then you know how he is. He needs people. He doesn't think he does, but he does. He can't be on his own. So, please. If you know where he is, you have to tell me. You have to. Before it's too late."

"I don't know where he is," Caesar said, "but maybe I can find him."

"You can?"

"I think so." He got up and faced her. "I don't know what the hell's goin' on with this book, but if Seb's in trouble, we gotta get him out of it."

"Okay," said Sarah. "Where do we start?"

Caesar hated what he was about to suggest, but there wasn't much choice. The one person most likely to have a pulse on Sebastian's location was Otto's right-hand man himself.

"The guy's name is Bless. But listen, lady. This ain't the place for you. I'll talk to him."

"No way," said Sarah. "I'm going with you. Whether you like it or not."

Fuck, Caesar thought. Stubborn like her brother. But he knew what she was feeling, or he knew what Sebastian was feeling at the very least. Alone, out on that curb in the cold, waiting for that monster to descend, its nails sharp, its tongue slobbering, its hunger beyond belief.

27.

Let me tell you about Marisa, a single mother who lived in Monterrey, Nuevo León.

Marisa was forty-five years old at the time of her death. Her older son, Marco, is twenty years old, attending classes in Mexico City. Her younger son, Andrés, was ten years old. Her first husband died in an automobile accident. Her second husband left her for a younger woman. For years, she worked two, sometimes three jobs to raise her sons. Marisa always thanked God for blessing Marco with a great mind. That mind won him several scholarships, enough to let him attend university. Doing so likely saved his life.

Marisa's days were consumed by stress, anxiety, and depression. She was always working, and exhaustion was her constant companion. There was very little about which to be happy. Even Andrés brought her little comfort. Everything appeared to her a dull, hard gray. Her home—small, cluttered, and rundown—felt suffocating.

Her one relief was retreating online. She spent many hours every night logged on to the web, immersed in a virtual reality that provided comfort, reassurance, and fun. Her old computer, despite its inactive disc drive and aging interface, was still able to take her away from the misery of her daily life. Her mouse became an extension of her body. Her headphones became her actual ears. She perused forums, played games, and made many profiles on all manner of dating and social media platforms. She could be whomever she wanted to be.

Her favorite pastime was inhabiting fully virtual worlds in which she could modify and adjust her online avatar. Through her avatar, she could be perfect, ideal, and complete. She was not restricted by the imperfections of the flesh or the strenuous demands of reality. Online, she was not an exhausted mother, but a lively vixen. Online, she was not a heavyset, middle-aged woman, but a young, coquettish girl. She was not shackled or chained. Her sessions became longer with time, and her craving for that escape deepened.

In that world, they found her.

Marisa had been playing a game when she encountered someone called "Jez." They played together briefly before Jez logged off. The next night, Marisa encountered Jez again, and they played another game. The following night, the pattern repeated, and such was the case for the subsequent nights. Soon, they were talking— or, more accurately, Marisa was talking, telling Jez about her life through chat and e-mail. She vented about the drudgery and depression with which she dealt on a daily basis. Jez was a good listener. She never belittled or demeaned Marisa. She never showed her anything but sympathy. Marisa found great comfort in talking with this new friend. She never realized that Jez said little, if anything, of her own life. Marisa knew nothing about her—not her real name, job, age, or even her favorite color. But this was unimportant. As long as Jez listened, as long as she was there, nothing else mattered.

One night, abruptly in the middle of a game, Jez told Marisa there was an answer. There was a solution to her problems. There was a way to be happy, Jez explained, a way to be free. But this solution came at a cost. Jez was part of a group, membership of which was only extended to those deemed worthy. There were many like her, online and in real life, working behind counters, serving beers, and teaching classes. They were the forgotten, she said, the oppressed, the forsaken. Society had left them behind, but they had not wallowed in pity or despair. They had united under a singular cause. They had become legion.

Marisa was curious. Despite logic telling her otherwise, she wanted to know more. She wanted Jez to be right. She wanted to believe. For so long, she had hungered for meaning beyond the mundane. For so long, she had hoped desperately for something to happen, for something to change in her life. So, she humored Jez. She asked to become part of this group. She asked to learn its revelatory secret. Jez complied and e-mailed her a file. She warned Marisa the file was not for the faint of heart. She stated the experience would be life-changing. Marisa doubted her, but she was excited nonetheless. She didn't know what to expect.

The file arrived free of fanfare. The name of the file was "happiness." Marisa hesitated. Was this a joke? A coy wink of the eye? But her curiosity got the better of her. She clicked on the file. She saw the portrait of a smiling young man. She saw his eyes.

The questions came like a flood. Jez calmed her. She explained their mission. She explained their cause. They served Him, she said. Who? Him. Look at the picture again. Marisa did. Indeed, she saw Him. She could not resist Him. She refused to resist.

What happened next is obvious. The descent. The downward spiral. Marisa did what they wanted very willingly. She compiled the words that came to her in the night. She kissed the pages. She prayed to them. Jez and the others provided her with names and locations. Marisa distributed the pages. She left excerpts in secret locations. Although she stopped eating, bathing, and working, she was happy. She was ecstatic. She was in total devotion to Him. She would have done anything—given anything— to please Him. And she did.

There would need to be one last thing, Jez said. One final act. A true and total release from the binding of the flesh. In order to cross the threshold. He was waiting beyond. Jez was waiting beyond. They were all waiting. There was no hesitation on Marisa's part. No remorse. She would go, and her son would go with her. They would enter the light and become one with the great dark. Andrés fought her, of course. He could not understand. He was just a child, ignorant and unaware. He struggled when she drew the marks around his neck, wrists, and ankles. He struggled when she held his face under the water of the tub. He struggled as she whispered to him that he would be all right. Soon, they would be gone. Soon, they would be safe, together with his father, whom she lost to mere chance. A worn brake. A rain-slick street. Marco would follow them eventually. But she could not wait any longer. She simply could not wait.

She cut her ankles afterwards. She cut her wrists. She sat in front of her computer as she faded. She stared at the boy's image with a smile, such a big smile. She looked into his eyes.

She had never felt so happy.

2 8 .

When Sebastian wasn't working on the manuscript with Miranda, he was out with Bless. The first night, he only watched as men and women alike were beaten, their bones broken, their faces slammed into brick and dragged across asphalt. He joined in after that. He dug his foot into ribs, swung pipes against heads. There were times when the violence didn't end with merely broken arms and bloody faces—sometimes, it ended with a bullet to the dome or the slit of a throat. Sebastian grew accustomed very quickly. The routine was comfortable, reliable. Watching Bless put on his brass knuckles—not his famous gold ones, though—became a guilty pleasure.

"Spooks," Bless called them. A way to control the population. The victims were usually two-bit competitors or traitors, but not always. One especially cold morning, lit pink by the dawn, they stood around an abandoned lot overgrown with weeds and dotted with discarded furniture and shattered television sets. Sebastian's breath came out in white wisps. His hand trembled around the gun in his pocket. The blare of a train horn broke the silence. Bless and a couple of other guys dragged a young man out to the middle of the lot. He screamed and struggled, but after repeated hits from a bat, he grew deathly quiet, his face bloated, his hands clutching his bruised, battered arms. Bless took out a thick, fat knife, one still caked with the dried blood of some other pitiful son of a bitch, and the kid screamed again—or tried to scream, given his swollen face. Bless strolled up to him, whistling, singing some song to himself. He took the boy by the hair, jerked him up, and slid the knife into his scalp. He carved the scalp right off, waved it around like a trophy. Don't fuck with us, it said. Don't even think about it. Junkies and dealers would fill the lot as the day went by. They would see the young man. They would know.

Sebastian told Miranda everything. He told her about the late nights and early mornings he spent with Bless. He told her about the killing of Polo and the death of Angel. He told her about Caesar and Sarah. He felt he owed her honesty. They were partners now, and she was the one who introduced him to the room of cloth in the first place. He was upfront: he had free reign around town as long as he did what Otto wanted. But it wouldn't be like that forever—they would get away somehow. They would protect the story. For now, it was a necessarily evil to get his hands dirty, and maybe it wasn't even an evil. Sebastian enjoyed it. He looked forward to joining Bless, even when he knew, more than likely, they were going to snuff out one more little life. But did killing somebody really matter all that much? What was one life, or two, or three, when the room of cloth was so close? When so much revelation was at hand? It was worth the sacrifice—and if Otto's wrath came down on Sarah or even Caesar eventually, maybe it was worth that, too.

Miranda was amazing. As much as she talked, she listened, too. She was his muse and his editor, his partner and his confidant, never preaching to him, never claiming to know the right way. She worked a certain type of magic, a bewitching veil, hiding behind smiles, putting forth laughter. His hunger for her grew, as much for her body as for everything she knew. "I've seen it," she said as they painted the walls of the apartment a dark red. "I've been in the room of cloth. I've touched his face." She described the experience as pulling back a curtain, glimpsing something amazing, before being ripped away. There were brief, jubilant peaks followed by long, painful lows. "You don't look at God and want to stop," she said. "You want to stare forever. And when you get taken away, when he leaves you—that's hell."

She was an expert on the manuscript. She knew about the Bretfords, about Terry, about Marisa, about most everyone who ever read or added to the story. When Sebastian asked her if the stories were true, if they all died, she laughed. "What's true?" she asked back. "What's a lie?" Truth or lie didn't matter. Only the story mattered. Fatten 'em up, she said. Make 'em gross. Make 'em spectacular, sensational, sublime. Every great myth or legend was a story. Every religion. Every way of life. They all started with stories. They all ended with belief.

With reality. Only the room of cloth was truly real, the stories concealing authentic reality. This was the veil, Miranda said, gesturing to her face, her body. The layers over the truth, hiding what was really there. We must remove them. We must set ourselves free.

Secretly, Sebastian still entertained his uncertainties. People had died. *He* could die. But then he would look at Miranda, see the certainty in her eyes, and he would know they were on the right path. They were totally, completely in the right.

One night, they sat in the living room, pages over the floor and pinned to the blood-red walls. Paint cans were stacked in the corner, surrounded by brushes and trays. The smell lingered long after the paint dried, mixing with the heavy scent of cinnamon. The aroma of the pages.

Sebastian typed busily on his laptop. His writing was getting better, or maybe the messages were becoming clearer. They came to him more quickly, more vividly. They weren't really his thoughts, at least not entirely. Maybe the manacled man fed him the images, or maybe the manacled man only represented something else, something that went beyond titles or names. All Sebastian knew were the words erupting from him. If he didn't let the words out, they jammed up, they hurt. Compared to this, going without dope had been easy. If he didn't write, the pain made him wish he would die.

Miranda sat against the wall, smoking. She eyed Sebastian's face locked on the screen, his fingers poised upon the keyboard. She smiled.

"You want to fuck me, right?"

He didn't turn around at first, didn't even hear her, but then she crawled over and pushed the laptop out of the way. "The fuck you doing?" he asked as she climbed onto his lap and slung her arms around his neck.

"You've been a hard worker," she said. "Harder than I thought you'd be. I like that."

Sebastian stared at her, stared at her lips, her neck, her tits. "But—"

She whispered in his ear. "Humor me, Omen. Let me give you a taste of it."

Of course, he gave in. He'd been wanting this all along, not sure whether to just ask or what to do, but here it was. Her pussy was sweeter, wetter than he had imagined. Her breath on his face, her teeth on his neck, her tongue—all of it like a wave, like his body breaking on the rocks. At first, she straddled him, held him down, totally in control, but then he pushed her onto her back, thrusting harder and harder until he couldn't feel himself anymore. Something snapped. He saw red—red over the walls, over the floor, over her face. Red leaking from his clenched fist. Red spraying from Polo's crushed head. Red trickling from between Angel's cloudy eyes. Red in him. Red outside him. Red everywhere.

Then it was over.

He lay atop her, shivering, his breaths short. She held him, her eyes following the spinning fan above, admiring the dark figures the blades cut into being.

They sat together in the morning and shared a joint. The hazy, obscured light from the windows was soft and gentle. Pretty, Sebastian thought. Heavenly. He looked at Miranda, touched her bare back, traced a finger down the tattoo of the indigo snake curving its way along her spine. He caressed faint, pink marks on the way down, scars from long ago. Joining with her had awoken in him feelings he had never felt. The violence with Bless was freeing, thrilling, but this was different. He felt attached to her suddenly, not just to her knowledge, but to *her*. Whoever that was. Whatever that was. He wanted her again. He wanted to keep having her.

"Snakes are holy," she said. "They were worshipped by all sorts of people. We look at them now and think they're evil. But they're better than us. Purer."

His fingers lingered on the scars. She blew smoke into the air.

"You want to know how I got them. It's not really a happy story."

"You don't have to tell."

She glared at him. "Don't bullshit me. Don't pretend like you care. You don't even know me." She took another puff. "Everyone just uses each other, Omen. You used me for sex. I use you for help. We trade things."

"That how you get around?"

"I use what I've got. Sex is the easiest thing. My mother taught me that. It's the gift that keeps on giving, and everyone wants it. Men. Women. It doesn't matter. Only they don't just want sex. It's always with strings attached. They feel too much, and feelings get in the way. That's why I don't feel, Omen. I never take my eyes off the big picture."

For once, her coy smile was gone. The mischievous glimmer in her eyes was nowhere to be seen. "You play a part," she said. "You change your hair, or your body, or your eyes. The way you talk. The way you move. You change into the person they want you to be. It's not *you* they want. People hate you. But they love who you can be. As long as you keep giving them what they want— what they really, really want—they don't care about the rest."

"You lie to them," Sebastian said.

"No." She was totally calm, totally serene. "I'm not a liar. When I'm someone else, I *am* someone else. It's not a lie. Nothing stays the same. The whole universe is changing, dying, giving off heat every second. Eventually, it'll go cold. And that'll be the only truth."

"But things can be true," Sebastian said. "People can. When they just act like themselves. When they're not trying to be something different."

Miranda laughed. "There's no real, Omen. No fake. There is no real self. There isn't something inside that was always there. We grow out of nothing, and then we change, and then we die. We pretend like it all means something, but it doesn't."

She took one last puff from the joint. "I'll tell you about change. My dad left when I was seven. I don't know why. He probably couldn't stand my mom. If anyone felt like they weren't real, it was her. She was a wreck. She could never get real work. She couldn't stick with anything. So, she brought men home, but, surprise, surprise, she couldn't even do that right. They hit her, took her money, and then one day, she married one of them, a real nice guy named Mark. Except Mark knew how to play the game. He could be all smiles one second, and then he could be beating you the next. And he did beat her. He beat her a lot.

"I'll let you guess what he did with the little girl. He beat her, too. She'd try to fight him, but what could she do? On the days when he was feeling really sadistic, he'd use his belt. Sometimes, the scars still hurt her."

Sebastian just stared.

"But it's okay. Because Mark taught that girl a very important lesson. He taught her the only lesson. You're alone in this world. Your father will leave you. Your mother won't help you. You will be used, abused, and thrown away. You'll be killed. Unless you wise up. And that little girl did wise up. She let Mark take her into bed, and then she cut his throat. She took all his money and ran. She shed her skin and became someone new."

She pushed the joint into her hand, studied the pink burn mark left behind. "That good enough? You feel like you know me? Like I'm real?"

Sebastian was quiet for a long time. "I killed my dad," he said at length. "I don't remember doing it, but that's what they told me. They said I got a knife and stabbed him—that I didn't stop stabbing him. All I remember is him yelling at me. Telling me I was good for nothing. Telling me I was stupid. That I shouldn't have been born. All the shit he always said to me and my sister. All the shit he'd say to my mom when he yelled at her, when he hit her. But something was different that night. I got real mad. Pissed. And the next thing I know, I'm in some place, some hospital, and my mom's there, my sister. They're taking me out in a wheelchair."

His right hand shook. "I don't remember it, but it happened. That make it real?"

"It's as real as you want it to be," Miranda said. "But the *real* truth? We'll never see it."

"Unless we go. To the room of cloth."

"Right. Unless we meet him."

They sat for a little longer, then went back to work.

2 9 .

"Oh, she's beautiful."

Sarah cradled the baby, cooed to her, stroked her cheeks. The baby was small, cocoa-skinned, eyes a light honey. Once, Sarah would have recoiled from holding her. She would have turned her head, winced. But now the child was a comfort, something heavenly, divine. A piece of light chiseled out of the sky and brought down to earth.

Louisa watched from her chair. "Amber's quiet," she said. "It's Nicole that's loud. Miracle she's asleep right now."

Sarah placed Amber back into her crib, squeezed her tiny hands, her feet. In the adjacent crib, her twin sister, Nicole, slept soundly, a thin line of saliva around her lips. Sarah admired them a little longer, took in the light of the window above them. She stepped back from the cribs.

"They're beautiful, Louisa," she said. "Really."

"You can have one if you like. Clay's already threatening to leave one in the garbage."

"The boys will warm up to them."

"Yeah. That's the way it is with family." Louisa joined her by the cribs. "You sure you can't stay for lunch? I know it's just tomato soup, but I think I make it damn good."

"I want to," Sarah said, "but I have to go."

Louisa studied her. She touched Sarah's shoulder, her hair. "Babe, is there something you need to talk about? You look awful. You said you were sick?"

"Yeah. It's just a cold. It'll pass."

"It's the stress," Louisa said. "You'd think I'd have it worse than you, but that brother of yours is equal to twenty of these. Let me guess: he run out on you again?"

"Something like that."

"You deserve better. Really, you do. I hope one day you realize it."

Sarah was quiet, still regarding the babies, the way they slept so peacefully. She wanted to tell Louisa everything, to lay bare all that had happened, all that was happening. But the longer she stayed there, the more danger there was of an errant word slipping through her lips or scratching itself onto a wall. And she wouldn't let that thing come into their home. She wouldn't allow it. As much to save them as spite that red-eyed monster in chains.

"I'd better go," she said. "I just wanted to check in on you. See how you were doing."

When Sarah got to the doorway, Louisa called to her. "Sarah, babe? You know this is your home, right? Always. You're family."

Sarah looked back. She smiled. "I know. Thank you, Louisa."

In her car, she clutched her shaking hand, wiped away her tears. She drove.

When she got to the diner, she waited in a booth at the far end, ordered some toast and coffee. Caesar was late. It had been his idea to meet somewhere safer, where there would be less chance to be seen together. Not that it mattered in the long run, he said. The dark man had eyes and ears everywhere. It was just a matter of time before the wrong person saw you, before someone let the secret slip. All bets would be off at that point. They would need to be ready to run, even if that meant abandoning Sebastian.

Run away, she thought, or die with her brother? Live with this thing crawling and breeding in her head? Or let a gangster take care of it for her? Would that even be the end? Why did it feel like death was nothing to the manacled man? Just another barrier to overcome, another wall to break down. Whittling her down to the bone, eroding her defenses—what other outcome was there? Kill her? No. Make her die. Make her *want* to die. Make her submit.

Fat chance. She held tight her ever-shaking hand. Don't think about it. Don't give it power. Distract yourself. Focus on other things. She looked around at the diner. The place was showing its age. The chrome, faded and foggy. The linoleum, cracked and dented. Sarah remembered coming here with her father. She recalled pancakes with chocolate chips, with smiley faces made of whipped cream and strawberries for eyes. "For the little lady," the chef said. They had been friends, him and her father. Another time, before the chef's lungs flooded and her father took even harder to the bottle. Another time, when she was small and pig-tailed and gap-toothed and ignorant of her mother's wasted, watery gaze.

In those moments, when Sarah recollected an instance of tenderness or affection on the part of her father, she considered the possibility of forgiving him. She considered analyzing his own life and circumstances—the military father, the late mother—to identify the point of origin, the seed from which the Creed family had sprung into manifold monsters, Cain-like and blasphemous. To pardon him would be the "correct" choice, the "good" choice, to hold true to what she told Sebastian: overcome the past and decide for oneself whom to be. But she could not forgive. And she hated that she relished that inability.

If only she could have wielded that knife herself.

If only she could have spared her brother that burden.

If only she could have indulged in that pleasure.

A waitress refilled cups and swept tables. An old man read the newspaper, ate an omelet. Sarah picked at her toast, but the smells—coffee, sugar, egg—made her nauseated. She had been scribbling mindlessly on a napkin in the meantime, and now she looked down at it. The pen had wandered onto the table, and more of those fucking words had followed. She folded the napkin and wiped away the ink as best she could. It only took one glance, after all. One harmless, little glance. Like touching a handrail. Like kissing a cheek. And there was no vaccine to protect oneself, no protective barrier to erect. The words found their way in and did their work. They seized control of the faculties of the mind and hijacked the rhythms of the body. Like any good virus, they replicated themselves with merciless, mechanical efficiency. They would bleed her dry, and then they would move on to the next victim.

But the current danger was more pressing. Both Paul and Caesar had mentioned this Otto character. The name was familiar—whispered by students in the hall, in the parking lot. Crime had always been bad in Lorraine, but lately? She heard the rumors that revealed what the news reports hid. Men and women beaten until their faces were gone, some with fingers cut off, others with slashed throats. That must have been the work of Otto and his men. Another cancer eating the kids. More trash polluting the world that deserved to be culled.

The door opened. Caesar entered, wearing sunglasses and drinking coffee. He sat down, took off the sunglasses, revealed a pair of bloodshot eyes. Sarah kept from cringing. He reeked of liquor and weed.

"So," he said, clearing his throat. "Sarah, right?"

"Yes. Thanks for coming."

"I had to. Seb—uh, Sebastian—he's in trouble. I know he is." He pointed at the napkin under her hand. "What's that?"

"Nothing." She tore it up quickly. "It's trash. You don't want to read it."

"Read it?"

She nodded. "It's the book. The room of cloth." Just saying the words made her stomach tighten. "Ever since I saw those pages, it doesn't stop. I get these impulses to write. It doesn't matter how much I put down—the words just keep coming. I tear them up, I cover them. Whatever I can do to get rid of them."

"So, the book Seb has," Caesar said, "you saying it's like magic?"

"I don't know. All I can tell you is that it's real. I can feel it inside of me, growing. I see things. I hear things. I feel like I'm going crazy." She clutched her left hand. "Sorry. I get this shaking, too. It's getting worse."

"I get it," said Caesar. "Ever since he got back, Seb was acting weird. I know dope and blow, but this was different. Like he was half here, half somewhere else. And always with this book. He wouldn't say anything about it, but you could tell just by looking at him. Whatever it was, he needed it."

"That's one thing," Sarah said. "You're saying there's something else. This Otto guy."

Caesar's face darkened at the sound of the name as though Sarah had uttered a curse. "Yeah," he said, voice lowered. "Otto Jackson. Sells all the product, runs all the muscle. You don't go on the street and not hear his name. He's everywhere."

"And Sebastian's involved with him? Why?"

"It's 'cause of me. Seb used to work for me. Little things. Taking packages, getting money. Nothing dangerous. He needed it. I found him sitting on the fucking sidewalk, looking like he'd come out a spaceship or something. So, I gave him something to do. There are a million other kids like him"

Sarah tried to listen, but all she could hear were nails on wood. Shuffling in the dark. A little voice begging to come in. All the sounds she tuned out as a young woman with her headphones and her boys and her cigarettes. All the sounds from which she ran away.

"But he never stuck around," Caesar went on. "He left all the time. And then he just took off for a year, didn't even say nothing. He comes back the other day, acts like nothing happened, says some shit in Boston didn't work out. I knew the guy he was with. Billy Tripp. What a fucking *cabrón*, that guy. What a piece of shit. I wouldn't have let him go, but Seb don't ask for advice. He wants it his way. So, he comes back, starts talking about wanting work, about finding this guy in Jersey. Says the guy has the rest of this story. But it ain't like it used to be, you know? Otto finds out I'm doing shit like that, it's my ass on the fire. So, I got Seb a meet. Otto said he'd help him if he just did a job. And I let it happen. I let it fucking happen."

"What was the job?" asked Sarah quietly.

"There was a guy. Pollito. Had his hair like a chicken and everything. He ripped a couple hundred off Otto—

or, fuck, maybe he didn't. Maybe that was just an excuse."

Sarah closed her eyes. It was hard to reconcile, her memory of the small boy from her youth, the little thing so meek and fearful. Hard to reconcile with the man he became. With the nightmare they were in now.

"Did he kill him?" she asked. "Did Sebastian kill him?"

"No," said Caesar. "I did. Seb was there, but I did it. I blew that guy's fucking head open." He reached for his coffee. "I keep seeing the eyes. Big and scared. I can't stop seeing 'em. All of 'em. Pollito and the others. But I don't got a choice. I don't do it, Otto finds out. He always finds out. And then I'm another body on the street with my head cut off, my fingers chopped off. Because they don't just kill you. They have fun with you first. They get off on it."

"Where is Sebastian?" Sarah asked.

"I don't know. But I think Otto got him to do something else. Seb wasn't right the last time I saw him. He blew up at me. Started yelling, started telling me I was trying to control him or something. But I wasn't. I was trying to warn him, trying to get him out before it's too late."

He sighed. "One of the last things he told me? Said I was like a brother. Said I looked out for him. But I just let those fuckers take him. I let him down. I didn't do shit. I *don't* do shit."

Sarah looked out the window, squinted at the glare. There was another thing hard to reconcile: this smelly slob of a man before her, supposedly some scary gangster, some killer, some pedophile. But there was nothing scary about the round, weepy face or the cut-up jacket and ill-fitting jeans. There was nothing frightening about the baggy, burning eyes and trembling, twitchy hands. No, Sarah was disgusted more than anything else, disgusted by the smell of alcohol she still loathed after all these years, disgusted by the helplessness, by the resignation. It was pitiful. Pathetic. But there was something else amid that pity and disgust. A resonance. In those moments of weakness when she held the bottle or the cigarette, in the brief seconds when she screamed or snapped, she was this man. She was this object of scorn.

"All this crying you're doing," she said. "It's not real. It doesn't mean anything. You're crying about someone who doesn't exist. And I'm doing the same thing."

Her hands knotted and unknotted. Her eyes glistened and glazed.

"I don't know if I love him. I don't know if I tricked myself into it, or if I lied to myself. Sometimes, I think I hate him, and the hate is so strong, it makes me sick— sick that I feel that way, sick that I *could* feel that way. But I don't know him, either. So, I'm no better than you. I'm loving and hating someone I don't know. Someone that I should know, that I could have known. Someone far away from me."

"You're crazy," Caesar said. "Crazier than him. You're out here right now, risking your neck for that fucking kid. You do love him."

Sarah said nothing. Caesar drank his coffee. He twiddled with the rosary around his neck. "Otto's guy," he said at length. "Bless. Piece of shit, but if anyone knows where Seb is, it's him."

Sarah nodded, more a confirmation for Caesar to continue than an acknowledgement of what she heard. Otto. Bless. They were names from some dream, not real life. From a nightmare she kept behind locked doors, behind walls of silence.

"I can set up a meet," said Caesar. "I can find out where Seb is."

"Okay." She nodded again, her eyes suddenly so heavy, her heart like lead. She struggled to say what came next. "I'm going with you. I want to be there when you meet him."

"I told you before," Caesar said. "You don't know this guy. What he does. He'll see your face. He'll know who you are."

"It doesn't matter." Sarah raised her shaking hand, so frail and bony, so small in the light. "I don't think I have a lot of time left. Not as myself, anyway."

Caesar was ready to refuse her, wanted to refuse her—after all, was this not Sebastian all over again, another sack of fresh meat he was delivering into the lion's den? But something in Sarah's eyes struck him. It was the same look he saw in Sebastian's eyes when he first found him on the street: dead, drained, exhausted. He knew then she wasn't afraid, and that thought scared him more than Bless ever could.

"Okay," he said finally. "We can do tomorrow morning."

Sarah smiled, relieved that something gave way, that the cosmic design shifted in her favor for once. Maybe this Bless guy would kill her, rape her, whatever. She knew his torture couldn't be any worse than what waited in the room of cloth.

"Thank you," she said, quietly, softly.

Caesar waved it off. "*De nada.*"

30.

One morning, in the red room of their own making, the walls so glazed by the light as to appear viscous, Miranda reached over and touched Sebastian's face.

"I have something to show you," she said, again with her mischievous smile. "For inspiration."

His muse. That's what she called herself constantly. The Beatrice to his Dante, though he didn't know the reference. Maybe Sarah did, reading all the time after he got back from the hospital, reading so much he wondered if she were herself trying to escape. Escape from what? The house? Him? She had gotten away before— no one asked her to go back. Not him, not their mother. Certainly not their fucking father. She did that shit to herself. Always to herself.

In the shower, he sighed, rubbed his eyes. Forget Sarah. Fuck her. But no matter how he fought to rid her image from his mind, she intruded. Her stupid, tired-looking face. Her bony, long fingers and gross, wispy hair. The annoying way her voice got shrill and squeaky when she scolded him. The goddamn self-righteous look in her eyes, the judgment, the contempt. More and more, he even thought he saw her in his periphery, around the corner on the street, behind the bend of hallways. Following him, waiting for him. Poised to pull him back into the shitty, life-ending cycle he was trying to escape. She was getting in the way of his writing—everything about her was ruining him—and he wanted her gone. He wanted to cut that weight loose.

Miranda saw it, too. Catlike, ever observant, she watched him and considered. What was she thinking? Was she planning to move on? Was she planning to work with someone else? Her look betrayed nothing, but suggested everything. Damn, he couldn't stand it! She and Sarah had that nosiness and smugness in common. But he was powerless to do anything to her, incapable of throwing his weight around. He had no leverage whereas Miranda had the keys to the kingdom. She was the link between him and what was on the other side. The room of cloth. The manacled man. The lightless, weightless realm of sweet-smelling gold they guarded and disguised. The real heaven for which his mother had prayed all those years. The real heaven for which she cried and pleaded on her deathbed. The real heaven that was forever out of her reach.

After they dressed, Miranda led him out to the street. Lorraine was bright that morning, glowing in a way that seemed to him deceptive. Like a fucking mirage, a trick as bad as a magician pulling a squirming rabbit from the pit of his hat. Lorraine was a pile of shit, and underneath all that was the garbage and blood in which he was already waist-deep. Otto. Bless. Caesar. No. Don't think about

Caesar, either. He betrayed you. He did worse than Sarah because he was the one person you thought had your back all this time. They're both the same. They want to keep you here, in this fucking fake place, this hall of horrors. They're blind. They're lost. They don't know it's all a front. They don't know it needs to be ripped away.

He followed Miranda into the shadow of an underpass, the concrete beneath their feet slick with recent rainwater. The wall before them was draped in oblong pinks and grotesque purples, cartoonish skulls and exaggerated devils. Sebastian looked upon the graffiti, faded and pointless, a cry at an indifferent world, and actually felt pity. He might have drawn something like this once, might have sat and moaned about how unfair everything was, how rigged. He would have thought he was actually fighting the problem when really, he would have just been slinging shit. How stupid. How fucking dumb.

"What are we doing here?" he asked. "This what you wanted to show me?"

Miranda smirked. She fetched a stone from the ground and etched into a blank patch of concrete one white, ghastly line, as tall as a person. Then she etched another a few feet to its right, a jagged copy of the original. The stone screeched like a knife on granite. A third line connected the two at the top. She stepped back, dropped the stone, dusted her hands. She reviewed her work with satisfaction, but Sebastian saw only the crude outline of a rectangle cut into the concrete. However, as he stared, recognition stirred within. Not just a rectangle, he thought, but a doorway. A passage. A portal.

Without realizing it, he was sweating. His hand shook.

"You're still scared," Miranda said. She held out her hand. "Here."

Hesitantly, he reached out, and with a sudden swipe, she slashed his palm with a switchblade. He reared back, clutching the hand to his chest, vaguely aware of how he always clutched it when it was hurt, when he slammed his fist against drywall or plunged it into glass. His heart was thudding now, his stomach plummeting. He wanted to puke. He was going to puke.

"What the fuck?" he stammered. "You crazy bitch!"

"Calm down. It's barely skin-deep." She ran a thumb along the edge of the switchblade and drew away a coat of red. That was his blood, his essence. She rubbed her fingertips together, seemed to play with it. Play with him.

"The fuck are you doing?" he demanded, watching her approach the doorway. "Stop!"

"Hush. I'm inspiring you, remember? I'm solving your writer's block."

She smeared his blood across the concrete, leaving a muddy thumbprint and a faint carmine trail beneath it. Nothing happened at first—only the wind blew, only discarded beer bottles rattled along the nearby gutter. Then the space within the lines *changed*. The concrete rippled and bled. The gray became black. Something in the darkness lurched and coiled. Something turned towards Sebastian. Something met his gaze, uttered his name. He heard the echo in that vast place, a place churning with blood and machinery, a place both threadbare and immeasurably deep. He knew they saw him, the denizens, those who had gone before. The ones who floated in the great dark. He knew they acknowledged him. Deep within, far inside, so did the manacled man. The red eyes found his own.

"Make it stop," he said. "For fuck's sake, make it stop!"

"You *are* scared. His chosen, and you're afraid."

"Just turn it off!"

"It's over. Look again."

He turned slowly. The concrete was indeed unchanged, the space enclosed by the lines flat and dead, no longer alive, no longer revealing dark depths and unfathomable reaches. Miranda watched him touch the wall and retract his hand. She smiled.

"You want to know why you can't write?" she asked. "Why you're stuck? You won't face it. You're thickheaded. You're stubborn."

"Fuck off. I'm not stuck. I'm not afraid."

"You're terrified, Omen," she said. "That was just a glimpse, too. We barely scratched the surface. You can't cross over unless you give it all up. He won't accept anything less."

Sebastian said nothing. He had been avoiding this dilemma since the beginning: eventually, his body would be forfeit. All the rumors and stories, however fucking insane or absolutely batshit, had that one inevitability in common. Everyone died. They hung themselves, cut themselves, drowned themselves. They killed their loved ones to ferry them across. Jim and the Bretfords. Terry. Marisa and her son. Hundreds, thousands, millions more. Miranda would die, too. She said this constantly, said she fantasized about it, how the manacled man would take her into his arms, how he would stroke her and fill her and render her saintlike. They'd paint pictures of her in the new world. They would chant her name. They would sing of her, the whore mother, the redeemed wife. She claimed not to believe in anything, but she believed in that well enough—her eyes couldn't lie, not when they lit up like Christmas lights in the dead of night.

But Sebastian couldn't feel the same. Death made his bowels clench, his head spin. Don't think about it, he said. Just like good dope, good blow. Let it take you away. Don't think about it. Don't feel anything. Let it go. It's not real. It can't be real.

"You're still attached," Miranda said. "You're still stuck on what's supposed to be."

"I'm not."

"You are." She faced the doorway, caressing the white lines with her eyes, sweeping lovingly the encompassed space with her gaze. "The ones who introduced me to the room of cloth, they understood what was at stake. They were willing to give everything, their bodies and souls, over to him. They knew the flesh is a cage, the skin a fragile fabric."

"They're dead?" asked Sebastian, his throat dry, his mouth like cotton.

She shrugged. "Who knows. The point is that death doesn't matter. The truth doesn't matter. What you think about the world doesn't matter."

They stared at the doorway, to anyone else just lines on rock, but to the initiated, a portal to a realm beyond comprehension, to a place of infinite love and endless belonging. Miranda wiped the switchblade on her jeans. She regarded the blemished steel.

"You want to finish the manuscript? Cut it all off. Everything. Leave nothing behind."

Was it that easy? Was it worth his fear? He had witnessed Polo's death. He had killed Angel. He had forsaken Sarah and Caesar. What was holding him back? His body? His genes, desperate to replicate, programmed to persevere? That programming was what they needed to destroy. That link to the body had to be severed. As Sebastian looked over his slashed palm, looked over the pages upon pages of the manuscript, he realized he was already partway there. After killing his father, where had he gone? A hospital he couldn't remember, a span of time that lasted years, but somehow felt like a seconds-long dream? Where had he gone in that interim, that dark space between the lines? Where did he go when he read and wrote, when the words transported him on waves of honey-hued light and wafts of cinnamon-scented bliss? He was marked. The manacled man had chained him. The burns on his wrists and ankles told the story. The rash on his neck said it all.

In the evening, under the twin covers of dark and rain, he stood at the foot of Sarah's apartment building. There was no light where her apartment was, and there never would be—Sarah already lived in a lightless world, but it wasn't weightless. Cut it off, Miranda had said. Feed it to the fucking dogs. Let them tear into the meat and lick clean the bones. The last tether, not the Sarah of now, he realized, deflated and decrepit, like an old stain on wood impossible to wash out, but the Sarah of his youth. The Sarah who rebelled against their dear old dad. The Sarah who mocked their bitch mother. The Sarah who did what she wanted when she wanted and took nothing from no one. The Sarah who broke free. That Sarah had been wild, like a goddamn mustang on the plain. He'd loved her, idolized her, had wanted nothing more than to be just like her. She was a blazing star in his mind, sharp-nosed, bright-eyed, eternally furious and frowning. She was full of hate, full of his hate, the hate that had led him to the room of cloth, the hate that had attracted the manacled man. He would've given anything to bring her back. His guiding star. His true muse. His icon.

But the truth was that he had already cut out that lionhearted Sarah a long time ago. When he stuck that knife into his father's back, when he stabbed him again and again, he had also driven the blade into that old

Sarah's breast. By murdering one, he killed the other. That Sarah could not burn without the toxic oxygen of their father. She had dimmed, faded, and withered into something cold and lifeless. Her light was gone. She left behind only a charred silhouette on the wall of his mind, a blackened reminder tough to scrape away, difficult to wash clean. But the burn would come out. The burn had to come out. The stain in the wood would be cleansed. Even if that meant lighting up everything else and leaving nothing behind.

That old Sarah was gone, banished into a dark place not even the manacled man could reach. There was no reason to keep a candle burning for her—because that's what he'd been doing. Waiting for her. Waiting for her to come back. Waiting for her to open the door. All this time, he'd been the sentimental fool, not her. But no more. There was no reason to stick around, no reason to fear. His family was dead, unable to come back, and only the room of cloth remained. Nothing held him back.

He turned away from her building and back into the night. He had a job to do. Something only he could do. Something even the old Sarah could never have done.

31.

For Bless, this was the life.

The night had been one part business and two parts pleasure. He'd finally found the hideout of some meth-heads who thought they could sell without paying Otto their dues. It always baffled him how these fuckers thought they could get away with that shit. They liked living, right? They liked having eyes and ears, right? Then again, the world was going to hell. Bible-thumpin' rednecks with AKs on their fireplaces. Pink-haired dykes cutting off their own pussies. Babies with sewn-up stomachs full of dope (this last one kept him up at night). Like, fuck. Sometimes, he wondered. Sometimes, he honestly fucking wondered.

The meth-heads had holed up in some slummy piece of shit filled with roaches and other nasty creepy-crawlies. Now, Bless hated bugs. Spiders, bees, cockroaches—it didn't matter. Fucking abominations with beady, little eyes and long, spindly legs and gross, hairy bellies. The worst was when the roaches gushed out all their guts, or when the eggs on the momma spilled out. It made him want to vomit. He killed them whenever he saw them, and that was all the time in this shithole town.

Back in New York, they had penthouses, they had bars, they had clean fucking facilities. Life was easy, and after years of scraping knuckles on concrete, it better have been fucking easy. Which was why he didn't understand Otto's decision to come to the boonies and throw down the law. It was batshit. Yeah, the old cunts up there gave the order, but Otto was Otto. And maybe that was the problem. Once, Bless saw Otto sit down and work on a jigsaw puzzle (of sailboats, fucking SAILBOATS) literally *all night*, just piecing it together, not saying nothing, just once in a while putting his hands together and gnashing his teeth. Otto committed, and that was his charm, his fucking aura, but committing to *this*? Bless didn't see the appeal.

Still, it wasn't all bad. The nights when he got to have fun, well, he had fucking *fun*. He liked to think of little shits like the meth-heads as though they were bugs—made it easier to root 'em out. Imagining them with giant ant heads and fly faces was fucking hilarious, too. Boom, there was a bat to the head, eyes popping out, antennae flopping off, guts and brains exploding. Bam! Wham! Pow! Them running around, tripping over themselves, scared shitless, hi*lari*ous! They were the pests, and he was the exterminator. The night prior was one of the best in a long time. He took a couple of guys, threw gasoline all over the place, lit a match, and just watched it burn. Smoke 'em out. That's what you do with fucking pests. Then they went in, bashing skulls and bobbing their heads and swinging their hips. Bless loved using bats. He loved his knuckles the most, but bats were up there. Such a satisfying *crunch*. Things fucking break when you hit them with a bat. It's not like a knife—that's pussy shit. A bat's a full-on slam. You don't get up after that. You stay on the ground. It's a great. Fucking. Way. To make. A point. . . . *A point*. There. Don't get up again, baby-cakes. Just stay where Momma Bless can keep an eye on you. Aww, don't bleed on the carpet again, boy. It's not good manners.

They hit up some girls after that, some fine, big-tit *mamasotas*. Bless loved the big ones—not the *fat* ones, the *big* ones. He loved burying his face into some angelic, perfectly sculpted mound of ass. It got his blood boiling. After the pest control, the night had been a revolving door of ladies, and he threw out each one who didn't meet his standards. He got a hotel room for slapping them around and making them gag on his cock. You live and you die, that was what he knew. If you weren't sucking up the moment, if you weren't just plain enjoying yourself, what the fuck were you doing? Have fun, bitch. Don't take life too seriously.

His morning quickie was interrupted by his cell phone blasting off. He fucking hated getting calls in the morning, and he *really* hated getting calls from pussy, faggot cocksuckers. Fucking Caesar. Fucking pedo faggot. He wanted to demolish the beaner's fucking face and leave him for the goddamn coyotes, but he was "too valuable." They needed guys on the ground, Otto said, guys who already had connections and reputations. Otto always went on about "good business"—you never went in with a scorched-earth policy. You did it slowly, quietly. Some shit about it being better to be both feared and loved. You killed a few to make a statement, to get some fear, but you didn't go overboard. And you definitely didn't reshuffle the deck. People like doing business with familiar faces. They like people they know. Remember, the goal's always to keep things calm and comfortable. Makes for more pleasant shopping that way. Like they were running a fucking department store!

Well, Bless didn't like the cocksucker telling *him* to meet. The little bitch didn't know his place, but as much as he wanted to throttle him, Otto would be pissed if he did. So, Bless put on a smile, stuck a cigar in his mouth. Don't worry, be happy! Why get mad about some fucking beaner? Caesar wanted to meet at some lot on the south side of town. Fine, Bless would meet. He'd play along. But maybe, just maybe, he'd get in a few kicks, too. Just for laughs. He had a heaven-sent bubble butt bouncing on him just fifteen minutes before. If he was getting ripped out of paradise, then he had better get *something* out of it.

At least the sunrise looked stupendous. Have fun, motherfucker! Life's a ride!

Caesar and Sarah waited for him in Caesar's van. The lot was mostly dirt, tires piled up in one corner, beer bottles rolling around another. Plastic bags rippled and flailed upon the chain-link fence. Sarah watched the road. Caesar drank long gulps from his flask. He held his rosary in the other hand. Funny how the little trinket could still make him feel better. The rosary evoked memories: his mother and his *abuelita*, their tiny house in Florida, the green-blue of the sea.

Once upon a time, he almost swore off his faith. He had wondered why God made him a faggot. He had wondered why his *abuela* had looked at him like he was a monster, like he didn't deserve to live. He had long wondered, in the clubs, in the brothels, in the hotels, why, why, *why*. But even at his lowest point, he could not shake the love he felt deep inside. He couldn't explain the feeling that swept through him in the early mornings, in the late nights. To this feeling, he prayed. To this feeling, he asked for help, especially now.

"Fucking demon," he muttered, wiping his mouth.

"Sorry?"

"Nothing. Nothing." Caesar looked at the woman beside him. She didn't smile much, but there was something admirable in her eyes. Something hard. Her brother she was not.

"You got some balls, lady," he said. "You know that?"

"What do you mean?"

"This. Coming out here."

"Oh." Sarah clasped her shaking wrist. "It's not like I'm not scared. But there isn't anyone who'd care if something happened to me. Not really."

"Nobody? Not even a boyfriend?"

"Maybe my friend Louisa." She paused. "And you. Thank you. For being here, too."

"*De nada*," he mumbled, eyes straight ahead, booze dribbling from his quaking lips.

A car peeled into the lot a few minutes later, kicking up dust. "Let me do the talking," Caesar said. He took out a gun from the glove compartment. "Just in case."

Bless sauntered up, puffing on a cigar and snapping his fingers. "Big Caesar! How the hell can I help you, sugar? What you need?"

Caesar got out of the van. "Sorry 'bout calling you so early," he said. "Need to talk."

"No problem, mama-san. I have a very flexible schedule. Very fucking flexible." Bless looked around the lot. "Coulda picked a better place, though, *mi amigo*. What, you gonna whack me? 'Eh, Bless, see, we're gonna pew-pew-pew ya, see? Pew-pew-pew!'" He laughed, but the look in his eyes was deadly. It took everything Caesar had not to turn away.

"I just wanna know where Seb is."

"Seb? Oh, the kid! What, you two ain't pals anymore? Broke up? Had a fight?"

"I just gotta talk to him. It don't got anything to do with Otto."

"No can do, *compadre*. Everything that kid does has to do with Otto. And if it's gotta do with Otto, it's gotta do with me. So, whatever you gotta tell the kid, you can just tell me. I'll relay the message. I got real good memory, too. Just don't tell me any numbers. I can't remember those for jack-shit."

"Just tell us where Sebastian is." Sarah was out of the van. "He's my brother."

Caesar turned to her, pale-faced. Bless grinned.

"Caesar, Caesar, Caesar! I thought you only liked little boys!" He licked his lips. "Yeah, yeah, yeah, the sister. You're a teacher, right? I should goddamn fucking salute you, ma'am. Dealing with the little shits every day. Me, I'd just pop 'em in the head. Do the state a favor."

"Look, I don't care about you or this Otto guy. I just want to see my brother."

"Your brother's on Otto Jackson's payroll now, baby," Bless said. "Didn't Caesar tell you? We're taking good care of him. Otto's got a real eye for talent. He picks 'em out bright and young. Your brother's one of the good ones. Real talented. He was born to hold a gun, sister. Born to be wild!" He laughed. "Here in the good ol' U-S-of-A, you gotta be able to shoot a gun. Wanna make money? Wanna live free? Shoot 'em, baby! Kill the fuckers that get in your way! It's real simple. It's the goddamn second amendment, isn't it?"

"No more bullshit," Caesar said. He stood between them, tried to keep from shrinking. "Tell us where Seb is."

"Ooh, look at you, Caesar, all high and mighty! I'm used to you shaking like a little bitch!" Bless turned to Sarah. "You could do better than this guy, sugar. You know he's into little boys, right? Yeah, that's what he's known for! Big Caesar! Fucks all the little boys around the block! Puts his finger up their assholes! Plays with their little cocks! Probably can't get enough of your brother's skinny white ass—"

"*Hijo de puta*!"

Caesar grabbed Bless by the collar and slammed him against his car. "I never touched him, you fucking rat! I never put a finger on him!"

"Whoa, whoa, whoa! Look at you, Caesar! Balls dropped at last! Did I touch a nerve? You in love with that little shithead? Kept him pristine, huh? So noble! So heroic!"

"Keep talking, you fucking trash! Keep fucking talking!"

"Oh, Caesar, you're making me blush! Go on, sweetie, do it! Show me you're not a little faggot pussy! Then you can see your white-bread honey again!"

Caesar held him against the car, breathing hard, fists tightening. He was about to shove that smug, shit-ridden face through the window, into the dirt, but Sarah's voice called him back.

"Enough! Caesar, let him go! Let him go now!"

With great effort, Caesar pulled away. "Motherfucker," he spat. "Trash."

Bless chuckled and dusted himself off. "Little, whipped Caesar. Can't even finish the job. But I gotta admit, that surprised me. Normally, I'd gut you for that, but I like the spirit. Maybe you're not such a fucking waste of space after all."

Caesar was ready to turn back around, but Sarah grabbed his arm.

"*Enough*," she said. "We're not here for this."

Caesar trembled, seethed, but relented. "You ain't worth it," he said. "I'm not like you. I wasn't made for this shit. I don't fucking like it."

"But you do it anyway," Bless said with a grin. "Look, you want the kid? Shit, you can have him. Otto doesn't care about the kid. He just wants the book."

"The book?" Sarah asked. "He knows about it?"

"I don't know what the fuck he knows. But it's what he wants. The kid's just a little insurance. We can always use extra bodies. That's what we deal in, mama-san. Bodies. Young, old, dead, alive, doesn't matter. Once he gets the book, the kid's old news. Yesterday's trash."

"So, let him go," Caesar said. "If you don't need him, let him go."

"He's got his uses, and so do you. Otto's got a job lined up for him right now as a matter of fact, a big ol' important job. He didn't even give it to me. He wants the kid to do it. But I bet you can go along. You do this for us, maybe Otto will give the kid up—if he gets the book."

"What's he want with the book?" demanded Sarah. "You people don't know what it is! You don't know how dangerous it is!"

"Listen, baby, I don't ask questions. I just do what I'm told." Bless turned back to Caesar. "So? Dump the girl and come back with me. We'll talk it over with Otto. Cross my heart."

"There has to be another way," Sarah said. "We can find him some other way."

"Nah," said Caesar. "We gotta play by their rules. They own the game." He pointed to his van. "Take it and get outta town. I'll let you know what happens."

"Caesar—"

"Just do it, *por favor*." He looked to Bless. "You won't hurt her?"

"That depends on you and the kid, but, nah, I don't think so. Up to Otto, of course, but he's got bigger things on his mind." He stepped aside. "After you, *amigo*. He should be at the club right now getting ready for tonight."

Caesar handed his keys to Sarah, then got inside the car with Bless. Bless flashed her one last, rotten smile before they drove off. Sarah watched them leave, then looked down at the keys in her hand. The golden chain of Caesar's rosary encircled them.

32

"We're making good progress." Miranda spooned lazily through a bowl of raisin bran and regarded the stack of pages in the middle of the living room. "You really picked up the pace. We might actually finish it at this rate."

Sebastian stood in the corner, putting on his jacket, staring down at the bright, morning-lit alleyway. The words came easier by the hour, as though a switch had been turned, a spigot loosed. He was setting fire to the walls in his mind, something he would never have been able to do before. Ever since he found the room of cloth, ever since Miranda arrived, ever since he started spending his nights with Bless, the awful anxiety he always felt was fading. That sense of unease was lifting. The entrapment. The dread. He was on the path. He had a mission, a purpose. For the first time in his life. If he had to die, if he had to cut it all off, so be it.

Miranda watched him, glimpsed the track marks dotting his arm. A dope fiend, she thought. Sebastian had told her how he went cold turkey after discovering the manuscript. The pain he described, the convulsions— just thinking about it made her skin crawl. She didn't have patience for drugs or booze. Too often they were distractions, roadblocks. Ugly and vile. If she took anything, it was always in the service of her mission. She lived in the moment, yes, but she also had an eye on the days ahead, the coming weeks, the coming months. She played the parts she had to play, whether the slutty whore, the classy escort, the kindly neighbor. She could change her hair, her dress, her accent. If the part demanded drugs, required sex, necessitated theft, that was all game, too. Maybe even killing if it needed to happen. But no matter what, she never got distracted. She never lost sight of the goal. Everything was in service to surviving today for the sake of tomorrow. For the sake of the room of cloth. For the sake of the manacled man.

She had been lost before. Wandering from man to man, from job to job, taking advantage of any kindness offered and punishing every abuse. No longer the hunted, but the hunter. Always strike first, she told herself. Never give an inch. Never show weakness. Never let them get close. As a result, she was never raped, never hit. She always came out unscathed. Had she even tortured once or twice? Yes, though she hadn't enjoyed it. There was no pleasure in hurting others—well, just a little. It was a fact of life. You were going to get hurt, you were going to be betrayed, so you had to do things you didn't want to do. You had to be frightening when necessary, charming when that was the better choice. You had to be ready for anything.

But simple survival didn't have much flavor. She woke up in trailers, in vans, in dirty rooms, her makeup hot and messy, her hair patched blonde or blue, her contacts falling out, her clothes disheveled and torn. There was no rhyme or reason. Until they found her.

She remembered the initial encounter so clearly: the chat window opening, the image file downloading, seeing his face, turning away from the screen crying, wailing. They let her into the group after that. Into the circle. Spread, they told her. Engulf. Infect. Disseminate. Propagate. Contribute to the message. Add to the fabric. The words came after that, filled up her being, became her blood. They left her with the complete manuscript, digitally and physically. She had opened the storage unit with trembling, anxious hands, breathed in the heavy smell of roses, just like the roses her mother always used to beautify the rooms where she lay with men, where she wiped away blood and turned over smeared coversheets. As a little girl, Miranda always admired the roses, always imagined them fresh and dew-covered, lining the path to a crystal castle, to a princess in a silver gown, to a prince, to a father.

She knew now that the roses had been her mother's little way of trying to dress up the ugly truth. Or the lack of truth, maybe. Denial. Blindness. There had never been a prince in a gilded carriage to free her. There was no father waiting in a sparkling castle. There would never be either in this place of flesh and bone and blood. Yet the scent of the roses remained, and she knew why. Because that smell pointed her towards the real place where she would finally be saved. Because even as a child, she knew this filthy, limited life was not all there was, that it could not be all there was. A true king commanded her. A true knight waited to spirit her away.

That had been her realization as she sifted through the junk within the storage unit, as she removed the nondescript binder from underneath planks of cardboard, as she allowed her eyes a glimpse of the grace therein. The crisp, pristine pages. The clean feel of the glossy sleeves. The others disappeared after that. Gone ahead of her, through one of the doorways. Through one of the celebrations. But she had been chosen to continue the work in the meantime. And she had. She would. Until it was done. Until it was finished.

Sebastian spoke. "I got a call. Gotta meet Otto."

"One of those jobs of yours?"

"Probably."

"Then go. Play his game a little longer. Pretend you're his bitch."

"I'm nobody's bitch."

"Whatever you say."

He still didn't like her knowing smile or her smug gestures. Like she knew more. Like she was better. As he drove to the club, her image kept bothering him. They were still so far apart. After the sex, after the talks, they were still strangers. More than anything, he wanted to know her. He wanted to know the real Miranda. They were both bound by the room of cloth, both constricted by the same chains. So, why was there such a distance between them?

But Miranda wasn't the only person he wanted to know. He wanted to know Caesar. He wanted to know Sarah. He wanted to know *everyone*. The more he thought about it, the more he realized it was possible. The room of cloth was the key. Everyone could share the truth. Everyone could share the light. The urge to possess the manuscript had been so strong before, but now he felt the opposite urge, a strong, powerful desire to spread it. The room of cloth could break open everything, blow away the fantasy! It could wake everyone up, drown the world in light! Yes! Everyone happy. Everyone loved. Everyone in a safe, special place. Together.

He could see it. On billboards. On marquees. On webpages. On the radio. On television. In books. In magazines. In the air. Everyone with joined hands, everyone a blip of light connected to one another. A grid of lights covering the world. All of them becoming a collective, loving *one*. Rising into the air, becoming cloud, becoming electricity, becoming spirit. He could see himself holding hands with Sarah and Miranda, could see their bodies disappearing, their fingertips fading into light.

He pulled over and looked at his hands. They were covered in tears.

33.

When Sebastian arrived at Otto's club, the staff were cleaning inside. They swept up cups and bottles. They wiped down tables. They checked equipment, tested lights and speakers. Otto surveyed the work from the center of the dance floor, hands on hips. He waved Sebastian over.

"Been waiting for you," he said. "Bless tells me you've been doing good work."

"I'm trying."

"Well, one way or the other, it's getting done. You're helping me keep balance. It's clean-up. Even this place needs it. It falls apart every night, and I gotta put it back together." He looked around the club. "That's why I came to this town."

"To clean it up?"

"Sure. I have to make things look a certain way. What you did with Angel was part of that. The picture I'm painting doesn't have room for her anymore. You understand?"

Sebastian shrugged.

"You understand," said Otto. "You want the perfect picture, so you rub out the things you don't like and leave the ones you do. You make a story."

For a moment, his eyes glinted with fire, like they had the first time Sebastian saw him. But then they were dark and glassy, almost watery. Like a candle melting.

"Angel made stories her whole life. She knew how things had to be. She was loyal. Not like these pussies today. They lie. They pass off dirty stories. They think they're good enough to get respect, but people aren't stupid. They only respect the picture that's cleanest. The story that's most honest."

He faced Sebastian, eyes lighting up again. "You're making your own story right now. But you know it's gonna be my story soon. It's *all* gonna be my story."

Like hell, Sebastian thought. Otto wasn't getting anywhere near the room of cloth. He and Miranda would play the game a little longer, and then they were gone. Then—maybe—Sarah could join them. They could start over, be a real family. He wouldn't have to cut her off after all. Maybe he could even turn her back to how she used to be. That blazing star in his mind.

A whistle drew their attention to the door. "Yo, mama-sans! I'm here!" Bless walked in, followed by Caesar.

"What's he doing here?" demanded Sebastian.

Otto only smiled. "Bless tells me you want to negotiate, Caesar."

"Yeah. I want you to let Seb go."

"Let him go? He's not mine."

"You're forcing him," Caesar said. "Saying you're gonna hurt his sister. Bless already told me you got a job. I'll do it. I'll do whatever you want. Just let him go."

"I do have a job, but I want Sebastian on it."

"Why's it gotta be him?"

"We have a deal," Otto said. "The story he has, the book—I want it. As long as he doesn't give it to me, he works for me. I give him a place to stay, food to eat, car to drive, and all he has to do is take care of things for me. And he just happens to be good at the job."

"You saying you'll let him go if he gives you the book?"

"It could be worked out."

"Don't I get a fucking say?" Sebastian snapped. "You're not forcing me to do anything. I'm doing it now, so just tell me what the job is."

"Seb," said Caesar. "Come on. Think about what you're doing—"

"I know what the fuck I'm doing. Stay out of it."

Otto smiled. "On to business. You listening, Caesar? You want to go, too?"

"I'm listening," Caesar muttered. "What's the job?"

"It's easy. We have a business partner up in Brooklyn. Mr. David Brenner. He's been a good go-between for me and the guys I work with. Very loyal. But the time's come to cut ties. He's getting one last package ready for us. You get that, and then you send him on his way."

"How do we find him?" Sebastian asked.

"There'll be someone waiting for you when you get there," Otto said. "He'll have everything you need. Money, info, tools. You'll have a place to stay, too."

"Kinda far," Caesar said. "Why don't one of your New York guys do it?"

"They want to make some distance. Brenner's not like other guys. Letting him go is gonna make some noise. Bad in the short term, but in the long term, we'll be better off."

"Whatever," said Sebastian. "I'm out of here. Just let me know when it's time." He walked out. Listening to them pissed him off. Bumping heads like they owned him, like he was their toy. They'd know soon enough. He was no toy, and he was no one's bitch.

Caesar watched him go, wanting to say something, wanting to reach out. Otto chuckled.

"So, the sister found you," he said. "Is that right, Bless?"

"Oh, yeah. Looked like she was pretty comfy with Caesar here. Guy actually put his hands on me." Bless laughed. "But I don't swing that way. The little teacher, though, definitely more my speed. Sometimes, I get hard for the bony type. Hard to believe, I know."

"You don't fucking touch her," Caesar growled. "You do *anything*—"

"Caesar, Caesar, Caesar." Otto placed a hand on his shoulder, wore his horrible smile. "Don't get so worked up. What we do to the sister or the kid or anyone— there's nothing you can do about it. We're gonna do it.

We earned that. Now, this past year's been good to us. To me, to Bless, to you. To everybody. But we only get to keep it that way if we work together."

Caesar looked away. Otto took him by the chin. "Hey. Look at me. Look at me, you fucking slob. I've been patient because you do good work. The shaking, the pissing your pants, the things you do with those boys—it's disgusting to me. But you've been a good worker. You've kept your nose clean. Now, you have a problem with me or Bless or anyone else, you can tell me. I won't get mad. But you decide to move against me, you decide to fuck up my business and screw with what I've been putting together, I won't be able to ignore all this disgusting behavior anymore. I'll have to take care of it."

Now was not the time to be scared, Caesar told himself. Not the fucking time. But looking into those eyes was like looking into a black hole. He could not prevent himself from shaking, nor could he prevent the sweat lining his brow or the chills running down his limbs. His soul was leaving him, being sucked away into some other dimension, some cold, dark place.

"Look at him!" Bless laughed. "He's gonna wet his fucking chonies!"

"I'm gonna level with you, Caesar," Otto said, not moving an inch, his breath hot on Caesar's face. "We got lots of willing workers out there. Year-round, we're never at a loss. You can thank Uncle Sam for that. The machine works for us. Keeps us gainfully employed, you might say. Now, Sebastian, I like him. He's a good kid—half-crazy, but I like him. He's a good worker. Better than you, that's for sure. But losing him won't be a blow. I can always grab somebody else, and then somebody else, and then somebody else. They're out there right now, ready to take the hits, ready to do whatever we need. And the job pays well. Hell, even before I got here, you had your game going. You knew the score. The problem is, Sebastian has something I want. And until he gives it to me, he's mine."

"You don't know," said Caesar. "You don't know what that thing is."

"I don't care what it is. I want it. There's power in it, I can feel it. Something like that doesn't come along every day. *That* is worth losing a good worker like Sebastian. It's worth twenty of him. So, I'm gonna give you an out, Caesar, as thanks for doing such good work for us. You get him to give me the book, and I'll let him go. You can take him back to his sister, you can save his soul, whatever it is you want to do. We all get what we want."

"It's a good deal, baby," Bless said. "I'd take it."

"You'll really let him go?" Caesar asked. "You won't come back at him?"

Otto smiled again. "I keep my promises, Caesar. You know I do." He spread his arms, gesturing to the whole of the club, the whole of their world. "I'm also very patient. And sooner or later, I will get what I want. I always get what I want."

He put his hand out. Caesar stared at it, saw the black claws, the purple fur matted with blood. Over and over, the same young, lost face appeared in his mind. The boy he found on that street corner, so pale and fragile, like a doll. The boy broken in a million ways, more sensitive than the others, more tender. Now, that boy was deep in the den of this beast, this monster in a man's skin. All Caesar could do was try to bring him back.

He shook the paw.

3 4 .

We have existed for eons, swelling in the darkness, defined by heat and fire, by blood and rust. We have swallowed pleas and prayers. We have gleamed in the black of the night and lounged upon the blue bed of the sky. In every culture, we have been given names and faces, yet we remain formless. Every attempt to make us less only makes us more. We have spread like shadows over waking and dreaming. We have cradled you since your birth. We have fondled your unchecked instinct and caressed your rampant ego. You desire death, destruction, dissolution, disintegration. You seek to reign down fire, blot out light, crush hope. Those are your fascinations, your wants. To those ends, we have nursed you. We have loved you.

You are consumed at all times by dread. You are forever uneasy, forever uncanny. You look about yourself and scream and flail. You cannot fathom the supposed void. You cannot comprehend the alleged absence. In despair, you perpetuate your fireside stories. In desperation, you invent evermore phenomena, evermore gods, with which to distract yourselves. But there is no need for fear. We will take you from this noisome senselessness. In the chain of being that led to you, we nurtured your salvation alongside your damnation. We knew your kind. What you would desire. What you would need.

We have in the world our agents. They glorify us. They pay us tribute. In our many names, they maim and slaughter. They spread disease. They wage war. They cause famine. Death trails behind them like sheets of locusts. They bleed out your small hope, your dwindling resolve. They are blades in the darkness, severing all ties with the world around you. They release you from your earthly bonds. They push you into our embrace.

We have watched our seeds grow. We have watched the roots take hold. We have watched the earth tremble and squeeze. We have watched the waters grow still. He has arrived at last to harvest you. You know Him. You have seen Him. We are Him. He is Us. He has wired you to one another. He has blinded you with radiation. He has alienated you with poverty and paranoia. He has deafened you with refuse on waves of sound and light. On all levels, you have been both isolated and connected. He has made you both one and all. With little effort, He will release you. He will grant you that beautiful, blissful escape you desire. He has come many times, and He will continue to do so, changing and transforming until the day He may finally emerge, unveiled, in all His splendor. He will shepherd you, and you will be grateful. You will thank Him. You will love Him. And He will love you. His little children.

35.

"It'll be a few days at least," Sebastian said, huddled in front of the laptop. The apartment was dark, some faint, orange light coming in from the alley below. He rolled another joint with shuddering hands. He was hungry. Anxious.

Miranda sat across from him. His little trip would be a good opportunity to plan her next move. It was up to her now. She made a promise to him, the one who brought her into the circle. He called himself "Jackal." Like all the others, he and his people only found the story—or it found them. They took it upon themselves to spread the message. But one lifetime wouldn't be enough. You had to plant seeds, he told her. And if something happened to Sebastian, if he got lost in this game between Otto and whomever else, she had to be ready to move on.

"You afraid?" she asked him.

"I shouldn't be."

"I think it'd be scary. Not knowing."

"Knowing what?"

"Who he is," she said. "Where he comes from."

Sebastian blinked, took a drag from the joint. This guy in New York was just like Polo. Just like Angel. They were all gonna die at some point. What difference did it make?

"You'll still be here?" he asked. "When I get back?"

"Why wouldn't I be?"

"I don't know. Just saying shit."

On the other side of town, in a dim, dirty motel room, Caesar handed Sarah a gun.

"*Mira*," he said, "that's the safety. You flick it off when you want to shoot."

"I got it." She sat on the edge of the bed, eyed her bag of clothes against the wall. "You really think this is necessary?"

"Yeah. Otto and Bless know you, and now they know you're with me. They know you want Seb. They probably got guys all around your place. I tried to be careful, but if they find you here, you take off. Use the rental car I got you. Hear me? Only shoot if you gotta."

"Why can't we go to the police?"

Caesar laughed. "They'll put me in a cell and throw away the key. Shit, they done it before. Besides, Otto's got 'em all in his pocket."

"So, he could kill us, and no one would know?"

"Yeah. Surprised he hasn't already."

Sarah placed the gun aside and rubbed her eyes. She was exhausted, but the thought of more terrible dreams, on top of the threat presented by Otto, kept her from even thinking about sleep. The bloody walls. The writhing bodies. Above all, that bound figure descending from on high, revealing himself. The manacled man beckoning her to join him. The call was disgusting, vile, but there were moments when its promise of relief eased her. Eased her greatly.

Caesar held out a thick, fat envelope. "Here's some more money."

"I can't. You've given me enough already."

"Just take it. You're gonna need it in case something happens. Me, I got more than I need. You know, Jesus wanted us to give away all our money. Two masters and all that. Funny I start doing it right when I could die. Fucking funny."

Reluctantly, Sarah took the envelope. Caesar looked around the room, kneaded his hands. "The gun, the money. You know what to do?"

"Yeah. I know what to do."

"Okay. Good." He gave her one last glance, then headed for the door. "Better go, then."

"Caesar. Wait."

He turned back.

"I wanted to thank you," she said. "What you've done for me, what you're trying to do for my brother, what you *did* do for him—I can't repay that."

"You don't gotta thank me. I'm the one who got him into this mess."

"My point is, what you're doing, not a lot of people would."

She paused, felt her wrists. They seemed so bony. So raw.

"I know what they say about you," she said. "I don't know how true it is, but I know I'm not looking at someone bad. You're not like Bless. Or Otto. And this"—she held up the gun with disdain—"this isn't you. You're not a killer. You wouldn't be helping my brother if you were."

He chuckled. "You sound like my *abuelita*. She said I was good, too. Her *hijo de oro*. But that was before she found out what I really was. God's biggest mistake. A faggot." He spat the word out, wiped at his eyes. "Maybe me and Seb are the same. Maybe that's why I gotta help him—one mistake trying to help the other."

"My brother isn't a mistake," said Sarah, "and neither are you."

"I am." The light from the nearby lamp cast half of him in shadow. The tears staining his face glimmered. "The other boys set me up. One of 'em promised to suck me off. Think about that shit. And I'm just a dumb kid, so I go along with it, and they're all waiting for me. I'm half-dead by the time I get home, and by then, my mom already knows. My *abuela*. I can see it before I even walk in. In their eyes."

"Caesar."

"I know what you're gonna say. It ain't my fault. I was just a kid. But you never think your own blood could stop loving you. And when they do, you know it's 'cause you're bad. And I know I'm bad because every-thing they say—everything you heard—is true."

"But you can stop," she said. Her eyes were soft, her tone tender. Out of the exhaustion came some sapling of strength, something that emerged in front of the students, that held fast in the long, quiet absences that constituted her life. "You have a choice."

He sniffled. He shook his head. "I can't stop. I want to, God knows, but I can't. I know what I do with those boys is wrong. But it's in me. That fucker put it in me. I know he did."

"Who?"

"His name was Rogelio, but he called himself Roger. He *knew* me. Just a kid, running away, and he knew right off. He was like me, another mistake, but I felt safe with him. God, he was beautiful. A blond angel with blue eyes. I went with him out of Florida, all the way to Philly. I really believed him when he said he loved me, that he'd take care of me. I really did.

"He used me. I didn't get a choice—he did what he wanted when he wanted it. Sometimes, it was him, and sometimes, it was others. He'd give me a few dollars and keep the rest. He could be so fucking ugly one second, and then he'd be nice again. I wanted to leave, but I didn't know where to go. And the way he made me feel when things were good—that's all that mattered. Then one day, he was gone. Left me in a fucking motel with no shirt, no money."

The memory of that time was so vivid. That morning and everything before, everything after. The blue carpet, like the fur of a slumbering beast. The morning wind, like the breath of a hissing serpent. Thin arms submerged in garbage. Bony hands hovering over fires. Bare feet padding lightly upon gravel, upon blacktop. The warm spices and red hue of the Miami kitchen always wavering in the distance like a mirage. During the cold, damp nights, when he lay starving in a tattered sleeping bag, he licked an imaginary, scalding soup spoon. He peeled invisible tamales. He fixated on the flames that flickered in the dark, the candles from which the Virgin Mary, the archangel Michael, the redeemer himself watched him. The sensations grew dimmer with each day, but the rosary in his fist remained constant. Remained real.

He unraveled that rosary now, the golden chain glistening in the lamplight, the miniature crucifix swinging to and fro. "Now, I'm the same as Roger," he said. "Using and throwing away. Using and throwing away. And I say he put it in me, but maybe it was always there. And he knew it 'cause it was in him, too."

Sarah watched him. She searched for words in vain. Indeed, the platitudes she gave her students—the platitudes she gave to Paul, Sebastian, even herself—seemed powerless in the face of Caesar's despair. But what else did she have?

She took his hands into her own. "You're not a monster. You have to believe there's good in there. Just like there's good in my brother."

Caesar looked at her, taken aback by the conviction in her eyes. But the conviction faded quickly. The strength turned to terror, the resilience to frailty. Her left hand trembled. She clutched her wrist, retreated from him, fell into convulsions atop the bed.

He watched her writhe and shake, shiver and scream. There were monsters in the world. He was one of them, he knew that. But as he watched her, he realized there were monsters out there somehow even worse than he was. Monsters that couldn't be stopped.

He thought about those monsters on the road, driving up the interstate towards Pennsylvania and eventually New York. White sky stretched on endlessly. Neither he nor Sebastian said anything during the drive. At a couple of pit stops, they bought snacks, ate quietly in the van. Always, the white sky beckoned them forward. When the day grew dark, they stopped at the prearranged hotel. Out smoking on the patio, in the lobby admiring the impressionist paintings and glass sculptures, on the balcony watching the dusk settle, Caesar thought about the monsters.

The world was full of them. Under beds, in closets, behind curtains. On street corners. In alleyways. Evil things. Evil people. Roger was one of them. Otto was one of them. He was one of them. But the monsters came in other forms, too. He didn't know what the book was—Sarah called it the "room of cloth"—but what the words had done to her reminded him of the exorcisms his *abuela* spoke about when he was very young. Spirits found their way into bad boys and girls, she said. They broke bones, scorched skin, twisted tongues. In stuffy, sweltering wooden houses, the victims convulsed. They cursed God, spat out black blood, laughed through mouthfuls of green, burning bile. Priests prayed, made the sign of the cross, scattered holy water. Sometimes, the possession lasted for weeks, maybe months. Often, the victims did not come out of the ordeal alive. Often, those who survived were left small and broken.

The stories scared him like they were intended, but he hadn't really believed in them. Not until now. Even when he prayed to God, even when he shivered before the many iterations of Christ on the cross, he never really entertained the notion of the devil operating among people, slithering about them in his serpentine way, whispering in their ears with his forked tongue. Now, he knew differently. Now, he knew, without a doubt, God was above, even if He wasn't watching. There were demons roaming the earth, having their way. They were winning.

He thought about Roger. He didn't want to remember, but it was good that he did. Good that he pictured the face again, burnt the image into his mind like a brand. That handsome, tan face. The blond curls. The blue eyes. The face of an angel disguising a beast. A horned horror turning him over, overpowering him, driving its cold flesh into his own. He had to remember. He had to feel that fear and pain as intensely as he first did. Those feelings would keep him alive. Keep him fighting. Keep him angry.

He tried to sleep, tossing and turning in the darkness, tormented by the snow flurries hitting the window, haunted by the howling wind. The anger he felt for Roger—anger tinged, nevertheless, with remnants of puppyish devotion—gave way to tremors in his chest. He traced over his cheek the spot where his grandmother struck him. With no words, disowning him. With no words, making clear how miniscule he was, how irredeemably ugly. His mother behind her, usually larger than the old woman, but on that night, so much smaller.

He tried desperately to replace their image with that of Roger—tried to superimpose the picturesque, unearthly beauty of that angelic face upon his grandmother's hard, hateful, human features. But again and again, he failed. The gaunt, wrinkled cheeks. The taut, pursed lips. The boiling, seething rage. Hard, calloused hands that once caressed his face and pinched his arms. Burning, steely eyes that once regarded him with the height of affection. Hands that tricked him into thinking they were soft. Eyes that tricked him into thinking they were loving.

At worst, Roger had looked upon him with pity, maybe mild disgust. Otto saw his worth as a tool even if he disregarded him as a human being. But neither had communicated with such intense fury as his grandmother the desire to kill. More than kill—destroy so utterly that no trace remained, no stain or burn mark or even cell. That pure hatred made him run from his grandmother when even the fear under his subsequent monstrous oppressors did not. At least the pimps and kingpins kept him alive. At least they saw some worth inside him, even if only to exploit and abuse.

He searched for the rosary around his neck. Tempted to tear its chain, tempted to throw it against the wall, he did not. Because there was still someone looking out for him. Still someone who had to love him. If there were monsters—if those monsters possessed people, if they wore human faces—then there had to be also a protective force, a benevolent force. For all the hate, there had to be love. Caesar could not conceive of the alternative. He would not conceive of it.

Sebastian awoke to flurries of snow hitting the window. He stared out at the white, at the dark clouds overhead, and listened to the wailing wind. Just like his dreams, he thought. More and more, his sleep was troubled by intense, unrelenting imagery. Scenes of cities collapsing into ashen rubble. Visions of tsunamis dragging crowds into the dark sea. Portents of a red star, a flaring dot against the black expanse of the night sky. A dot that grew larger and brighter with each night, approaching steadily, unhurried, bringing with it an unfathomable, inevitable end.

He sat on the edge of his bed, arms and legs thinner than ever, skin paler, eyes darker. Shaking again, not just his hand, but his whole body. Fucking shaking again. Why? Why was he scared? Because he had to kill again? He had done it before. He would do it again, as many times as it took to bring the room of cloth into the world. But the fear found him in those rare moments when his confidence waned, when there was no Miranda to support him, no Sarah or Caesar to conveniently scorn. He had doused his mental theater in gasoline, set fire to the upholstery and the curtains, bleached the stage, shattered the lights, and yet the stains of his tethers remained. Faint memories of the cold and the dark and Caesar bringing him into warmth. Vague recollections of the shadowy labyrinth of the old house and the rebellious visage of Sarah like a beacon somewhere within. He killed them again and again in his mind, burnt them, smothered them, drowned them, but they kept coming back. Was he doing something wrong? Was he really not supposed to kill them, but save them? Like in his vision of them all rising into the sky, becoming electricity, becoming air?

Miranda's devious gaze and mischievous smile flitted before him. No doubt she would tell him otherwise, remind him that all of it was by design. He wanted her in that moment, in all those moments of weakness—no, he *needed* her. She was his anchor, what kept him grounded and unafraid. Her skin and her bones and her breasts and her legs. That snake coiling its way up and down her back. The chipped paint on her nails. The colored streak in her hair. All of her shrine and sacrifice, tribute and temple. As he pictured her, as he felt his groin tighten and his face flush, a brutal thought intruded and dropped his gut to what felt like his toes. His anchor. His weight. Would he have to cut her loose, too?

No. No, he couldn't. Besides, she was chosen, too. They were united by their shared suffering, links in the same chain that was bound to the room of cloth. If she anchored him, he anchored her—if he cut her loose, she cut him loose. They would go together. That was their promise. The manacled man would welcome them both into the room of cloth, take them into his embrace at the same time. Together. One and the same. Wrapped up. Bound up.

He dressed in the cold light, throwing on the extra jacket he bought along the way, wrestling on the boots he borrowed from Caesar. The laces fell again and again between his trembling fingers. He struggled so much to wear his sunglasses that he nearly snapped them in two. Jesus Christ, he was fucking scared. Miranda. Miranda. Why the fuck wasn't she there? Why wasn't she helping him? Why was she gone when he needed her so goddamn bad?

He poured a line of coke on the restroom sink, looking at the powder as though it were sediment from Mars or residue from the bottom of the ocean. Supposed to stay clean, keep his head clear, but here he was again, always here again, still using like the lowlife he was. You're weak. You're scared. Fucking pussy. Fucking dog. Weren't you chosen? Aren't you the big bad hero? The one who's gonna save everybody? Tear down all this bullshit?

You have to go in first. Even if you are supposed to save them—save her—you have to go in first. Still too connected, he thought, looking up from the coke and wriggling his nose. Need to break free. Need to separate. Separate to become one. Break to become whole.

Somewhere beyond the raging white outside was that red star, summoning him, beckoning him. Already, the chains were coming undone, the shackles breaking apart.

Were the words in his head his own? Were they the drugs? Or were they the manacled man? He wrote on his hand with a pen, smearing and smudging ink over his knuckles and fingertips. With each word, the shaking subsided. The fear became distant. The confidence returned. Yes, drawing a line down his forearm, encircling his wrist. Yes, hatching blue lines across his throat and behind his neck. Break free. Separate. The flesh a silent cage. The skin a fragile fabric.

He met Caesar outside. Caesar was also bundled in coats, boots, and gloves. Again, they said nothing to each other. They continued driving. At length, Caesar spoke.

"Your sis," he said. "Sarah. She found me."

Sebastian said nothing.

"She's worried about you," Caesar went on. "She's not doing good. That book you got, it did something to her. It's driving her crazy." He turned to Sebastian, saw the vacancy in his face, the apathy. "You hearing me, Seb? Your sister needs help!"

"It's her fault," Sebastian said. "He didn't pick her. She wasn't supposed to read it. At least not yet."

"It's fucking evil, Seb. Nothing good does that to people. You hear me? Nothing good. She's your sister. You should help her."

"She has to help herself. She has to open up. I can't make her do that."

"And you're better, huh?" asked Caesar. "That why you're with Otto? He made you his bitch, Seb. He turned you into one of 'em. But you give him the book, and it all goes away."

"He's not getting the book. And I'm not his bitch. Don't fucking say that again." Sebastian stared ahead. "Just drive. I'm not talking about this anymore."

When they got to New York City, they stopped at a bar, some small, dark place with low lights and no music. The bartender led them into a back room, revealed two handguns and two silencers encased in bubble wrap. He handed over a folder filled with photographs: the row house where David Brenner lived, his blue sedan, Brenner himself. Caesar lit a cigarette and flipped through the photographs. Brenner was tall, white, scruffy. There he was buying a coffee, walking in the crowd. Sitting on a park bench. Waiting at a streetlight. Somewhere in his forties. Dressed decently, so he had some money.

"Any family?" Caesar asked.

The bartender shrugged. A couple of guys in black had swung by with the materials like they always did. They just said to give their regards to Otto. Caesar nodded, put out the cigarette.

Afterwards, he and Sebastian bought some hotdogs, then parked on the pier and looked out at the cold, gray bay. They ate silently in the van, the hotdogs big and fat, their fingers dripping with mustard and ketchup. Caesar tried the radio. He listened to some crackling, static-ridden punk rock, some seventies pop, then turned it off.

After what seemed like an eternity, they drove up to Brenner's row house. "This the place?" asked Sebastian. Caesar nodded. He held up the photo for reference.

"It's green in the picture," he said. "Leaves and everything. They must've been planning this for a while." He turned the van off. Sebastian reached for his door handle.

"Hold up." Caesar lit another cigarette. "You want one?"

"We're wasting time. What if he leaves?"

"He won't." Caesar blew out smoke. "He's done this tons of times. He knows there are guys coming for the money. He won't leave." He held out his carton of cigarettes. "Take one."

Sebastian hesitated, then did as asked.

"Usually, I got some whiskey," Caesar said, "but not this time." He looked up at the smoke hanging over their heads. "I remember my first cig. Must've been eleven or twelve. What about you?"

Sebastian dragged deep. "I don't remember."

Caesar nodded. He crushed the cigarette into the console.

They approached the row house, the walkway slick with melted snow. With every step, Caesar felt the weight of the gun against his hip. He felt the finality, the inevitability. He drew a breath and rang the doorbell.

A minute later, Brenner stood in the doorway, just as he looked in the photos: tall and unshaven, wearing a fleece sweater, toting a cigarette.

He narrowed his eyes at the two men. "Nick and Bob?"

"They couldn't make it," Caesar said. "I'm Caesar. This is Sebastian."

"Hmm." Brenner studied them, the cigarette simmering between his fingers, the nearby trees, dead and black, ratting ominously. Caesar waited, conscious always of the gun at his side, but also conscious of the one on Sebastian.

Finally, Brenner stood aside. "Well, come in. We can't stay out here."

They followed him into the foyer, which was lined with boxes of books and documents. Photographs on the walls depicted a younger Brenner and a woman. There was a little girl in a tutu with a gap-toothed smile. There was a young woman's graduation portrait.

"Sorry about the mess," said Brenner. "Company wants me out in Chicago, so I've been packing the whole week. Should be gone by the end of the month."

"That your wife?" asked Caesar.

"Ex-wife." Brenner pointed at the graduation portrait. "That's Samantha, my daughter."

The kitchen was small, composed of white wood and cracked tile. A plate of pink-frosted doughnuts lay on the table. A pot of coffee bubbled on the countertop. Brenner cleared the chairs of newspapers and wiped the table off. "Help yourself," he said. "Nick loves these."

Reluctantly, Caesar sat down and broke off a piece of doughnut. Sebastian lingered by the sink. Brenner sat and resumed studying the men, flicking his eyes between the two. He crossed and re-crossed his legs. He tapped his ashes into an overfilled ashtray.

Caesar bit into the doughnut. "It's good," he said. "*Muy bien.*"

Brenner focused on him. "You speak Spanish? Where are you from?"

"My *abuela*—my grandma—she's from Cuba. I grew up in Florida."

"Florida," said Brenner. "Been to Miami a few times, myself. Too hot down there for me. But the language is something else. No offense, but your people are taking over. It won't be long before Spanish and Portuguese and even Mandarin are required learning. But I guess America belonged to you guys first. Now, it belongs to everyone."

Caesar shrugged. "We all come from somewhere."

"That's true." Silence ensued as the men shifted. Caesar took another bite of the doughnut. Sebastian glared out the window. Brenner re-crossed his legs. He tapped his ashes into the ashtray. He sniffed the air. "You smell that? Smells like rotten meat."

"I don't smell anything," Sebastian said.

"I guess not. I probably have something dying in the fridge." Brenner smiled and stood up when the coffee pot beeped. "It's decaf. Don't know if that's a problem."

He poured some mugs, handed one to each of the men. "I'm working my way down from full black. Nice to actually sleep for once."

Caesar smiled. Sebastian snorted.

"So," Brenner went on, "what's the story with you guys? Maybe I shouldn't ask."

"It's okay," Caesar said. "Not much of a story. We're from Maryland."

"They got you guys running around like ants. I'm the same. Have to go where the bosses tell us. You know, I used to feel guilty about cleaning the money, but not anymore. It's not my fault the system's broken. Besides, I'm done. Going to Chicago means cutting ties."

There was a pause. He threw the cigarette into the ashtray and set his mug aside. "Well, I guess we should get to business, right? I've got the money in the back."

Caesar and Sebastian followed him to a small office, a cramped space with a desk and a laptop. A window overlooked an abandoned lot down below. Brenner withdrew a silver briefcase from underneath the desk. "Here it is. Seven-hundred-fifty." He unlatched the briefcase. Inside, clean and neatly packed, were bundles of hundred-dollar bills.

"Looks good," said Caesar softly. He motioned for Sebastian to take the briefcase.

"That's a weight off my shoulders," Brenner said. "Last thing I had to worry about. Weird request, but it's done."

Caesar was quiet, an elbow propped against the doorjamb, his eyes on the floor, his jaw shifting from side to side. Sebastian waited behind him with the briefcase. Brenner stared.

"What's wrong?"

Caesar sighed. He took the gun out of his coat.

No one spoke. Brenner looked at the gun. His shoulders slumped. His gaze fell.

"So, that's how it is. I thought as much."

"It's not personal," Caesar said. "It's just a job."

"No, I get it." Brenner drew a breath and leaned back against the desk. "I thought about suicide once. I bought a gun—a Python. Overkill, I know, but I thought if you're gonna do it, you might as well go all the way. I got as far as sitting in my tub with the fucking thing in my mouth. I think my teeth were clamped down on it, I was so scared. I even wrote a note. I told my ex-wife to go fuck herself. I told Sammy I loved her. And then I threw it away. I sold the Python. I was a coward. I guess I've always been one."

Caesar raised the gun. "Might be easier if you turn around, keep talking."

"Yeah. You're probably right." Brenner gave his back to him. He waited. "You're a good guy, Caesar, you know that? Anyone else probably would've come in and just blown my head off. Just splat, and then I'd fall to the ground like a ragdoll, and that would be it. You'd leave, maybe take some of the doughnuts with you, get the money, and then go off again like you were never even here. Go back to Maryland, right? Party it up. Anyone else probably does this every day. Goes out at night, shoots some guys, beats some up. I bet there's a lot of people like that. People just disappearing. There one day, gone the next. I heard about a case once, maybe five years back, some girl. She was white, of course. What about all the other ones? The women and the men, black, Hispanic like you, the Asians. Where do they go? Who looks for them? What about the homeless? No one would even notice. You're just there, and then you're not there anymore. Dead. Or worse. Maybe someone has you chained up in a room, and you're trapped, and there's no getting out. That's what happened to that girl. Stuck in a tiny room just like this one. Raped, beaten. Trained. When they found her, she'd already been there for years. She couldn't say her name. She didn't know it anymore. She couldn't even speak. Whatever that fucker did, he turned her into something else, something less than what she was. Imagine that's your whole life. All you see are the walls, the door. If you're lucky, there's a window. Fuck, what if you can't see at all, right? What if the lights are off all the time, and all you know is the dark, and the guy coming in, just this thing hurting you, and you're screaming, and you don't even know what a scream is, or how it should sound, or if there's anything else but the screaming and the pain and the thing in the dark and the hits and the exhaustion and sleep and eventually the sleep is no different than the being awake it's all dark and it just goes on and on and on and on and on and on—"

Brenner kept talking, going faster, starting to stammer, starting to slur. The barrel of Caesar's gun trembled, followed by the gun itself, then his hand, his arm, his whole body. He saw Sarah in Brenner's place, her agonized face in the dim light of the lamp, her small, frail body curling and twisting on the bed. What had she told him? He wasn't a mistake? He wasn't a killer? Oh, what a joke. He did kill people. He did take advantage of those boys. His grandmother had been right. He was a monster. He was a mistake. He deserved what Roger had done to him all those years. He deserved his grandmother's wrath and scorn.

The gold of her rosary glistened from underneath his glove. He kept looking at it, moving his eyes from the gun to the rosary and back again. He carried this fucking thing around, said his prayers, put on a good show. But it was all a lie. His prayers weren't stopping anything. His weeping and wailing, when the boys lay naked atop his bed, when the weight on his chest nearly suffocated him—what good did any of it do?

Sebastian's voice sounded behind him. "What the fuck are you waiting for? Do it."

Caesar shut his eyes. He needed a drink. He needed the shaking to stop. The shaking in bed as he stroked a pale, flaccid arm. The shaking in the back of the van as he heard the boots approach, the belt unlatch. The shaking in the shadow of that wooden, bloody-faced Jesus as he watched the withered fist of his grandmother come down upon him. The shaking as he lay awake at night in that tattered, rotten sleeping bag, terrified of the shadows around him.

"My Sammy, my baby Sammy, God I wish she was here, I wish she was here—"

The shaking as he watched Sarah writhe on the bed. The shaking as he watched her eyes.

"Just fucking do it!"

She was fighting it. The book was driving her mad, but she was fighting it. Why? Why was she fighting when she was going to lose?

"Oh, Sammy, my Sammy, oh God, oh Sammy—"

"Do it!"

Caesar opened his eyes. Brenner was still talking, mumbling, making no sense. Sebastian kept hissing behind him. The gun remained in his hand, his finger still on the trigger. Just one push, one light tap, and it would be over, all of it would be over—but he couldn't. He wouldn't.

Caesar lowered the gun. His breath left him in one great sigh. After what felt like an eternity, Brenner turned around. He looked at the gun, looked at Caesar. His eyes questioned.

"I won't do it," Caesar said. "I don't care what happens. Otto can go fuck himself."

"Holy shit. You sure?"

"Yeah. We're gonna go. After that, take off. Don't go to Chicago. Go somewhere else. Stay low. They're gonna look for you."

"Fuck. I don't know what to say."

"You don't gotta say anything. I didn't wanna do it, so I'm not gonna do it."

Brenner fumbled with lighting a cigarette. He offered one to Caesar, but Caesar refused it.

"Nice meeting you, man," Caesar said. "You should talk to your girl."

"Yeah. I'll do that."

Caesar returned to the foyer. Sebastian trailed behind him. "What the fuck are we doing?" he whispered. "What about the job?"

"We got the money."

"They'll kill us. Once they find out, they'll fucking kill us."

"No," said Caesar quietly, "not if we kill 'em first. We kill Otto, Bless, all of 'em. You and your sister get out. You keep going, you don't look back. I'll take care of the rest."

"You keep doing that," Sebastian said. "Both of you. You keep making choices for me. I can take care of myself, Caesar."

Caesar whipped around. "Oh, yeah? Who do you go to if it's not me or her? You think Otto's gonna take care of you? He's gonna throw you away when you ain't useful anymore!" He turned to the door. "Now, come on."

Sebastian stood still. "I know what's really going on. You're scared."

"What?"

"You're scared. You've always been scared. It's why you weren't chosen. Why he didn't pick you. You don't have what it takes."

"The fuck you talking about?"

"I'm saying it's me. I'll do whatever it takes to get in. Shit, I want to do it. It makes me feel alive. Like I can be whatever I want."

"Seb," said Caesar, "Seb, *no*—"

But it was too late. Sebastian marched back into Brenner's office. Brenner barely turned around and opened his mouth when a bullet broke the skin above his left eye. A mess of bone, brain, and blood hit the window with a splat. Brenner fell like a ragdoll, just like he said he would. He crashed against his desk, head to one side, eyes wide open, lips slightly apart. The still-burning cigarette rolled from between his loose, limp fingers to the toe of Sebastian's boot.

Sebastian looked upon the flap of skin where the bullet entered, upon the trail of blood, upon the glassy eyes. Brenner didn't look dead. He just looked stuck somehow, frozen in time. Gingerly, Sebastian nudged the silencer of the gun against a cheek, against the forehead. No movement. No response. He was dead. He had to be dead. All the talking and fidgeting and fucking crying and now nothing. Wait. His eyes. They were moving. They were staring at him.

Sebastian reared back, pulled up the gun. The eyes followed him. The lips spread out into a grin. "Omen," said the body, in Brenner's voice, in the voice of his mother, in the voice of his father. In Miranda's voice. In Sarah's voice. "Omen, you're here at last. At the door."

"What the fuck?"

He fired twice. One cheek blew apart in a spray of red. The nose disappeared. Still, the eyes followed him. He turned in panic, but the walls were gone, as were the floor and ceiling. He stood in a void, an abyss, a pure darkness, and when he looked back at Brenner, he saw Angel instead. She sat on her sofa, sifting listlessly through the bowl of popcorn in her lap. The twin trails of blood, like a serpent's tongue, ran down her face from the bullet hole between her eyes.

"You're so close," the voices said. "One more step."

"The fuck is this?"

"You know. You feel it. He's waiting for you, Omen. We all are. Look."

The eyes rose. Sebastian followed them. He screamed. From the darkness above, *he* was descending. Chains binding him, his bound legs and arms twitching, eager to break free. A leather muzzle over his face, burning and dripping with froth. Broken fingers and toes. Hooks buried into flesh and muscle. Eyes red and furious, hating him, hating him with such intensity, there could be no mistaking the intent.

Never had he seen something so pure and true.

Sebastian fell to his knees. His screams turned to laughter, his horror into bliss. He dropped the gun and raised his hands in beckoning. Just take me, he thought. Take me, for fuck's sake! Just take me! *Take me now! Please fucking take me away*—

"Seb!"

Caesar grabbed him, shook him hard. "Get a grip! Calm the fuck down!"

The trance was broken. Sebastian fell forward, drenched in sweat, shivering. Dazed, he grabbed his gun and climbed uneasily to his feet.

Caesar regarded him. "Goddamn it, Seb! We coulda just walked out!"

Sebastian turned to him, wiped away the saliva lining his mouth. "He chose me," he said softly. "He showed himself to me, Caesar. Don't you get it? I'm on the path."

"Seb, listen to me. You're fucked up. You hear me? You need help!"

Sebastian laughed. He picked up the briefcase. "I'll take it back if you're so scared. Otto can't do shit to me anymore. Neither can you. Neither can Sarah."

"Seb," said Caesar, but he couldn't think of anything to say. As angry as he felt, as confused, looking at Sebastian was almost comforting. For the first time, the boy didn't look lost.

Caesar stood alone in the office. He stared at Brenner's body. "Sorry," he said. "I didn't want this to happen." He closed Brenner's eyes, and then he picked up the phone, dialed 9-1-1, and left the receiver off the cradle. Outside, Sebastian stood smiling, like he'd just won the lottery, like he'd just made it big.

3 8 .

Sebastian wrote for a long time that night. During a pit stop at a corner store, he bought a cheap, wire-bound notebook, special only because it could be special, for the moment his pen touched its paper, the notebook's mundane, mass-produced existence became sacred. His vision after killing Brenner awoke something inside him. He was inspired, possessed, the words spilling out of him definitely not his own, certainly not even of this world. They belonged to something else, something bigger, some deep swell of darkness in his subconscious mind, in that of all people. More and more, he felt himself less cohesive, as though he were disappearing into a roaring sea. Was it him he saw in the mirror? Was that his hand, his arm, his face? When he moved his fingers, when he smiled, when he frowned, when he tugged at the skin on his chest and arms, was that Sebastian? Or was that something else? Were invisible wires tucked into his flesh, tethered to a master? He knew he was fading, but he couldn't stop it. He didn't want to stop it.

Caesar sat awake in the adjacent hotel room, listening to the intermittent hum of the air conditioner, holding the silenced pistol before him. He had failed. He missed his opportunity to save Sebastian, if such an opportunity ever existed. He failed to save Brenner. All the supposed courage, all the shit it took to put the gun down, hadn't done a damn thing. Now, he was heading back to that hell, back to Otto, back to this madness with the book.

The book. What the fuck was it? Sarah forbade him from looking at the words that came out of her, and he gladly obliged. Sweating and shivering like that, screaming from the pain, she seemed worse than any addict, worse than even the possessed girls he imagined while listening to his grandmother's stories. No drug he knew did that to a person. No demon he knew, either.

What would she say when he got back? Would she be disappointed? Would there even be enough of her left to care? Would she even be alive? He didn't want to picture her pale skin in the tub full of blood, didn't want to imagine her limp body hanging from the ceiling fan. An angel to greet him, to welcome him home.

Back in Florida, when he was still a boy, not even nine, the kids had run up and down the block one morning, whispering to one another, congregating. Marco said he was the first to smell it—that he threw a baseball over a fence, went to get it, almost doubled over from the smell. Like rotten meat, he said, worse than a pig or cow cut open. Even worse than your mom's *culo* after getting plowed by the neighborhood. Fucking Marco. Always something to say.

They picked straws to see who would go into the shed. Of course, Caesar picked the shortest straw. He wasn't the youngest of the bunch, but he was the smallest. The other boys had no idea of the real monster lurking inside him, the beast they eventually exposed and ridiculed and maybe even feared, but the difference in size was enough reason to lord themselves over him at the time. When they pushed him towards the door, what was he supposed to do? Maybe another monster was inside the shed, like the ones he knew hid in the closet, but he was more afraid of those grinning faces and sweaty hands behind him. Always egging him on, always judging him. So, he went in, little Caesar, and he *was* judged.

He remembered the slant of light coming down on her face, on her one open eye. He remembered the pasty, white skin, remembered the cracked, saliva-encrusted lips. The flies buzzing around the head, around the exposed guts. The maggots squirming in the caked blood, in the crevasses of the bruised face, under the grimy fingernails, throughout the disheveled hair.

The little boy standing in awe of that spectacle pissed himself, almost collapsed on the spot. When he walked out, the others laughed and shoved him, called him a pussy, a *maricón*. That word haunted him in the years after, when he knew full well what he was, but then, at that moment? The sight of that thing made him deaf and mute, and he stumbled off, unaware of their taunts and jeers, to shiver away the rest of the day in his bedroom, unable to sleep, unable to escape even briefly that lone, awful, silver eye.

It didn't matter if he avoided the words. It didn't matter if he covered his ears and closed his eyes. Whatever was in that book was already inside him. Whether from God, Roger, his grandmother, the dead whore, it didn't matter. The monster inside grew, calling out to the other monsters like it, searching for its whole, craving a return to its darkness.

He downed his flask, clutched his rosary. The night was long. The day would be longer.

39

The next morning, they rode back to Lorraine. Once again, the drive was silent. Caesar glanced over at Sebastian, saw the ink stains on his hands, the serenity in his eyes. Like a good high—no, the best. He imagined briefly driving Sebastian to the motel against his will, knocking him out, taking him and Sarah out of the town, far away—but that dazed, peaceful look numbed him. That look, and the gun sticking out above Sebastian's beltline. There was still too much at stake to risk something like that.

"You can drop me off here," Sebastian said, gesturing to a vacant street corner once they were back in town. He stuffed the briefcase into a travel bag and dragged it with him out of the van. "I'll take it from here. Don't worry, they won't know shit."

"You just gonna carry it around with you?"

"Yeah. You got a problem with that?"

Caesar sighed. "Seb."

Sebastian waited, but no words came. Caesar only fingered his rosary and tapped the steering wheel. All of that stress he'd been feeling, and for what? To go from a sidewalk on some cold, bitter night to the essence of a black hole. To realize one's life was rigged from the start. There was no choice, only the illusion thereof. In trying to help Sebastian all those years prior, had he merely brought the kid closer to Otto, to the book? Brought him to this moment?

"I'm good, Caesar," Sebastian said. "Everything's good. You can tell Sarah that."

Caesar watched him go. Maybe he failed Sebastian, but there was still someone else waiting for him. He put the van into drive and headed for the motel.

In the meantime, Miranda was there to greet Sebastian when he got back to the apartment. He looked like shit, hair frayed, eyes bloodshot, hands ink-stained, but he was smiling, smiling like he'd just eaten a good meal or had a good fuck. He wasn't twitchy or nervous. She was surprised, but also excited. Sooner than she expected. Maybe even better.

She pointed at the briefcase. "What's that?"

"The money we got," he said. "I gotta get it to Bless. I gotta take a shower. But first"—he gave her the notebook—"read this."

"You wrote more?"

"I wrote it all. I barely remember it, but I know I did. It's all there. Everything. I think it might even be the ending."

Miranda's eyes flicked up to him, then back to the notebook. "An ending?"

"Yeah. I think so. Read it. Fuck, I just need a shower."

He shambled away, shedding his coat as he went. Miranda opened the notebook. Indeed, the pages were full, replete with words upon words upon words. She started reading. Down the hall, the shower shot on. Her eyes widened. Her pulse quickened. Maybe not an ending, she thought, reaching the end of the first page, but something inspired. Something true. Not bullshit thought up by human minds, not weak, frail ideas, not just syntax and symbols masquerading as meaningful. This was *it*. Coughed up out of the dark, drawn from the depths. Actual revelation, the word of the one true god translated by human hand. His gospel. His *Logos*.

Omen had been the best one for the job after all.

Miranda put the notebook down and went to the restroom. Sebastian stood in the gray cube of a shower, the old showerhead spitting out water, the air around him warm, thick, and suffocating. She slid out of her clothes, came up quietly behind him, linked her arms around his waist, pressed her cheek against his back. "It's perfect," she said. "It's everything we need. Everything we've been looking for."

"We're gonna finish it," he said. "And then everyone will read it. Everyone will know. They're gonna be so happy when they read it."

She brushed her lips against his skin, planted a trail of soft kisses. "You're tired. Going up there, doing all this. You need to rest."

"Yeah." He felt her touch, felt the liquid pleasure wind its way from his stomach up to his chest, throughout his body. "I'm tired, but I feel good. Like I'm in a dream."

"It's all a dream, and it's all real." She turned him around. "It's fantasy, Omen. It's pleasure and pain. And you're in the middle of it."

He kissed her, was inside of her, felt at home in her arms. He slept soundly afterwards.

40.

An hour later, Miranda was at the back of a café, the notebook open in her lap. The wind outside rattled the windows, threatened to blow over the umbrellas on the patio. The sky was a dark blue turning black. Change coming, she thought with a smile. A purge.

What was in the notebook surprised her. The words were even more vivid than she hoped, more resonant than she expected. She had done well picking him. That was her job, after all. "You'll watch," Jackal told her over the phone so long ago, his voice ridden with static, as though coming from somewhere else. "You'll wait. You'll be both his mother and lover. When the time is right, you'll act. Do you understand?"

She mumbled a "yes," felt her face grow hot, her knees go weak. They found her not long after that. Hands had grabbed her from her bed, dragged her into the dark, through the rain. Vaguely, she recalled their faces—or more accurately, their lack of faces, as though they wore masks, as though they had no eyes, no mouths. Stripped, cowering, she had winced at the candlelight, the heat, the stench. A man emerged, hooded, garbed in black, the specter from her nightmares realized like an oath fulfilled. With a gloved hand, he had taken hold of a soft, slim neck, a neck throbbing with life. The orange light had gleamed in an arc off his blade like a comet streaking across the night sky. The torrent of blood had drenched her face, her hands.

She could admit she had been afraid. Just like Omen, just like Bryan, just like the rest of them. Even Jackal said he had been afraid once, long before, when his attachment to this life was too great, when not enough had been taken away. She had tried to run, slipping on bare feet, stumbling against wood, screaming, screaming endlessly. They held her down, pulled back her hair, unclamped her mouth. The rim of a goblet, overflowing with that girl's blood, had been held to her lips. She drank and choked, nearly suffocated. Worse than whiskey, more vile than vodka. Like ingesting liquid metal.

They left her squirming in a pool of bile and blood. Left her to scream and cry, thrash about like a frightened child. Around her, the darkness had swum with life. That was the first time she saw them. The ones already taken. The ones already crossed over. His thralls. His children. They watched her. They laughed. And then they turned their eyeless, mouthless faces upward. They heralded the coming of her new god, who descended on a figurative chariot of rusted steel, who confirmed to her via his enraged, red-eyed glare everything she knew about the world but had secretly never wanted to accept. No, those eyes told her. She was right. The world was wrong. And there was only one corrective.

Her screams had turned to laughs. She had never felt so happy.

She woke up the next morning convinced the entire experience had been a nightmare, but the key on the nightstand suggested otherwise. Initiated, she thought. A life exchanged for new blood. A door closed so another could open. A vision of the truth, of the only way forward. That key led her to the storage unit, to the binder inside with its glossy sleeves, to the smell of roses that drifted out. That episode had been her beginning. Maybe this was close to the end.

She put the notebook in her backpack along with the rest of the manuscript and the money she took from the briefcase. At the counter, she ordered a cappuccino. One for the road. It was going to be a long trip.

41.

Sarah stood outside her motel room, hugging herself, wiping her eyes. The sky was a monstrous blue-black, webs of lightning cutting through the dark. A heavy wind blew by, shook the trees, clattered the wind chime hanging from the awning.

It wasn't wise to expose herself, but she needed the air. The fits were getting worse. She woke up in the morning to a section of the wall covered in scrawls, to the motel Bible filled with more hellish words. She burned the Bible, plastered newspapers over the wall. She couldn't let it out, couldn't let other people see it. But it was only a matter of time. All it took was one word. One letter. Then it would find its way into someone else. Then it would start again.

Her hand twitched. She held it tight.

Headlights appeared on the rise coming into the parking lot—Caesar's van. She went to him immediately. "What happened? Where's Sebastian?"

Caesar got out of the van. He shook his head.

"What does that mean? Is he okay?"

"We gotta get ready," Caesar said. "I can't stay for long."

"What are you saying? Where's my brother, Caesar?"

Caesar stopped at the doorway to her room. The sheets on the bed were strewn about, the pillows scattered over the floor. Newspapers had been taped to one of the walls, like a bandage dressing a wound. And there was a *smell* hovering over everything, so rancid it almost brought him to tears. He knew the smell, too. The same stench hung over that shed with the dead whore. The same stench had filled his nostrils whenever Roger descended upon him. The same stench had haunted him in his tattered sleeping bag. The same stench had swelled in the nights when a boy's arm lay over his chest.

He turned around to Sarah, noticing at last how much paler she looked, how much frailer. "We gotta do something," he said. "Get you to a hospital, or—"

"*Sebastian*, Caesar!" Sarah cried, shoving him back despite her stature, surprising him with her strength. "Where is he? What happened to him?"

He watched her. The shove alone doubled her over, made her break into a coughing fit. He touched her shoulder, but she swatted his hand away.

"Just tell me," she said, getting her breath back. "Just tell me where he is."

Caesar stood there. He reached for his flask.

"He didn't want to come back," he said. "You didn't see him, Sarah. The way his eyes looked. After he went in there and shot Brenner, it was like he changed."

"What?" Sarah looked up at him. "What did you say?"

"Seb shot him. I was just gonna get the money and leave, but he shot him. And it ain't the first time. He likes it. Said so himself."

Sarah's mouth went dry. Her skin tingled. "My God."

"Listen, Sarah—I wanna help him. But as long as he's with Otto, you ain't safe. So, I gotta get Otto out of the picture. He's gonna be at his club tonight, same with Bless, some of their other guys. Seb's gonna take the money eventually, and I can be there. If I can surprise 'em, that'll buy you time. We get Seb after. When you're safe, I take off. I take all the heat with me."

"What are you saying? What are you going to do?"

"Only thing I can do," he said. "Kill them. Otto and Bless. Anyone else. Everyone in that club if it comes down to it."

"That's insane, Caesar. You won't make it."

He was quiet. Just sat on the bed and drank from his flask. He gestured at the patch of newspapers on the wall.

"That what I think it is?"

Sarah looked at it. She turned away.

"Yes."

"Seb was talking about it. Didn't want to give it up, no matter what I said. Thinks he's chosen or something. Like he's special."

"That's what it wants you to think," Sarah said. "It whispers to you. Sings to you."

Caesar kept looking at the patch of newspapers, straining his eyes, scrutinizing, studying. "Maybe this thing ain't evil," he said at length. "Maybe it's just something else looking in, something we don't want to see. You know?"

When he turned to her, his eyes were pleading, begging for an out. What could she say? What could make it right? She had no answers for him, no answers for herself. When she looked at the patch of newspapers, she saw no signs or portents. She saw only a flimsy veil covering something too horrible and grandiose to be contained. An inefficient, ad hoc solution—a bandage over a gunshot wound. There wasn't meaning there. Only fear. Only desperation.

Caesar left not long after. Watch your phone, he said, and she tried, but the longer she sat in the silence of that motel room, the longer she flipped through the same five channels on the television, the more her eyelids dipped, the more the darkness fell around her. In the fuzzy, color-drained game shows and interviews of the television, shadows grew long and faces turned pale. Just as she fell asleep, she swore they were looking at her.

42.

His food always tasted like mud.

Didn't matter what it was—chicken or beef, broccoli or carrot. The sweetest white wine was indistinguishable from the most dour red. The most delectable lamb turned into dust, the most heavenly fish into ash. Again and again, no matter the class of the neighborhood or the caliber of the restaurant. His whole life, running from those early days when hunger—gnawing, agonizing, inconsolable hunger—had driven a boy of six to seek out worms and maggots in the ground and among the garbage.

His story wasn't any different from those of the deadbeats and fools, the bottom-feeders and ankle-biters. Father behind bars for murder or possession or theft. Mother slave to the dragon or the crystal. But what did separate him from the rest was discipline. Commitment. Perseverance. Even while pawing in the squirming dirt or pushing aside black plastic, he had looked around at the slums of Brooklyn and felt stomach-churning, chest-tearing disgust—no, hatred. Hatred for the slate sky and the congested tenements. Hatred for the addict and the whore. Hatred for weakness and pity.

Use them. Use them. Those were the words that came to him even then. Bless complained of his single-mindedness, but Bless was pleasure-drunk, too used to the abundance of flesh and drink they had accumulated. Once, Bless had been just as hungry, just as hateful, but success had made him soft. Fucking and killing were all he was good for now, as if all the blood and struggle had only served to buy him license to be more animal, not less. Sweaty, pungent, vulgar—Bless's type only worked to be free of work. They had no vision. They waited on word from the real prophets. The real storytellers.

Otto had not allowed his trade of the street for the suite to soften him. He had grown to appreciate the mud in his mouth. The muck kept him sharp, kept him strong. As did the knife, blackjack, and chain. Rest was death. Sleep was eternal. There could be no stopping, would be no stopping. Unless he was ready and willing to die.

Over the many years, his lack of taste had refined his smell to a supernatural degree. Like a bloodhound, he could catch whiffs of fear from across rooms, could sense desperation and pain from down multiple city blocks. But one smell was strongest above all, most unmistakable—that of death. That stench clung to the damned like a shroud, one he could almost visualize as the clichéd cloud of flies above the head or the stereotypical specter of the reaper hovering over the shoulder. Without fail, the ones marked by that smell ended up dead, either by Otto's hand or that of another. He thought of the stench as their weakness made manifest, their doom like dress. Something in the gut recognized that odor, some instinct that compelled the earliest men to abandon their most cherished kin or ally with their most hated enemies. Evade that reek, elude that stink, until the road ran out and the clock struck twelve.

But now that smell was everywhere, stuck on everything, draped over everyone. He no longer tasted mud, but rotten meat. He had hardly eaten, in fact, such was the overwhelming, vile taste. And he knew where it was coming from, too. The kid. Caesar's pup, stupid and feral, biting at all the hands, snapping at all the fingers, chasing all the cars. The pup on his own would have died long ago if not for some type of intervention. Something steered him. Something had taken up residence in his corner, had perched itself on his shoulders.

Otto should have been afraid. He should have burned his club to the ground the second the kid walked in with his pollution. But a stench that strong, so absolutely overpowering, was as much a high as it was a repellant. For an old dog like Otto, little engaged the senses anymore. Little got the tail wagging or the tongue panting. He sat in the club, his latest castle, hands laced beneath his chin, rings jostling restlessly. The stink filled the office, evoking images of jail cells, dumpsters, freshly dug graves. Even those smells redeemed themselves with hints of life. The jail cells stunk of sweat and semen. The dumpsters radiated with the heat of rats and strays, buzzed with the flutter of flies and the mingle of maggots. The graves, especially before dawn, smelled of sweet dew and rich soil. But this new smell, so intensely, undeniably dead, seemed incapable of any life at all. Even the scavengers avoided it. No buzzards picked at that blackened meat. No wolves approached that profane carcass. Yet there was an appeal, like a call from deep inside. The body recognized something in that smell. An end. A release.

"Just cut him loose," Bless had told him. "Him and that cocksucker Caesar." But Otto was nothing if not curious. And he could not abide a power like that to exist without his knowledge. A book, the pup said. A book. More like a bell. A dinner bell for the greatest of feasts. For the last. The last supper for everyone and everything.

Otto stroked his rings. He waited.

4 3 .

What had there been before the room of cloth?

Nights roaming the streets, whether those of Lorraine or Boston, staying warm with only a pint of liquor, the flickering flame of a lighter. Crouched amid overturned garbage, watching with fidgety eyes for the next customer he could swindle. In dingy, amber-lit bars, the air thick with smoke and dust, he provoked beatings and endured thrashings. Many mornings, he crawled from the pitch-black recesses of an alley into sunlight, pummeled and battered, chewing stale bread with fewer teeth, pinching bruises he could have avoided with fewer insults. He always ended up back in his hovel of the day or nest of the week. He preferred the seclusion of isolated underpasses and overgrown public parks, but occasionally, fellow sellers spotted him a corner of a filthy apartment or let him squat on the outskirts of a trash-strewn lot. When he sold for Billy Tripp, he'd enjoyed his own room, his own square hole of sunlight in the ceiling through which he could smell spring and admire the shapes of the clouds. How often he lay there, coiling his belt around his arm slowly, deliberately, anticipating with quiet excitement the prick of the needle, the warmth of the dope. A little slice of heaven, nice and quiet. Away from the world.

That year in Boston had been revelatory in many ways. The longest time he'd spent on his own, without the guidance of Caesar or the policing of Sarah. The longest time he'd been able to think without the heavy hand of one or the other dictating what was right, what was acceptable. The freedom was intoxicating at first, better than the dope or the cocaine. The fights and the highs, the whores who did whatever he wanted as long as he produced that extra bill. But the sex quickly lost its appeal, and he looked to them for different needs. He sat with them, waxing and waning about the injustice of the world, the cruelty. How couldn't he? His own parents had forsaken him. His sister scorned him. And always there were rules, codes about this, protocols about that. Live this way, the world commanded. Perform that way. Otherwise, get lost. Otherwise, *be* lost. That was why he chose the name, he said. LostOmen. Wayward, wasted, but nonetheless, a sign of what was already here and of what was to come.

They entertained his rambling—that was their job, of course, what they were paid to do—but he knew those bitches mocked him in private. Little puppy, he imagined them saying. Poor, little puppy. Roll over, puppy. Go fetch. Play dead. Follow the rules because you have nothing else. Follow the rules because you *are* nothing else. You are nothing. No one shaped you. And that's what you want more than anything. That's what you cry for in your disgusting little bed. That's what you wish for as you fondle your puny little dick.

Their lips pursing as they cooed. Little puppy. Poor, little puppy.

I'm not lost, he would tell himself. I am *not* lost. I'm no one's bitch. But he looked around and saw no evidence of that. The whores looked down on him. The fucking tweakers and fiends took him for an idiot. Billy talked sweet, but offloaded everything onto him constantly. You're the boss, Billy told him. A fucking legend. I ever tell you that? A fucking grade-A legend. And then he would take off with his girls to New York or Philly for days or even weeks without so much as a word. The freedom from Sarah and Caesar and all the chains of his old life had been an illusion. The chains followed him, hooked into his flesh, tethered to his core. If he resisted too much, they pulled back. They threatened to tear him apart.

Hence the late nights in front of the computer. Hence the enraptured clicks of the mouse. Every artifacted video and pixelated photo led him deeper into a realm of acknowledgment, desire, and mystery. The allure of the blue light, the ecstasy of the next lurid image—eventually, not even dope could compete. And then there was the biggest dragon of them all, an elusive white whale with a serpentine shadow that left a trail of rumors and dead ends in its wake. He searched for clues everywhere, finding in each lifeless, years-old forum thread and bastardized, half-legible testimonial a breadcrumb. He asked questions. He sent messages. His pursuit never slackened—his dedication never faltered—and eventually, he no longer went outside at all, no longer prowled the streets, no longer peddled product or collected cash. One night, in frustrated fury, he toppled furniture and shattered glass. He broke windows and cratered walls. He turned the flat Billy left him into his own glorified punching bag. But no matter the damage he caused, he found no relief. He collapsed in the center of the carnage, weeping, begging for his mother, his father, Sarah, Caesar, anyone. And then the computer chimed. He sat up, wiping his tears, swallowing his snot. The first of many messages waited for him.

Hello. Are you looking for the truth? :)

Miranda. His muse. His Beatrice. His Cheshire Cat. She called herself so many things, each identity another wall through which he had to break. He sometimes felt close to her, thought he started to understand her, but then she was gone again, hiding behind another obstruction. As they were, wrapped up in their bodies, trapped within sinew and skeleton, any attempt at understanding was doomed to fail. Arms and legs entangled in awkward knots and curls. Words were misconstrued and misapplied. Eyes revealed either too much or too little. There were too many layers in themselves, let alone between them. He needed a leveling force. He needed her to see him for whom and what he truly was—he wanted to see her the same way. He wanted the same for Sarah, for Caesar. There was no need to hide in the room of cloth, no reason to be afraid or misunderstood. All would be revealed. All would be accepted.

He was crying again, blubbering like a baby. Mom. Dad. Feeling hands through his hair, on his skin. Sarah. Miranda. Warmth like a blanket over him. Words in his ear, soft and sweet.

Almost there.

Nearly there.

Waiting for you.

Always waiting for you.

"I'm coming," he said, feeling himself rise from his sleep on the floor. Breaching the cover of his body. Transcending the barrier. Reaching that hallowed place.

But not quite. Not yet.

44.

Sebastian awoke to the sounds of thunder and rain. He sat up, rubbed his shoulders and sides—his muscles ached as if he had been asleep for years.

He walked out into the hall. "Miranda?"

The apartment was dark. She had taken the laptop, probably to work on the story elsewhere. He stood there in a daze, listening to the patter of the rain outside, the distant wail of a police siren. Headlights from the street below cut underneath the garbage bags over the windows and illuminated the room briefly. He caught sight of the briefcase.

He called Bless and told him he had the money. "'Bout time, baby!" Bless said. "Been waiting for your call. Haven't heard from Caesar. Something happen?"

Sebastian thought about Caesar's outburst, his refusal to kill Brenner. If he told Bless and Otto, who knew what would happen—Caesar hunted down, beaten into the pavement, definitely killed. Bad as it was, as many their differences, Sebastian still wanted a chance to show Caesar the manuscript. A chance to save him.

"Caesar's fine," he said. "We did the job, got the money. Came back. Nothing special."

"I don't know about that. Guy was going on about getting you out. But I don't think you'd be dumb enough to give up all the perks, huh? Come on, sweetie—we're good to you. Give you everything you want. Everything you need. You're happy, right?"

"Yeah. I'm happy."

"Good, good. I need to talk to Caesar. Guy's getting ideas in his head. Starting to think. But, baby, we're not paid to think. We're paid to work. Ain't that right?"

"Yeah."

"Yup, yup. But anyway. How about I swing by in fifteen minutes? Grabbing some food at the *momentito*. Noodles, orange chicken, chi chong fu shit. You want something? Some fucking cream puffs? Egg woll?"

Sebastian waited for the laughing to subside. "I'm good," he said.

"Whatever you want, baby. See you in a bit."

Bless drove up a while later. He was digging through a carton of noodles when Sebastian got inside the car. "Gimme a sec," Bless mumbled. "Almost done." The car was thick with the smell of oil and soy sauce. Egg rolls lay beneath the console on a piece of tinfoil. "Take one," Bless said. With a belch, he threw the empty carton to the back of the car and gulped down some beer. "Don't be shy, sweetie."

"I'm okay. Not really hungry."

"Okay, okay. Don't get mad about it." Bless grinned and slapped the briefcase. "Let me take a look. Gotta verify."

Sebastian opened the briefcase. Bless chomped down on an egg roll and looked closely at the money, eyes scanning, teeth grinding. He gave a thumbs-up. "Looking good, mama-san," he said through a mouthful of fried dough and cabbage. "Very clean. Otto's gonna be happy."

"We're gonna see him?"

"Yeah. He wants to know what went down. Seems like the po-lice found Brenner real quick. We were thinking it'd be quiet for at least a couple more days."

"I don't know. We didn't stick around."

"Yeah, no problem, sweetie. It's all good."

Otto's club, Rhapsody, was as loud, noisy, and bright as it had been when Sebastian first visited. He followed Bless inside and up the stairs, cringing at the red and purple lights, the ear-splitting music. His stomach twisted. His breath quickened. Something was wrong. He felt great just hours before with Miranda, but now the anxiety was coming back, the ever-present, ever-escalating dread. He couldn't leave with Bless so close. It was all the excuse they would need.

"Hold up, baby," Bless said at the top of the stairs. He took the briefcase. "I just need a sec with the boss." He disappeared into the office. Sebastian waited and watched the dance floor below. There went his hand again, shaking. He looked over his shoulder. He could make it. All he had to do was run, head straight for the exit. Go back, get Miranda, take off—

"All set!" Bless grinned at him from the hazy darkness within. "Come on in, sweetie pie."

Sebastian entered. Smoke filled the room just as before. Men sat on either side of the office, some smoking, some drinking. The briefcase sat open atop Otto's desk—he sat behind it. The lights of the club flared intermittently behind him. Yellow. Orange. Red.

"Still with us," Otto said.

"I did the job. There's your money. Why'd you want me here?"

"I was curious. I sent Caesar up there with you because I wanted to see if he'd convince you. You give me the book, I let you go. But I guess it didn't work. Here you are. Still stinking just as bad as you were the first time." He sniffed the air. "Hell, worse."

The men laughed. Sebastian swallowed down some bile, tried to control the chills spreading over his arms and legs.

"You don't even know what it is," he said. "The room of cloth. You want it, but you don't know what it is. You can't know. It's not for you."

Otto leaned forward, licked his lips. "The room of cloth, huh? Just hearing it feels like a thousand volts." He chuckled. "I think you got the wrong idea about me. See, I'm not a monster. I'm not a king. People like me, we're really servants. Hell, we're slaves. We're the ones breaking our backs for everyone else. Making their stories. Framing their lives. Ain't no one doing that but us. You're a part of that, too, Sebastian. Well, were a part of it."

He raised his hand. "Bless."

Bless stepped forward, swung Sebastian around, and plowed his brass knuckles into the gaunt, pale face. Sebastian hardly hit the floor before Bless pulled him up and hit him again. Blood stained the tile. He punched him a third time, nearly busted his eye. A fourth time. A fifth. The brass knuckles came away darker and wetter each time.

Otto watched, listened to the groans and whimpers. "Look at you. So high and mighty before. Lording over me with your secrets. Acting like you deserved the help I gave you, like it was your God-given right. You really thought you could pull a fast one on *me*? After everything you've seen? You thought this room of cloth made you that powerful?"

"I don't know what you're talking about!" Sebastian sputtered, seconds before a boot wedged itself in his ribcage. One rib cracked. Two. He cried out, rolled over, received another boot to the face, a kick to the back, a stomp to the head. The other men had joined in.

"You really lying to me?" Otto asked. "You won't admit it?"

"I didn't fucking do anything!" Sebastian cried, strings of saliva and blood dripping from his mouth. Bless grabbed him by the hair and punched him again. The others kicked him. They beat into his back. He turned over, face bruised and bloated, blood running freely down his brow. He spat out another wad of red.

His teeth hit the floor, slick and slimy in the crimson light.

"It ain't good to lie, baby!" Bless laughed. "Honesty's the best fucking policy! Don't you know that, sweet cheeks?"

"You can't deny the proof," Otto said. Bless yanked Sebastian up to the briefcase. He stared at the money, eyes blurred by sweat and blood, failing to understand.

"Doesn't look like anything's missing," Otto said. "Would've fooled someone not paying attention. Would've been enough time for you to run. Just a few thousand, you were probably thinking. Not a lot. Not a big deal. But a few thousand is worse than the whole thing. If you took all of it, at least you wouldn't be insulting my intelligence. That's how I know it wasn't Caesar. Faggot's too much of a coward, but he's also little. He's small. He doesn't know arrogance. But you? You're hungry. You're lazy. You think you can take everything we earned and not work for it? All because of some book? Some delusion? Or maybe that's just the way you've always been. A little white-trash kid who thinks selling some dope makes him big."

Even in the dark, Otto's eyes glimmered. "I know about you, Sebastian. I know what you did to Billy Tripp back in Boston. I don't blame you for not wanting to tell me. Tried to kill the poor fucker. Stabbed him, right? With a piece of mirror? A bad deal, I guess? Or just fucking him like you're trying to fuck me? Taking what's not yours."

"I didn't take the money," Sebastian murmured, shaking violently. "You gotta believe me! I didn't fucking take it! And Billy, that was—"

Another kick sent him back to the floor. "I don't care about the money," Otto said, "or your dumbass dealer. The money's just a means. We'll always get more."

"I didn't do it," Sebastian said. "I didn't do it. It wasn't me—"

Miranda's face appeared to him, floating amid the shadows and blood. She had vanished. She had taken the laptop and the manuscript. She had taken the money. She had taken everything.

"It was Miranda!" he yelled. "It was her! She has the money!"

Bless shoved him down. "Miranda? Oh, that bitch been hanging around with you. Makes sense, baby—she was too fine for your skinny ass."

"Doesn't matter who did it," Otto said, rising from behind the desk. "You were responsible. And you fucked up." Sebastian saw two copies of Otto coming around the desk, three, four. He saw something in Otto's hand, something gleaming in the lavender light. A blade. A machete. He started shaking again, his right hand worst of all. The swinging blade was all he could see, all on which he could concentrate.

"Scary, isn't it?" said Otto, rolling up his sleeves, brandishing the weapon. "Better than a gun. Bigger than a knife. Something about skin getting cut, bone getting broke. A gun can't do the same. It's clean, but it's too far away. For someone who doesn't want to get up close and personal. I know I say it's all business, that it *isn't* personal, but what good are you at your job if you don't take it all the way? If you don't have the balls to get your hands dirty?"

He pressed the tip of the blade against Sebastian's cheek, traced it around his mouth, dragged it along his jaw, slid it down his neck. With every new move, the machete dug deeper. "I was like you once," he said. "Exactly the same. Hungry. Proud. Full of myself. Then they had me just like this. Only I was naked, a fuck-all knife going around my dick and balls, teasing me, ready any second to take 'em away. They took two of my toes instead. The balls would have been next, though. Then the dick. Then the nose, ears, tongue. The less important things first, the things you don't really need. You like having cunt? Tasting food? Like to see? Smell? You don't need those things. They're luxuries. The things we love, but they're not necessary. What's one less eye? One less hand? One less foot? One less ear? Why have two? One's just as good."

He moved away. "Bless."

With a cackle, Bless dragged Sebastian forward and pinned his right arm upon the desk. The other men came around, held his shoulders, his head. Someone spread out his hand, peeled out the fingers, held the palm flat against the wood.

"Stop!" he screamed. "Please! Please, just fucking stop! I didn't take the money!"

"That's what I don't like," Otto said. "All the lying. I don't give a shit about the money or the product or anything else. But the *lying*. The *bullshit*. I can't fucking stand it."

He held Sebastian's wrist down. "Here's the deal. You're gonna admit you took the money. You're gonna tell the truth. If you don't, if you keep lying, I'm gonna cut off your fingers one by one. Not all at once. In pieces. It'll go long that way. I'll start with the one you need least." He grazed the edge of the machete back and forth across Sebastian's little finger, teasing the skin. The hand trembled uncontrollably.

"You took the money. You thought you could screw me."

"I didn't, it was Miranda—"

The machete came down. Sebastian screamed. The top part of his little finger rolled across the desk, followed by a rivulet of blood. Otto tapped the machete against the next section.

"You took the money."

Sebastian kept screaming. Tears, blood, and snot ran down his bloated, purple face.

"*Fuck—*"

Another thud. An even louder, more pained scream. A second piece rolling, more blood flowing. The flare of the lights, the beat of the music.

"You took the money."

Sebastian only screamed and shrieked and wailed, tried vainly to break free, let out another string of desperate curses.

"You took the money," Otto said, and then he chopped three times, took the base of the little finger, the top and middle of the ring finger. The screams were somehow even louder, but the music drowned them out, beat them down.

"Almost two gone. What good's a hand with no fingers?"

Sebastian looked up, squinted through the sweat and lights, saw his mangled, bloody hand. He sputtered and spat.

"I'm sorry, I'm sorry, for fuck's sake—"

Otto raised the machete.

"*I did it! I did it! I fucking did it!*"

The blade hovered just inches above what was left of the ring finger.

"You did?"

"Yes! Fuck, yes! I did it! I took the money!"

"That's all I wanted to hear. Let him go."

The men released Sebastian. He rolled over, cradled his hand, whimpered and cried.

"Dumb kid," said Otto. "You're just like the rest. Stupid, dumb, useless. Can't do a thing for yourself. Can't take care of yourself. Just a bag of meat and bones. Another mouth to feed that can't contribute. Another mouth out of a thousand."

Sebastian hardly listened. He was dizzy with pain, his whole body aching, burning, throbbing. He wasn't hot, but cold, his teeth chattering, his bones rattling. Black came down over him. What was left of his right hand twitched against his chest and soaked his shirt with blood.

Otto stood over him. "You belong to me, you little shit. You and your book. Whatever I want, I take. I don't hide or lie. I don't need to. You hear me? You understand?"

The words were muffled to Sebastian, far away. The tremors in his hand spread throughout his whole body. He was disappearing, losing himself that much more with each drop of blood. Dripping away, draining into dark.

"Put him in a room," Otto said. "Still got a lot to talk about, after all. Like that book." He smiled, licked his lips. "The room of cloth. I like the sound of that."

Drowning in darkness, naked in the red room, Sebastian heard it clear.

The bell.

One of the men reached out, touched Sebastian's shoulder, and in that moment, Sebastian let out a deep, primal cry. Otto turned, but he was already too late. Sebastian wrenched the machete from his grip and sunk it deep into Otto's skull. Screaming, bleeding, eyes dark and dead, Sebastian brought the blade down again and again and again, mashing the flesh and bone into bits, spraying blood and brain everywhere. The other men watched, unable to move. Bless took out his gun, but Sebastian moved too fast, driving the machete into another man's neck. The head fell sideways like a tree cut at its base. Then he was on the others, howling like an animal, tearing through them, hacking them apart. Hands flew into the air. Feet rolled away. Tongues and ears lay smashed in glistening pools of blood. Noses collapsed. Teeth shattered. Eyes popped. Bones broke. Screams stopped short.

Suddenly, Bless was all alone. Suddenly, the blood was splashing, the machete was coming his way, the music down below was louder than ever, the lights flashing pink, flashing red. He pulled up his gun. He saw straight into the hollow pits of Sebastian's eyes—because they *were* pits. Black, vacuous pits. For the first time in years, decades, he felt something unfamiliar, almost alien, something he had not felt since the moment he was just a boy on the streets with busted lips and bruised knees, the moment he swore he would never be weak again, never need or want or care. The same thing he felt when they dragged his mother away. The same thing he felt when they found his brother in a garbage can.

"Jesus," he said.

The machete split his head in two.

When it was over, Sebastian stood in the middle of the mess, his whole body numb. The machete slipped out of his hand. He looked around at the blood covering the floor, the arms and legs surrounding mutilated torsos and smashed faces. For a moment, he didn't understand what he saw, what he had done, but then the scene hit him hard, sent him reeling. The pain of his hand reappeared more intensely than ever, and he clenched the raw, bleeding stumps where his fingers had been. He was lightheaded, drained, empty, and then more flashes hit him.

He remembered what happened with Billy. The fucker promised him easy millions. A quick and easy ride to huge riches. And what happened instead? They wasted months in Boston, Sebastian selling the meager, weak heroin Billy cooked up while the guy went off and spent the money on whores and poker. Sebastian dealt with it, kept thinking a payoff was coming, until the night one of Billy's dumb-shit girls called and asked when he was going to pick her up for their trip to Vegas. "Sorry, Seb," the asshole said. "Gotta move with my girl. Gonna hit it big this time! I'll come back, man, I'll give you your cut—"

Sebastian hadn't listened. His right hand shook, and the next thing he knew, he drove a fist into the restroom mirror, broke off a piece of glass, cut his hand almost to the bone, and thrust that dagger deep into Billy's gut. The pig screamed, squealed, and Sebastian relished tearing through his skin, feeling his hot, rich blood stream over his hand. But the trance didn't last long. Within seconds, his eyes cleared up. Within seconds, he ran, grabbed the manuscript, escaped with all the cash he could scavenge. For a couple of days, he lay low in a hotel room, thinking through his options. Not much time passed before he was on his way back home to Sarah. All because of Billy, that fucking weasel—

Remembering it brought so much pain, like his head was going to split apart, like his eyes were going to fall out. No. He didn't have time. He had to get out. He had to take care of his hand. He had to find Miranda. *Miranda.* Just the name made him clutch his stomach, made him retch. Why did she do it? Why did she fucking do it? He had trusted her. He had fucking trusted her, and she betrayed him, she *betrayed* him—

Another wave of fresh pain rolled through his head, like his skull was melting, his brain steaming. She had the book. The bitch had the book, and he wasn't going to let her take it. He looked around the room again, still dazed, still lightheaded. No one had come in yet. No one had heard anything. The music had been too loud, the violence too short-lived. It didn't matter. Just looking at the bodies tore him up. And then there was his head, as if a thread had been plucked, a peg clipped. When he blinked, he saw not the bloody office, but the fat-splattered, grime-ridden walls of the room of cloth. That red room, wet and dripping. He swore he heard whispers obscured by static, heard the heavy, rusted chains of the manacled man coming down.

The rain came down harder as Caesar drove to Otto's club, several guns stowed in his coat. He didn't need any weed, didn't want any drink. For the first time, he wasn't afraid. He wouldn't be putting a gun to his head over these guys. They weren't the type to be scared shitless. They wouldn't be running away or begging for their lives. They were monsters who chewed on bone and spat out skin. Besides, his hands were already dirty. What were a few more bodies?

But something was up. The usual line outside the club was nowhere to be seen. Inside, the club was in chaos, bouncers and guards running down the stairs and out the door while dancers and waitresses funneled out. He caught the arm of a server amid the commotion.

"What's going on?"

"Otto," said the man breathlessly. "Someone did him."

"What?"

The man was gone before Caesar could say anything else. Dazed, he looked up at the office. Otto? Dead? It didn't make sense, didn't feel real. But maybe that was just the old fear talking. The feeling he got every time he walked into that fucking office, every time he looked into those pitch-black eyes. He'd get so scared, so choked up. He'd lie awake in bed, sometimes with the bottle, shivering like he did when he was a kid, lying in the backseat of Roger's truck, hoping the monster was too tired to open the door, too tired to turn those ice-blue eyes upon him.

He felt for the guns. No, this was real. This was happening. He went up the stairs, opened the door, nearly toppled over from the smell.

Red all over. On the floor, on the walls, on the desk. On the money. He stepped inside, boots splashing, hand over his mouth and nose. The *smell*. Just like his personal angel stewing in that shed. Just like the bodies that slumped before him in an alley, in a doorway. No amount of whiskey or coke could scrub away the scent. No amount of flesh.

Bless. Otto. Other guys he'd seen. All of them smashed and cut to pieces, floating on a sea of red. And the money. The same bills. The same briefcase. The sight of it brought on a cold chill. No doubt about it. Seb had done this.

Shit had gone bad, and it would only get worse. The guys above Otto would come to clean up the mess, and if the streets weren't in meltdown already, they would be soon. A star had fallen. The lights were going out.

He ran back to the van.

Miranda sat in the bus station, watched rain pound the windows. The televisions warned of continued thunderstorms throughout the night, but she was calm in spite of the worried phone calls around her, the crying babies, the agitated pacing and anxious looks. She had everything she needed: the notebook, the duffle bag with the manuscript, another bag with some clothes, some food, the chunk of money she took from the briefcase.

When was the last time she slipped away with so little trouble? Over the years, how many nights of halfhearted sex and obligatory blowjobs had she tolerated? How many accents had she perfected, how many odd jobs suffered? How many spoiled, bratty kids entertained, their rich daddies all too happy to shower their latest side piece with gifts? How much money had she taken from them? How many clothes, pieces of jewelry, account numbers? How many of those men had she wished she poisoned or strangled? How many had she actually killed?

Not all of those experiences had been without some genuine pleasure. She recalled with limited fondness the occasional dinner under the stars or the sight and smell of roses atop a glass table. Those wretched men and women could once or twice betray kindness or vulnerability. But their instances of grace were as fleeting as the ghosts she sometimes saw, the phantom emissaries of the manacled man. All was illusory. A penthouse was no different than a mobile home. Glitter was no different than dirt. The drunkard was as vicious and cruel whether he wore slacks or jeans, ties or boots. The child was as neglected whether she lived among mountains of garbage or mountains of toys. The dress always came off sooner or later, and underneath would be the quivering, violet walls and reeking, purple mist. The tendon and artery would always reveal themselves. And she would always disappear.

Compared to all that, her time in Lorraine had been a vacation. Maybe the town was a shit stain, but at least she had done relatively little to get free food and a roof over her head. And the cash had been a nice surprise. The dream was always to splurge and relax, ideally away from people. But she couldn't afford to get too comfortable yet. For now, she thought about her next role. Perhaps a student or waitress. Maybe even a writer, however much that was on the nose.

From afar, Sebastian watched her.

He wore his hood up, his cracked, broken sunglasses across his nose, his face bruised and bloated, his right hand wrapped haphazardly in a bundle of paper towels. He had stumbled through the rain, had almost fainted, but something kept him going all the way back to the apartment. Something kept him clear after he dumped what was left of the liquor on his mutilated hand. Something kept him awake despite the pain he felt all throughout his body. Indeed, he was very familiar with this feeling spreading through him like fire. The same feeling had burned towards Billy Tripp, towards Bless and Otto, towards his father.

There was hurt, too. How he had howled, screamed, *raged* at losing the manuscript. How he had hit the walls, stomped his feet, rolled across the floor, flailed and convulsed. But it was more the betrayal than the pain. Everyone betrayed him. Everyone tricked him. Miranda, Caesar, Bless, Otto, Billy. His parents. Sarah. Everyone used him, threw him away, thought him less, wrong, defective. But he *wasn't* less. He *wasn't* wrong. He *wasn't* defective. He was chosen. He was holy. The manacled man had visited him, graced him, shown him the way. Even now when he closed his eyes, if he didn't focus his anger and keep his head clear, he would see the room, feel its warmth, sense its closeness, its comfort. They were calling to him now, begging him to come, to join them, to leave all this pain behind. And he was going to. But first. First.

He sat down behind Miranda, watched her for a few minutes longer, stared with barely-contained fury at the notebook on her lap. *His* notebook. *His* writing. *His* vision.

He leaned in, his face inches from her ear.

"Viper."

She didn't turn around. She just closed the notebook and sighed.

"Omen. How'd you find me?"

"You're not the only one who likes to run away."

"Oh. Makes sense." She kept her eyes on the rain outside. "So, what do you want?"

He leaned in closer. "*Why?*"

"You really need to ask? We all just use each other, Omen. I told you that."

"But we were together," he said. "I told you things. I told you everything!"

"What did you think? That we were in love?"

The words cut deep. They hurt in a way he hadn't expected. They took apart the anger and left something else behind, something tender, like scorched skin exposed to air. Her tone wasn't smug. There was sympathy there. Maybe even pity.

"You're sweet, Omen," she said. "I didn't have to pretend too much with you if that makes you feel better. I could be myself. As much as there *is* myself. You bought it all. Even when I was just words on the screen, you bought it. I could tell you were lonely. Looking for friends online. I used to do the same thing."

Sebastian's throat grew thick. His eyes glazed over with tears. He let out a long, wheezing breath. "But why? They almost killed me."

She turned around, saw his battered face, his butchered hand. "Sorry," she said. "It's everything I told you. At first, I needed money, food, a place to stay. But then it was about keeping him alive. Keeping the story going. See, if you write, it starts to pull you apart. That's what they told me. But you *have* to write, or else it just keeps bottling up. It gets inside, eats you, sucks you dry, and when you're done, it moves on."

Sebastian looked at her. He remembered. She never touched the keyboard, never lifted a pen. In all the nights spent around the glow of the laptop, she sat apart. Listening. Suggesting.

"I wrote for you," he said.

"You did. They taught me how to control the urges. If I could find someone to write for me, I could pour the words into someone else. And it worked. You weren't the first. There was Bryan, others before him. All of you are the same, you know that? You all think a pretty girl who lets you fuck her is going to fix everything. But that's what makes you perfect for it."

She raised the notebook. "This? I never could've done it. I don't know why. Maybe I'm dried up already. But you? You still have that sweetness inside of you. You act like you're cool, like you're badass, but your sister? The way you talk about her when you're comfortable? You really think you can save her. But you can't. There's no saving anyone. We're all just floating through the bullshit, tired of living, too afraid to die. The room of cloth can take that fear away. You know it can. You've seen it."

She smiled at him, her eyes aflame with some hidden, horrifying wonder. "If those gangsters had killed you, would it really have been so bad? You would have been free. Gone. Doesn't that sound amazing? Just floating into the dark, all of who you were, everything you thought, just gone. And then imagine that happening to everyone. *Everyone* going to the room of cloth. *Everyone* gone. Nothing left on this piece-of-shit planet but the animals, the trees, the water, and we've already killed those. Who's going to keep the nuclear waste from spilling out? Who's going to take care of the electricity and the oil? All the machines? It'd just be a matter of time. Everything drying up. Deer falling down. Birds dropping from the sky. The ground radioactive. The air filled with smoke. The literal end of the world. Just a cold, dead rock going through space. Everything gone."

She caressed the cool, purple plastic of his bruised cheek. "*That* is the room of cloth, Omen. And *I* was chosen. They picked me. *He* picked me. Jackal told me everything. They went on ahead, and they left me to do the work. I have to keep it going until it's finished. When it's finally done, then we can show everyone. We can stream it, air it, broadcast it, whatever. But until then, I'm his mother. His lover. Whatever he needs me to be."

She stood up, put the notebook in the duffle bag, pulled the bag over her shoulder. "You should be glad," she said. "You saw him. You felt him. How many people can say that? But that's the thing about God. You can't hear a voice like that and not pay a price. Our bodies, our brains—they aren't meant for that. That's why we have to get rid of them."

Sebastian just sat there.

"Well, anyway. I guess this is goodbye. Take care of yourself, Omen. If I were you, I'd run away again. Find someplace new. Start over."

She walked off and went into the restroom at the far side of the station. Sebastian didn't do anything at first. There was pain, confusion, paralysis—and then something else. That feeling again, bright, red, and hot. Furious.

His right hand trembled. He followed her.

She was washing her hands when he walked inside. She saw him in the mirror. "What else do you want?" she said. "Let it go. Go back to your sister."

"He didn't pick you."

"What?"

"He didn't pick you."

The tremors reached his shoulder, his neck, his head. Miranda backed away.

"Omen—"

"*He didn't pick you!*" he yelled, grabbing her by the hair and smashing her face into the mirror. She fell to the floor, bleeding, moaning, grasping at the shards of glass embedded in her cheek. Reflected in the shards were gray, hollow-eyed faces. Laughing, screaming faces.

"*Fuck*, you fucking—"

Sebastian reached for her again. He slammed her head against the tile, beat her with his fist, slapped her. He wrapped his good hand around her throat and pressed his mangled one over her mouth. "He picked *me*!" he snarled, sweat running down his face, veins and tendons bulging in his neck, spit flying from his mouth. "He picked me, he picked me, *he picked me*!"

He thrashed her, bashed her, throttled her. He saw only red, felt only immense, monstrous anger, rage, fury, fucking madness. He was *not* a tool. He was *not* a doll. He was *not* lost. He was *not* lost! He was *not* fucking lost!

"He picked me, he picked me, he picked me, he picked me—" He kept chanting the words, squeezing harder, hitting harder, long after she went limp, long after her eyes went dark. Finally, he stopped and looked upon her face. What was left of her face. More bone than skin. More blood. He didn't understand, couldn't comprehend—and then he did. Pain shot through his skull, more intense than he ever felt. He fell over, cried out, saw red, blood, guts, tissue, flesh, fat, fire, bone, metal, rust, concrete, cement, brick, steel, corrosion, acid, dying, barren land rotting away like bleached bones picked clean by vultures, rotting underneath a white, burning sun, a sun that was too big, too hot, too close. Everything simmering, melting, cooking, boiling. People. Animals. Mountains. Oceans. Everything drying out. Not a cold, frozen planet, but one that was on fire, literally burning, flying through the cosmos, annihilating everything in its path.

A red star emerged, churning not with volatile gases, but with masses of blood-drenched bodies, an amalgamation of hands and arms and feet and legs and torsos driven by an engine of rotating, grinding metal. Where the star passed, all disappeared, all vanished into an event horizon deeper and vaster than that of the most colossal black hole. Sebastian, floating, weightless, lightless, beheld the star loom over him, beheld its ever-shifting interior, beheld its infinite core of flesh and blood and rust and metal, an endless passage through its gargantuan middle. He flew into its gravity like a mote of dust into a vacuum, stretched to an unimaginable length, compressed to an unthinkable size, his every thought crushed, his every feeling inflated. Far above him, far above the chaos, a bell tolled. A door opened.

He went into the room of cloth at last. Inside, he came before his new god.

<h1 style="text-align:center">47.</h1>

There was some trashy reality show on the television, something about practical jokes, guys dressed in drag. As usual, the father belched and laughed and yelled his obscenities. He stank of beer. So many cans lay on the carpet, and another fell out of his hand, newly opened and frothing. He reached for his side, no longer laughing, but hissing, wheezing, his fingers drenched in blood. When he got up from that wretched chair, the one that stunk of him for years afterwards, the knife went inside him again. Into his back, his kidneys, over and over, until the man lay prostrate, gasping for breath. Blood pooled around him. The knife fell to the floor with an almost inaudible thud. The boy stood over his father, impish and pale, small and shivering. He said nothing, would say nothing. The father fell silent.

Everything happened so quickly after that. The mother screaming, falling to her knees. The boy standing there, mute. The police handcuffing him, demanding things of him. The emergency responders wheeling away the father on a stretcher. A flimsy, yellow tarp covering his girth. The boy put in a room, questioned, tested. No response. Never a response. Repression, the doctors said.

IED. Catatonia. Always a new label. Always a new excuse. He was in shock. He wouldn't remember. The mother asked questions, first to the doctors and then to her daughter. Why? Why did he do it? Why was he born? No answer. Never any answers.

Sarah woke up. She listened to the pouring rain outside, the hard wind. Just more dreams. More pollution in her head. She hadn't been there the night her father had been murdered, but somehow, she saw the scene clearly, as if she had stood in the room along with Sebastian and their mother and witnessed the grisly particulars firsthand. Maybe it was her brain working overtime, piecing together a story she heard about time and again. She knew every secondhand detail by heart—how could she not, the way her mother went on and on, the way the doctors and police insisted on repeating the episode at every possible opportunity? How many times could one entertain the same story and get nothing new from it, glean no additional insight? Here was the takeaway: her father was dead. Her brother was a murderer. What was the point in trying to understand why when nothing could be changed?

At the time, she had been far away partying. She remembered that spring break well. Waking up to blue-gray dawns, to the salty sea breeze, the strong, clear air. The last fresh air she ever breathed. The last free wind she ever felt. The wind, the seagulls, the sand, the water— and then the call. Like Hamlet, forced to return home, forced to reassemble the pieces of a life thought left behind. Only there was no treachery, no ghost, no villain on whom to exact revenge. Just a broken, dead-eyed brother. Just a miserable, self-righteous mother. Just the old house, inescapable and eternal. For Sarah, the night of her father's death had never ended.

She got a water from the mini fridge beside the bed and held the bottle to her head. The dull throb was getting worse, persistent and annoying, like a mosquito bite that never stopped itching. Just leave me alone, she thought. For one second, just leave me alone. Let me rest.

Her brother. Her mother. Her father. The perpetual riddle. The unsolvable mystery. So much cruelty and frustration, abuse and pain, yet there were moments when their family had been functional, even loving. She recalled one vivid memory: Sebastian nestled against their mother, no more than five or six, a little, skinny boy with short, blond hair and wide, gray eyes. Historically, their mother had been a weak, petty woman, critical and judgmental, but she could be soft, too. She had dreams and passions, worries and anxieties. Before their father had beaten and belittled the figurative life out of her, she had been capable of real love. And especially when Sebastian was young, when he was just a boy, long before the night that changed everything, Sarah could remember her mother extending kindness to him, kissing him on the brow, lying with him as he drifted to sleep. Did he remember that, too?

But even her memory was corrupted now. The golden light in the room bled red. The hand of her mother became gnarled and withered. The young boy turned into a doll, his eyes black pits, his plastic face a mockery of innocence.

She looked at her hand. Shaking again. Fucking shaking again. "Were you always there?" she asked. "Or did someone put you there when I wasn't looking? You son of a bitch. Aren't you tired yet? Haven't I given you enough? No? You're still hungry? You want to take more? Well, fuck you! Leave me alone! You hear me? Get the fuck out of my head!"

She threw the bottled water at the wall. The water spilled out, ran over the newspaper she put up, blurred the ink, revealed the words underneath. "*Goddamn you!*" she screamed. Her knees gave out. She crumpled to the floor. She wept. "Just go away. Oh, God, just go away."

Miraculously, the shaking stopped. She curled up into a ball, smelling the must of the carpet, hearing the thunder and rain. Her eyes were warm and wet. So heavy.

"Go away," she murmured, closing her eyes. "Just go away."

Darkness came down. Then, later, a buzzing. A warm, blue light.

She looked up. Her cell phone vibrated from across the room. The sight and sound broke through her daze. It must've been Caesar. Was he okay? Was it done? Was it over?

She picked up the phone. "Caesar? What happened?"

There was a tired sigh, a hoarse breath. A long pause.

"Caesar? Are you there? I can't—"

"Sarah."

Her breath caught in her throat. "Sebastian? Sebastian, is that you?" There wasn't a response, just more labored, exhausted breathing. "Sebastian, say something, please—"

"Sarah." His voice was far away, muffled, as if there were many walls separating them. "Sarah, where are you? You aren't here. I need to show you. I need to show you."

"Where are you, Sebastian?"

"You're not here. You're still away. Far away. I need to show you."

"Sebastian, just tell me where you are. I'll come get you."

"No one's here. Mom. Dad. Where are they? It feels like I was gone a long time."

His voice was farther away, interrupted by static.

"Sebastian? Sebastian, are you there?"

A high-pitched whine. More garbled noise.

"Sebastian?"

Something in the static. Laughter? There was too much noise, too much distance.

The line went dead.

She threw the phone to the floor. Was it taunting her? Did it get off on that, leading her around like a mouse in a maze? Fucking thing! Fucking monster!

But if it wasn't a trick? That meant Sebastian was looking for her, but where was he? Her apartment?

No—he mentioned their mother, their father. The house?

Her hand shook. No, this wasn't the time to be afraid. This was the time to act. To be courageous. To choose to be courageous. What she hadn't chosen all those years.

The rain came down heavy and cold. She drove fast, recklessly, barely able to see through the black. Her phone lit up at a stoplight.

"Sarah? You okay? Been trying to call—"

"Caesar? Caesar, he called me!"

"What?"

"He called me. Sebastian called me. He's at the old house, I know it."

"Sarah, listen, Seb's in trouble! Some shit went down. Otto, Bless—they're all dead. They're gonna be looking for him. If they find you—"

"I'm going, Caesar. This might be my only chance. The house is on Bradbury Street. He doesn't sound like he knows where he is, and that whole area's been condemned. I have to find him before something happens."

"Sarah, you gotta wait for me!"

"I can't wait. You know I can't. I'm sorry."

She clicked the phone off. Just mentioning the street took something out of her. The house. Years had passed since she'd been there, and she never thought she would go back. When it was just her and Sebastian, it made sense to downsize to the apartment, but it was just as much about cutting off that history, that cancer. Of course, the cancer had never really gone away. After eating their mother, it had waited patiently. Now, the cells were growing again, reasserting themselves, spreading their grotesque mass wherever they could.

She turned onto Bradbury Street. Hard to see through the rain and dark, but there were the old, familiar houses, emptied out, falling apart. Once, those houses had been places of comfort, respite, love, but now they were relics literally fading away. All those families. All those lives. Her family. Her life.

She parked in front of the house. The headlights illuminated the ruined mailbox, the overgrown lawn, the trash-strewn driveway. She turned off the car and sat there in the darkness, listening to the beat of the rain, trying to imagine how things used to be, as though that would be comforting somehow. But there wasn't any happy memory on which to look back. Maybe when she had been that little girl with the pigtails and the missing teeth, that quarter-person, that tiny angel. Maybe things had been better then. But try as she might, she couldn't slip into that small body, couldn't inhabit the headspace. That little girl grew up. She changed into someone else.

There was one comfort, though. She felt for the gun Caesar gave her. The weapon couldn't protect her from the things in the house, from the words in her head, but at least it was something real, something present. Neither a memory nor an illusion.

Up the steps, onto the porch. A flash of lightning exposed the decrepit doorway, the warped woodwork. She held her phone out for light, but the small, blue glow was less useful than even a match. The shadows were too dense, the blackness almost impenetrable. At the door, she recoiled. An intense, dead heat radiated from within and smothered the chill of the rain, accompanied by the nauseating stench of dried blood and rotted meat. The same goddamn smell.

Some primal instinct kicked in once Sarah was inside. She jumped at every creak, swung the gun around at every groan. "Sebastian? Are you here?" Her voice shook and cracked. Something lurked inside the house, watching, listening, like a lion eyeing its prey, biding its time. She could sense its hunger. Ravenous. Insatiable.

She raised the gun. "Where's my brother? Is he here?"

No answer. Just the rain. Just that stench.

"Answer me! Is he here?"

A sudden gust of hot, stale wind. Distant, heavy laughter. Forms shifted in the weak, blue light of her phone. Black, grimy grins. Gray, bruised knees. White, sickly fingers. So many. Too many. Pointing? Pointing to the hall? To her room?

Her room. Of course. Of course.

She followed those miserable fingers, endured the ghoulish gaze of each phantom. She felt a thousand hands grope her in the darkness, a million feelers touch her, a hundred chains graze her. Her arms and legs trembled. Her eyes watered. She opened the door. She gasped.

Sebastian sat in the middle of the empty room, shirtless, covered in cuts, a knife loose in his hand. All around him were the pages. His face was bulbous and blue. His eyes. God, his *eyes*.

"Sarah," he said, his voice quiet and low. "Sarah, you came. Good. Now, we can go. Together." He stood up, swayed on his feet, held out the knife. "I was waiting for you. I called you, just like you told me to. Remember? Before you went to school, you told me to call if I ever needed you. You actually answered this time. You really came. I'm so happy, Sarah."

She stood there, rigid. She lowered the gun.

"I need to show you," he said. "I need to make you see it. The room of cloth—we can be safe there. You and me. And Caesar. Everybody. We can be safe there."

That look in his eyes, the one from so long before, when she sat down in front of him at the psychiatric hospital and realized he was gone. That peaceful, dead-eyed look, as serene as the trees had been that day. The flesh a silent cage, an empty room. The skin a fragile fabric.

"Sebastian," she said softly, though the name sounded wrong, sounded alien. Was this really her brother? Had the room of cloth done this to him? Or had he always been like this?

"We need to give up something," he said. "We need to make him happy. Then he'll come down. He'll save us. He'll take us away. We can be happy in our own special place." He laughed. "You just need to read it. You just need to see him."

"Sebastian."

"He's all around us. He's in the paper, in the words. He's in me. In my skin. He needs to *come out*." He cut into his arm, drew fresh blood. "Maybe it's the wrists. Where the chains are."

Sarah watched as he held the blade over his wrist. She couldn't speak, couldn't reach out and take the knife from him. All she saw was that small, pitiful, half-formed thing from her youth. That tiny face with its big, hollow eyes. That shadow peeking around corners. That little creature shambling after her in the dark.

He slit the wrist. Blood ran out.

"That's good. Now, I just need the other one."

Sarah closed her eyes. She prayed halfheartedly, despairingly.

"We'll go together," Sebastian repeated. He struggled to move the knife to his other hand. "But first I need to let him out. I need to finish the story."

Gently, tenderly, Sarah took the knife away.

"I'm sorry," she said. "This is my fault. It's all my fault."

She hugged him, held him tight, stroked his hair.

"I'm sorry. I'm so, so sorry."

"Sarah," he said, nestling against her, closing his eyes. Oh, it was so good. Just like long, long ago. The hand in his hair. The warmth. The smell of the cinnamon candies his mother loved to eat. The golden light coming through the window—

A bang, a splatter. He slumped against her. The gun hit the floor. Her ears rang. Her head pounded. "Oh,

God. Oh fucking Christ." She cradled him, caressed his hair with bloody hands, gasped through thick, choked sobs. Just like that, the light out. The door closed forever.

All around her, the voices laughed, celebrated, welcomed their newest addition. She looked down at her brother's lifeless face and screamed.

She had never seen him so happy.

She turned the gun on herself, pulled the trigger. Nothing. Nothing, nothing, nothing. Jammed. Useless. She threw the gun aside, grabbed the knife, pressed the blade against her throat—

No. Not yet. It wasn't going to win. It wouldn't get what it wanted.

She took the nearest page and ripped through it with the knife. She tore through one after another. She cut them apart, attacking the words, slashing the letters, stabbing until nothing was left but shreds, until the knife dug only into wooden floor, into blood.

But the shadows only laughed. The faces in the dark only grinned.

Sarah peered at them through her tears. "What's so funny? You think this is a joke? You think this is fucking funny? Stop laughing! You hear me? Stop it! *Just fucking stop it!*"

Then she saw them. Chains. Red, rusted chains unfurling, snakelike, out of the black. Chains hooking into Sebastian's skin. Chains pulling him down. Chains taking him away.

"No! Let him go! It's not his fault! It's not his fault!"

But he was already gone. Those pale, ghastly figures emerged from the darkness and surrounded her. Her father was there, his stab wounds fresh and wet. Her mother, skeletal, consumed by the cancer. Others. Countless others. Retching from poison. Shivering from exposure. Groaning from starvation. All of them with that awful, black grin. All of them laughing. All of them crying. All of them screaming.

"No, no, *no!*" she cried. "Let him go! Please, let him go! Take me instead! I'm the one you want! It's my fault! It's because of me! It's all because of me! It's me, not him! It's *me!*"

The black coughed something out. A notebook. The pages turned on their own, beckoned her. The blood, they said. The blood. Your fresh ink. Your flesh and your blood.

"No! I won't do it! I won't do it, you *fucking monster—*"

Her hands suddenly fell flat upon the floor, clamped by steel shackles. Searing pain flared through her head. Rivers of blood brimming with corpses, with hands, arms, and legs. The oceans turning red, sharks and fish and whales and all the others down below rising to the surface, all of them floating, decaying. Forests burning to soot. Cities crumbling to ash.

"I won't do it! You can't make me do it!"

A light in the sky, shining brighter than the sun. A bell tolling. A spreading, collective cry of euphoria. Bodies coming apart. Skin sloughing off. The whole planet peeling like an orange, its molten center gushing out like sweet juice.

"I won't! I won't! You can't make me, you son of a bitch—"

Sarah saw herself take the knife to her arm. Saw the skin come off. Saw the muscle drip away. Saw the coarse, white bone underneath. Saw the knife move up to her face, saw the blade dip under the chin, the cheek peel away, the nose swing on a tether of loose skin—

Her hands moved on their own, the fingers wet with blood, clawing hungrily for the exposed pages of the notebook. Finish it, they said. Finish it.

"Go to hell," Sarah muttered, pulling back with all her strength. She could hardly move her hands, barely feel her fingers. "You won't use me!"

Louisa. Paul. Janette. Caesar. Her students. All of them wading through a sea of blood. Chains around their arms and legs. Black pools where their eyes should have been.

She screamed, roared, took hold of the knife. Laughter all around her. Screams.

"I won't do it!"

The knife moved, broke flesh. She screamed.

She was in the den of the house—not the waterlogged, condemned hell through which the ghosts led her, but the den as she remembered it from her adolescence. Just another kind of hell. The musty, mustard-colored carpet. The grainy, blue-tinted television. The trashy reality shows. The crosses on the wall. The reeking, bleeding girth of her father at her feet. She stood over him with bloodstained hands, in bloodstained blouse. In the mirror across from her, she was not the Sarah of now, but the Sarah of then, the lionhearted Sarah her brother idolized, the wayward Sarah she had renounced. The long, bright hair. The fierce, shining eyes. The smooth, rosy skin. The fury. The rage. The impossible, unstoppable hatred. Nostrils flared, eyes burning, she raised the knife again.

"Fuck you! Fuck you! Fuck you!"

She stabbed him, not once, not twice, but ten times, twenty times, thirty. She didn't stop stabbing. The carpet grew moist with his blood. Her knife nearly slipped from her hands. "I hate you," she said through gritted teeth. "I hate you, and I hate this, and I hate everything! You're a monster! You're a fucking joke! You should have never been born! You should have never existed! You're better off dead!"

It was only as her stabs slowed, as her arms trembled with exhausted tremors and her eyes watered with frustrated tears, that she heard the sobbing behind her. The wretched, hysterical sobbing of the nighttime arguments, the midnight beatings. The weak and pitiful sobbing of the brittle doll that went insane with anxiety and terror at the sight of her own son. The sobs—no, the wheezing, the crackling, constricted wheezing—of the shriveled, shrunken shrew in the hospital bed. More corpse than body. More dead than alive.

"You killed him!" her mother shrieked. "You killed him! You killed him!"

Sarah turned, lurching as though drunk, intoxicated with bloodlust, high off the smells of metal and rust. Recklessly, furiously, she slashed her mother's throat open. The woman staggered back, hands over the gushing gap, lips flapping like those of a fish out of water. She fell and lay twitching in her own blood, gasping for air, with each failed breath pumping more blood down her neck and chest, across her torso, towards her legs. Sarah approached, sneakers sloshing, arms drooping, and stood over her. She stared with hard, pointed anger at the stupidly innocent face. She once more raised the knife. She removed the eyes, detached the tongue. She sawed at the wrists and ankles, grinding the knife through skin and against bone, pushing with all her might to sever the ligaments and break the tethers. She returned to the throat and sliced until the last of the meaty threads connecting head to neck and neck to body were undone.

Grunting, pawing at the mangled flesh and exposed bone, she sniffed the air. Not enough. Not enough. Her tongue wagged, withdrew. Her ears perked. There, deeper in that stinking hell of a house: the patter of socks on wood. The scurrying of small feet. The whimpering of a tiny mouth. The slamming of a door. She raced into the darkness on all fours, hurtling into wood, crashing through plaster. The little, big-eyed imp had no chance. She grabbed a clump of his hair, bit into his neck. Her teeth pulled out skin and muscle in long, red, warbling strings. She ripped arms and legs from their sockets, ran her tongue over scapula and skull until the bone shined a sparkling, pristine white. She burrowed her snout into his collapsed chest cavity, lapping at the overflowing blood, chewing at the miniature lungs and diminutive heart. She picked and pulled at bits of skin, spat out nail, gagged on hair. Finally, her claws roamed on bloodied, rotted wood. Her eager fangs found no more meat to devour. There was nothing left of him. All had been consumed. All had been eradicated. No longer would the small, socked feet scamper on wood. Never again would the tiny, feeble hands slap at her door.

The ferocious hunger waned. The animalistic heat cooled. She touched her arms and face, smearing his blood and their mother's blood and their father's blood over her pale skin. Where were they? Where was he? Sebastian? Sebastian, say something. Answer me. Come out. Come out, please. I'm begging you.

He's gone.

Where is he? Tell me. Please, tell me.

He's gone. They're all gone.

No. He was here. They were here.

Not anymore. You killed them.

I didn't.

You did. Look at yourself.

The mirror again. Her face as though she wore a red mask. Her hands as though the skin had been flayed. She saw them now with clarity: her slain father, her butchered mother. But her brother was gone. Only a patch of damp, reeking wood remained in his place. Only an ink-blotched, rain-doused notebook. A notebook filled with his words. His last will and testament.

She took a page between her fingers, lovingly caressing the paper as though the interweaved fibers were his hair, his skin. She inhaled the scent of the pages, so vaguely like cinnamon, and nestled her cheek against the ink. Her tears finished the job of the rain, smearing the words, blurring the sentences, ruining the paragraphs. But the damage was done. Your fresh ink, the pages said. Your flesh and your blood.

The toll of the bell. The laughter of the damned. She looked up and saw them, the legions of the eyeless, the hosts of the black-mouthed. All pointing. All waiting. The notebook before her, demanding her contribution. The words in her head. Your fresh ink. Your flesh and your blood. Your fresh ink. Your flesh and your blood.

"Sebastian," she said, but he did not come. She tried to visualize him, but not even his wretched, doped-up face appeared to her. Only the patch of damp, reeking wood. Only his gaunt form on the autopsy table, chest folded out, entrails sloughing out in piles of mashed, pulverized meat. Only the hole in her life, the black hole where there should have been a person. Only the fringed absence in the magazine page, large enough for a finger to push through.

She screamed. Screamed longer than she thought possible, even longer than when she spent the nights in the tub. Screamed louder than she could remember, even louder than when the shock of the phone call faded and she realized with crushing certainty that with the end of her father's life came the end of her own life as well. All around her, they laughed. They pointed. They called to him. Their god. Their king. Their savior.

She plunged the knife into her neck.

Everything went silent. She lay on her side, shivering, hazy-eyed. Was that her blood oozing out? Were those her arms she couldn't move, her legs? Why were those horrible things still standing there? Why were they still smiling? Why were they still laughing? Why were they still pointing? Wasn't it enough? Wasn't she dead? What was that noise? What was that light—

Blinding, steaming, scalding, erupting from above as though the ceiling exploded and the sky tore open. She couldn't move, couldn't scream, but she could see the chains, hear their rattling. Static. White noise. Something coming down from that blazing light.

Him. Wrapped in chains, suspended by hooks, descending from his throne on high. Red eyes manic above the writhing, froth-dripping muzzle. Hands and feet swinging on shattered wrists and ankles. Fingers and toes bent upwards, downwards, the bones snapped in two.

The others followed him with their black pits. They raised their ashen arms in adoration. Their moans became hymnal. Sarah flailed and flopped, but her body was like lead. He was getting closer, closer, close, too close, too fucking close, trumpets in the air behind him, clouds parting, the bright light turning red, brown, black, black like an eclipse, like a red giant, a brown dwarf, no, a white dwarf, no, no, a black dwarf, no, a BLACK HOLE no no no nothing. NO. NOTHING. No, no, please, *please*, she just wanted to go, she just wanted it to be over, why was this happening, why wasn't it enough, why are you DOING THIS GOD-DAMN YOU I WANT HIM BACK I WANT MY BROTHER BACK he didn't do anything wrong he didn't do anything you monster you monster and—wait, what was that? What was that little thing, that tiny, little thing, that small, gray face, those big, black eyes, those hollow eyes—oh no, oh God, oh please no, oh no let him go, let him go let him go let him go LET HIM GO YOU FUCKING MONSTER she screamed, was screaming, but no words were coming out, no voice, no sound, just that horrible, awful thing descending, just that burning black light, just that *smell*, just that little thing, that little imp coming closer, coming closer, saying something, touching her face—

—she opened her eyes. She screamed.

Nothing.

No pale horde. No great light. No black hole. No manacled man.

No imp.

She lay in the back of a van, aching, caked with dried blood. She could move, flex her stiff fingers, lick her chapped lips. Her neck hurt. She felt a piece of gauze on the side. She had only grazed the skin with the knife.

The door was open. Outside was dark, wet. Sweet-smelling. The rain had stopped. There were the sounds of traffic, the blare of a train horn. But no trumpets or bells. No rallying cry. No laughing or howling.

Caesar appeared before her, a cigarette in his hand. "Sarah? You okay?"

She lay back down. Closed her eyes.

He took a drag. "You been out for a while. I went to the house, but when I got there, you were—I thought you were gone. And Seb. He was gone."

He struggled for a moment. She didn't say anything.

"You don't need to say. I'm gonna take care of this, Sarah. I'll take care of it."

She couldn't keep her head up, couldn't keep her eyes open. She just wanted to sleep. Just wanted to forget. Forget about the old house and its endless shadows and its host of phantoms. Forget about the world turned red and then black, all life extinguished, all potential erased. Forget about her own bloodstained hands, her own dripping, insatiable maw. Because that was her, she realized. That was her. Always had been her. Always would be her.

But no matter how hard she tried to erase those images, how hard she tried to relax her muscles and will herself to sleep, there was an inkling of something she could not shake, a vague sense of something warm despite the cold. Like a child's hand on her face. Like a gentle caress.

49.

The cool wind of the beach, wet with the ocean spray. The blue-gray of the morning, soft like watercolor. The light on the water, glistening. The call of seagulls above. Everything fine on the surface. All at peace.

Sarah lit the lighter underneath what remained of the manuscript. The flame licked and ate. She thought she heard laughter, thought she heard cries, but there was nothing. No awful chorus of the manacled man's captive followers. No rustling of a hundred chains. No apocalyptic tolls of a bell heralding the end of the world. Just the quiet of the empty boardwalk. Just the fresh breeze and strong air.

She dropped the folder into a trash can and went back to the van. Caesar was waiting for her. "*No más?*" he asked. "It's over?"

"No. But it's all I can do."

She felt the traces of a tremor in her hand and pulled it tight into a fist. "Who cares if I burn it? It got him. It got all of them. And it's still out there. Even if we got everything in the house, it's online, it's in the air. It's everywhere."

She couldn't hold back the laugh. "I guess I got what I wanted. I'm free. The one thing I wanted for years, and now I have it. Funny, isn't it? The joke that never gets old. The joke that just gets funnier and funnier."

Caesar wanted to tell her it wasn't funny at all, that it was wrong, awful, horrible. But anything he tried to put into words felt empty. He had lost Sebastian, too, had seen what the boy had become when he found him and Sarah inside the house. The image of the lacerated, bloody body had stayed with him for days, stained his dreams, haunted his waking hours. There were no words or sentiments that could wipe that away. His and Sarah's trail could be made clean with enough favors and elbow grease, but the rest of it? That stayed for a long time. Maybe forever.

So, he didn't say anything. Instead, he held out his rosary.

Sarah looked at it. "What are you doing?"

"Take it."

"But it was your grandmother's."

"*Sí*, and she's probably dead by now for all I know. Been holding on to this thing for a long time. Thought I needed it, like it kept them with me or something. I don't feel like that anymore. You know she named me? César, like my grandpa. She named me, and she unnamed me. She said I was touched by the devil. And I was."

He placed the rosary in her hand.

"Maybe I give you this, and it starts to make up for it."

She stared at the rosary, at the light gleaming off it. Like all the crosses her mother used to keep on the wall. Christ with his crown of thorns and bloodied, sweat-ridden face. Silent, never saying a word. Suspended. Held down by the weight.

"I looked up there, Caesar," she said. "It wasn't God. It wasn't anything. It was nothing. It was *worse* than nothing. And it's inside me, too. Always has been. So, you tell me. What good is this supposed to do?"

"I don't know."

He took out his cigarettes and offered her one. She took it. Her first cigarette in years. Funny how the body remembered. Funny how everything else faded in that moment, that little escape. Right then, it really was just her in that van, not far from the shore. Her adolescent dream, her teenage fantasy. Liberated and weightless, in her own small world of light and air. At peace. Quiet. Removed from it all.

"Caesar," she said. "Thank you."

"*De nada.*"

They rolled the windows down, finished their cigarettes. Long after they left, the pages were still burning, still trailing up to the sky in wisps of smoke. Eventually, they were gone.

0.

He was nervous, sitting at the back of the restaurant. Actually, he was scared out of his mind. He had been there for an hour already, watching people eat, watching them talk. At any moment, he expected the place to explode, the patrons to go up in flames, the ceiling to collapse. He couldn't help but knead his hands together and kick his feet. He had turned down the waiter three times already. He was expecting someone. For now, he would just busy himself with a beer, maybe an appetizer or two—

"Crispin?"

He looked up. A woman stood beside his booth, slim and beautiful in a white dress, wearing a hat and sunglasses. She smiled, revealed stunning white teeth. Her blonde hair curled down her neck. She looked as though she had been taken from the pages of a storybook, from a painting, but he couldn't see her eyes. The sunglasses were too dark. Almost black.

He stammered. "Delilah?"

"That's right." She sat down, removed her hat. Honestly, it was hard to look at her. He had never spoken to a girl this pretty before, had never even gotten one to look at him, much less smile. He was a loser. He didn't shave much, had a face full of pockmarks, wore thick-rimmed glasses. He couldn't even afford a pair of slacks. He was the sore thumb in the room, the weird, skinny guy in sneakers and jeans. The ratty sport coat was a relic of his grandfather. But despite all that, here was this woman sitting across from him, shining like an angel. Maybe his luck really *was* changing.

"I'm glad to finally meet you," she said. "How long's it been? Six months?"

"Seven," he said, maybe a little too quickly. He hoped he wasn't blushing. He wanted to ask her, wanted to bring up the whole reason they were there, but it seemed too soon. Maybe she saw it in his face because she reached into her purse and brought out the notebook.

"You must be curious," she said, placing the note-book on the table. There it was, what he heard so much about, what he had dreamt about the last seven months. Right in front of him, almost literally within his grasp. All he had to do was reach out—

"Not so fast," she said. "You can't look at it yet."

"I can't?"

"No. First, I want you to remember. I want you to remember that you were chosen. He picked *you*, Crispin. Out of everyone, he picked *you*."

She was right. *He* had been chosen. *He* had been picked. Him. No one else. Someone had finally taken notice of him, finally given him a purpose. No longer was his life going to be a shitty cycle of fast food, work, and porn. Now, his life had meaning. Now, his life would change.

"Before you look," she said, "you have to promise me. You have to promise you will never forget. You have to promise you will do what we need you to do. Whatever we ask. Whenever we ask it. That's your duty now. What you're meant for."

Of course. He didn't need to give it a second thought.

"I promise. Because I'm chosen. Because he picked me."

"Good. Go ahead and open it."

Continue reading for the first chapter
of R. H. Gründ's upcoming novel:

SIMULACRUM

Laura was dead.

Kelsey hardly heard anything else Pete said, such were the tremors in his voice, the tremors in her chest. In the dark of her bedroom, she clutched her throat. Laura. A name she hadn't heard in so long. A name she had refused to remember. A name she had willed away.

In the kitchenette, she cradled the phone in the crook of her neck and scrounged for a glass in the cupboard. Pete had not stopped talking since he woke her up with his call. "She thought about calling you," he said, "about getting back in touch. I told her she should. After she got really sick, I kept telling her. 'Call Kelsey. Call Kelsey.' But she didn't. I know she wanted to. I thought she wanted to. You were like sisters. That's how she always said it. But she never told me what happened. Why you stopped talking. She never mentioned it. Even when it was really bad, she didn't tell me. She wouldn't say."

Kelsey stood on the balcony of her Houston apartment and watched the pre-dawn sun shimmer across the skyline, felt the morning breeze on her face. Traffic flowed below in rivers of red and white lights. An ambulance sped through, siren wailing. Crows scattered overhead.

She sipped her bourbon. Her voice shook. "When did it happen?"

"Just a few hours ago. Listen, Kels, you have to come. I want you to come. She did."

After Pete hung up, she returned inside and refilled her glass. She left the excess bourbon where it spilt.

Pointless to go back to sleep, she thought. Pointless when every thought would be of that head of blonde hair, those eyes of ocean blue. Pointless now that Laura was dead.

The memory of Laura had disappeared slowly over time, consumed by the stress of today, the minutiae of now. How strange that her image came back so forcefully now upon news of her death, so vividly, as if the two women had never parted ways. Kelsey would be checking a patient's teeth, filling a cavity, scraping a retainer, and then suddenly, her hands would lock, her eyes glaze. No matter where she excused herself, whether the sterile-smelling lobby or the sunlit breezeway, memories surged. Studying in their cramped dorm. Drinking in the field. Crashing the old Chevrolet. Watching one of Laura's performances. Waiting in the hospital. Wheeling her around. Helping her walk. Holding her by the waist. Smelling her hair.

Anthony came over that night, and they talked about the upcoming funeral.

"You want me to go with you?" he asked, pulling the lasagna out of the oven.

"You don't have to."

"You sure?"

She gulped down more red wine. "Yeah. I'll be okay."

When they had sex later, Laura's smells kept coming back. Lilac and rosemary.

Kelsey hadn't seen Laura in years, hadn't spoken to her, hadn't even sent her an e-mail or text message. Once upon a time, they slept in the same bed, shared the same meals, told each other every secret, every smallest detail. Laura had something to say about everyone—if a girl's skirt was too short or her hair too dark, if a guy walked too straight or slouched too deeply. But there was always warmth in her voice, as though she weren't criticizing, but just poking fun, prodding at the quirks and defects, the lovable imperfections. "Now, it's your turn, Kels," she said one night as they lay beside each other. "Tell me what's wrong with me." Kelsey had tried, tried very hard, but she couldn't come up with anything. "You're too perfect," she pouted, and Laura laughed. She said she wasn't, but she knew she was. Kelsey knew she knew.

When Kelsey first met her, Laura had been unearthly in her beauty, as though cut out from a magazine or commercial, every bad hair day air-brushed, every pimple erased. She could wear anything: skirts, jeans, heels, boots, mascara, lipstick. Nothing looked bad. Everything just accentuated her. She was already bright, but she had a way of making herself brighter. You knew she was in the room the second she walked in, all smiles and laughs. She knew you knew.

She loved flowers. She would doodle them in the margins of her notebook, draw them in pink and purple on her arms. Sometimes, she had Alia paint henna on her hands. Other times, she stamped peace signs and smiley faces on her palms and cheeks. She painted her nails red, yellow, and green. She wore her silver rosary around her neck and never took it off.

And the way she smelt! Lilac and rosemary. Always lilac and rosemary. A couple of puffs around the neck, a dollop of moisturizer on each wrist. Those smells followed her around, coalesced, became her. In the dorm. On the stage. By the hospital bed. Like a springtime field wherever she was, however light or dire the situation.

With each recollection, Kelsey's smile inevitably faded. Every memory of Laura terminated with the cancer, the cancer that changed everything, the cancer that robbed Laura of herself. She became Laura with cancer, who couldn't grow her hair because of cancer, who couldn't dance because of cancer, who couldn't finish school because of cancer. By the end, she wasn't Laura at all. She became something less. Like a painting with its colors dulled. Like a broken reflection on the surface of water.

Kelsey was on the highway the next day, radio turned low, wind whistling through the open windows of her car. She recalled what Pete said, how Laura had just fallen suddenly, how the family had shuttled her to the hospital, how the doctors found out the cancer had reemerged. "Kidneys," Pete said. "Liver. Getting to the lungs. She'd been clean, Kelsey. She'd been fine. Nothing for so long, and then it just hit her like a train."

That was how it was in the beginning, Kelsey thought. From one day to the next, practically, as though the cancer appeared from nowhere. As though some power up above realized a mistake had been made and sought to quickly correct it. What did that mean—that

Laura herself was a mistake? Maybe not a mistake, but too good. Too unbroken.

When Kelsey arrived at her hotel later that afternoon, she unpacked her suitcase, hung up her black blouse and pencil skirt, put aside her high heels. Everything was ready for the funeral. The funeral. God. How surreal to remember Laura after so long only to bury her again. She fished out the half-pint bottle of liquor stowed away beneath her jeans and twisted off the cap.

She spent that night driving around Laura's hometown of Ranger's Field, trying to restore her mental map of those old stomping grounds. She remembered the town being so much smaller, so much more dirt and crop. A new strip mall was going up. The high school was being renovated. The paved roads outnumbered the unpaved. She and Laura would laze around there during the summers, watching movies, looking up at the stars. The same stars were still out now, still shining. The same stars, but no Laura underneath them. No Laura to look up with her eyes sparkling. No Laura to breathe out in wonder, even though she had seen them a thousand times before. No Laura to help her see Leo and Virgo.

No Laura.

The funeral parlor was packed the next morning. Ranger's Field was still a small town at heart, and Laura's family was well known. Kelsey signed her name in the guest ledger, then looked at the adjacent portraits. Seeing Laura's face was like seeing a literal ghost, an angel pulled down from heaven, a spirit dragged up from memory.

The glossy black and shining silver of her homecoming dress and coronet. The silky blue of her graduation cap and gown. The dark red of her flamenco dress and lipstick. The gossamer white of her wedding dress, purple wrap around her pale skull, eyes duller, smile more muted.

Kelsey touched the eyes, traced the lips. Her fingers lingered on the canvas.

A hand found her back. "Kels, that you?"

She turned around. "Pete."

He pulled her into a hug and kissed her cheek. "I'm so glad you came," he said, eyeing her. "You didn't say when I called, so I wasn't sure. But here you are. Almost didn't recognize you. You look terrific."

"You, too," she said. She hadn't seem him in years, but he did look good. Cropped beard, parted hair. His hazel eyes were red, wet from recent tears. A white rose was in his breast pocket.

"When did you get in?" he asked.

"Yesterday. I thought about calling, but I don't know. I guess I wanted some time."

"You should come in. Angela's up front. She'll be happy to see you."

"I don't know."

"You have to. Come on."

He led her by hand into the chapel. The smell of flowers hit her immediately. Red, white, and yellow roses surrounded the casket at the far end of the room. Lilac, too, and moonflowers. Blue and purple light came in through the stained-glass window—Jesus on the cross, dripping blood—and spilt over the white of the casket's interior and the pale face inside. Kelsey kept her eyes away as they got close.

A short, older woman stood at the front pew receiving guests, trading hugs, exchanging kisses. Pete touched her arm. "Angela," he said, "look who's here. It's Kelsey."

Laura's mother turned and stared at Kelsey for a moment, her swollen eyes cloudy and dim. Then they lit up. She took Kelsey's hands into her own and clutched them tightly. "Kelsey," she whispered, another wave of tears sliding down her weathered cheeks. "Oh, my Lord, Kelsey!" Angela embraced her, touched her face, stroked her hair. "Kelsey! I don't believe it!"

"Angela," Kelsey said, just above a whisper. "I'm sorry. I didn't know."

"I called her," Pete said. "I told her to come. That Laura wanted it."

Angela nodded. "She was talking about you. Wouldn't say a word for so long, and then she just started talking. Oh, Kelsey. She just started *talking*. The life came back into her."

"We fought about something," Kelsey said, "and we just—"

"Never mind about that. She didn't care. She was talking about you, sweetie. Smiling and laughing like she used to. She didn't care." Angela brought her over to the casket. "You have to see her. Please."

Kelsey wanted to turn away, leave, but being so close, with the blue and purple light coming down, the scent of the flowers around her, she had to look. Laura lay inside, hair bundled up behind her head, hands clasped over her stomach. Her skin was so pale, her limbs so slim, her face so gaunt. She was so small the blue dress seemed almost like a blanket. She was like porcelain. One touch and she would break.

"She didn't want it," Angela said. "She didn't want the medicine again. She didn't want the radiation. She wanted it dignified. The chances were too small. So, she just wanted to wait. She just wanted it to be over."

"I'm sorry," Kelsey said again. It was all she could say. She didn't feel anything, somehow. Ever since Pete called her, she hadn't felt anything. What was this waking dream, erupting like a volcano and scattering her life like ashes? What was this unearthed grave, flooding and over-flowing with water and dirt? Why was it happening? Why to her?

She sat silently through the Mass. She watched quietly as they laid the casket into a plot at the local cemetery, as Pete and Angela and others threw roses onto the satin pall. Perhaps Kelsey would have been among them with a rose of her own, had she and Laura never fought, never separated. Perhaps she would have wept and wailed, felt something, felt anything. All she could think as the casket disappeared was that Laura was truly gone, not just forgotten, but dead, reclaimed by the earth. Sun-bright Laura, then a feeble shadow, now an ashen corpse. No more dancing. No more singing. No more praying. No more.

Pete walked over once the crowd dispersed. "Come by the house," he said. "The reception's not for a few hours. We can talk. You can see Hunter."

"Hunter?"

"Our son."

She followed him to Laura's family home. As with the portraits at the funeral parlor, her memories came to life as they parked in the driveway. The green lawn was as expertly manicured as ever. The single oak tree was as dominating as she remembered, eternally large and imposing. The cherry brick was as warm and inviting as when Laura first brought her to the house during that long-ago spring break. Kelsey would have believed that Laura was waiting for her at the door. She did believe it, in fact, until Pete led her into the orange-smelling foyer, the wooden floor recently waxed, and no Laura greeted her, no Laura took her hand.

"Bernie," Pete called, "I'm back. I have a friend with me."

"We're in here!" In the den, a young woman sat with a small boy. "Look, Hunter," she said, "your daddy's back!"

Kelsey lingered in the doorway and watched Pete take the boy into his arms. He must have been two at the oldest, tiny compared to his father, but with Laura's hair, her eyes. He stared at her from over Pete's shoulder.

Kelsey looked away. They were definitely Laura's eyes.

"Hey, buddy," Pete said, kissing the boy's brow. "I brought a friend with me, an old friend. This is Kelsey. See her? She was good friends with your mommy. Good friends with me."

The boy just stared. Kelsey cleared her throat.

"I figured you two got married, but I didn't think you'd have a kid."

"You know Laura. She always wanted kids. It was all she could talk about after they gave her the all-clear." Pete paused, struggled to maintain his smile. "Oh, yeah. Bernadette, this is Kelsey Hernandez. I don't know if you ever met."

"I think we did," Bernadette said, shaking Kelsey's hand. "Laura's college friend, right? It's just been so long. How was the burial?"

"It was fine," Pete said. "A lot of people were there. It's going to be packed later."

"No problem. I'll keep an eye on him."

"Thanks. Could you take him up to his room? I wanted to talk to Kelsey for a bit. She's not going to stay for the reception."

"Oh, I'm sorry to hear that."

"I'd like to stay," Kelsey said, "but I'm always so busy at work. You know."

Pete put Hunter down, and Bernadette took his hand. "Okay, Hunter. Let's go play with your toys. Let Daddy talk to his friend."

They went up the stairs in the foyer. The boy looked back at Kelsey. She turned her head.

Pete smiled. "He's something, isn't he? I didn't want to take him over there. Didn't want him to see her. She actually said goodbye to him weeks ago, when she had to stay in the hospital. He didn't understand, and he won't really have to. He won't remember."

"Pete, maybe I shouldn't have—"

"I thought I was going to lose it back there," he said. "I keep thinking I'm going to lose my shit sooner or later, but it hasn't happened yet. I got close the night I called you—the night she went. She was already asleep. At least there's that. No more pain, right? We'd found your number, been thinking about it for a while. She got close, but she wouldn't. She was stubborn about it. Forget it. Whatever happened between you two, it doesn't matter anymore."

He went over to the bar at the other side of the room and pulled down a couple of glasses. "What are you drinking?"

"I really shouldn't."

"Kels, come on. For me."

She sighed. "You have bourbon?"

"Damn. You really took it up a notch, didn't you?"

As he filled the glasses, she regarded the room. Much was the same—the brickwork fireplace, the wildlife decor, the brocade carpet—but there were many more photographs upon the mantel. Beside the pictures of Laura as a child and teenager were now portraits of

Hunter. His first birthday. His first visit to the beach. There was again Laura in her wedding dress. There were Pete and Laura exchanging their rings, their vows. There was Angela smiling over her grandson. There were photos of the entire family, so apparently happy that one would never think anything amiss if not for the wrap around Laura's head.

Hidden within some of the photos, hard to spot at a distance, was a small, sweater-clad girl in blocky glasses. Hiding behind Laura's radiant smile. Cowering between Laura and her mother. Laura's little shadow. At one time, long before, her other half.

"Feeling nostalgic?" Pete handed her glass to her. "A lot changed."

"Yeah. She was happy?"

"Oh, yeah. Happy as she could be." He downed his glass. "You know, I'm really glad you came. I thought it would be awkward, talking to you again, hearing your voice—but it wasn't. It was like nothing changed. And you look so good. So different. Even so much better than when I last saw you. You're so far from that nerdy girl Laura brought down with her that first time. You remember? You were so shy. Always hiding behind her back. I'd take one look at you, and you'd curl up into a ball. Not anymore. Not for a long time. I bet men are the ones who hide now. With just a look."

Kelsey drank her bourbon.

"It hurt," he said. "When you just left. When you stopped calling, stopped answering. I couldn't show it to

Laura—I had to be there for her—but, Jesus, Kels, I never thought it would hurt so much. I never thought it would hurt *this* much.”

“Pete.”

“Was it because of me that you two fought?”

“Pete.”

“I have to know, Kels.”

She finished her glass. “No, it wasn’t because of you. It was something else.”

“And did you think about me? Because I thought about you. Every day. Christ, I thought about both of you. It wasn’t supposed to be like that. It was supposed to just go away. But it didn’t. It hasn’t.”

Suddenly, roughly, he pulled her close. “You’re fucking beautiful.” His breath stank not only of the drink he just had, but of the many he had over the last several days. His eyes, no longer watery, but hard, locked on hers. “Like you took it all from her. Like you sucked her dry.”

He kissed her hard, ran his hand over her back. He moved the same way even after so many years, took hold the same way. Instinctively, she opened her mouth, pressed herself against him—then stopped. She eased him back.

“Pete, you just put her in the fucking ground.”

“You think I’d be doing this otherwise?” The force was gone from his voice. Only a pleading, plaintive whine remained. “I need you, Kels.”

"I can't." She wiped her mouth, straightened her skirt. "I'm not the backup anymore. I have a boyfriend. You have a son. We can't."

"Kels, please."

"We can't, Pete. I'm sorry."

He backed away. "You're right," he said at length. "I'm sorry. I just saw you, and it felt like it used to."

What Kelsey didn't say, she thought: Go fuck yourself, Pete.

That night, she drove around Ranger's Field again, stopping finally at the bar she would frequent with Laura, Steely's. It was still the same, and she was grateful for that. Pool tables underneath a persistent haze of smoke. Confederate flag draped across the wall. Jukebox in the corner that played Led Zeppelin or AC/DC. She took a seat at the bar, ordered one beer, then another. She half-expected Laura to appear out of the dark, coming back from the restroom after fixing her hair or makeup.

But it wasn't Laura who eventually, inevitably walked up. No, it was some good old boy in his ten-gallon hat and croc-skin boots, plaid sleeves rolled up, jeans starched stiff. He was young. No one she ever met. No one she would ever see again.

"Hey, there," he said, tipping his hat.

She stifled her laugh. "Howdy."

Back at her hotel room, after they were done, he rolled onto his back and let out a long, drained sigh. "Holy shit."

She pulled on her bra. "Glad you liked it."

"You were like a hurricane. Goddamn."

She almost considered another round, but suddenly, she didn't see him lying there, bare chest covered in a sheen of sweat, jeans like fetters around his ankles. All she saw was the open casket. Jesus on the cross, blood running down his brow. The blue and purple light awash over that soft, porcelain face. That face poised to fall apart at any moment.

"I gotta see you again," the young man said. "What's your name?"

Shakily, Kelsey buttoned her blouse, straightened her hair. Sex was always easy, abundant, reliable—but the casket and lights and smells overwhelmed her. Lilac and rosemary. The glint of the silver rosary around that thin neck. The lurid, oppressive light through the windows when she saw Laura in the hospital bed the first time. The gentle, waning light as she left Laura on the porch after their last conversation. After their one and only true fight.

"My friend died," she said. "Did you know her? Laura Brooks? She used to be Brackett."

"What?"

She imagined touching the porcelain face in the casket, the last image she would ever have of sun-bright Laura. She imagined smudging the rouge and smearing the chalk. But it wasn't just the makeup that came away on her fingertips. It was the skin, muscle, and fat, all of it sloughing off in strings. There was only dull, gray bone underneath—only maggots crawling through the eye sockets, out the mouth, around the nose. She imagined tearing the face away, smashing it, cutting it apart. She imagined poking holes in the portraits, taking out the eyes, ripping out the mouths. Trying to find her. Trying desperately to see more than just her back on that warm-lit, lonely porch.

"Sorry," she said, willing back her tears. "I'm not in the mood anymore."

She left Ranger's Field in the morning, before dawn. Pete tried calling a few times, left a voicemail, but she deleted it. She didn't think anything as she drove. Didn't feel anything. The steel-blue sky waxed on. The crop fields spread to the horizon. The highway snaked ahead.

It was only when she got home, when she dropped her keys, kicked off her shoes, and slid into bed, that the tears came in force. They had been building with each passing day, with each passing hour, but now the flood-gates broke. All of a sudden, she was crying, wailing. She couldn't stop it. Her arms convulsed. Her legs trembled. She hugged the pillows, punched the mattress, seized the sheets, but nothing helped. There was just Laura. Laura passing her a note during a lecture. Laura praying at her bedside. Laura dancing under spotlights upon a stage. Laura drawing kittens on a friend's cast. Laura lying be-side her. Laura holding her in the dark.

She spoke her name as she once did. Laura. Laura. Laura.

At the most painful moment, her every limb like stone, her chest constricted, the last utterance of Laura's name left her as though it were her final breath, so potent as to be visible, a multi-colored, opalescent wisp, gleaming like a gemstone, that vanished into the air. Drained, exhausted, she fell quickly into a child's deep, unbreakable sleep.

ABOUT THE AUTHOR

R. H. Gründ is the author of *Room of Cloth* and the upcoming *Simulacrum*. Apart from writing and publishing, he has taught composition at both the secondary and postsecondary levels. He lives in South Texas with his family. You can follow him on social media at @rhgrundwriting and find more information on his website at www.rhgrundwriting.com.